The Border Rifles
A Tale Of The Texan War

By

Gustave Aimard

Double 9
BOOKS

The Border Rifles
A Tale Of The Texan War
by Gustave Aimard

ISBN: 978-93-62200-85-3

Published by

DOUBLE 9 BOOKS

2/13-B, Ansari Road
Daryaganj, New Delhi – 110002
info@double9books.com
www.double9books.com
Tel. 011-40042856

ABOUT THE AUTHOR

Gustave Aimard wrote multiple volumes about Latin America and the American frontier. Oliver Aimard was born in Paris. As he previously stated, he was the offspring of two married individuals, "but not to each other". His father, François Sébastiani de la Porta (1775-1851), was a commander in Napoleon's army and a representative of the Louis Philippe government. Sebastiani was married to the Duchess of Coigny. In 1806, the couple had a daughter, Alatrice-Rosalba Fanny. The mother died shortly after she was born. Fanny was reared by her grandmother, Duchess of Coigny. Aimard was placed as a baby with a family that were paid to raise him. By the age of nine or twelve, he was sent off on a herring boat. Later, about 1838, he served briefly with the French Navy. After one more trip to America (when he claims he was adopted into a Comanche tribe), Aimard returned to Paris in 1847, the same year his half-sister, Duchess de Choiseul-Pralin, was cruelly killed by her noble husband. Reconciliation or acknowledgement by his biological family did not occur. After serving briefly in the Garde Mobil, Aimard returned to the Americas.

CONTENTS

PREFACE

In the series commencing with the present volume GUSTAVE AIMARD has entirely changed the character of his stories. He has selected a magnificent episode of American history, the liberation of Texas from the intolerable yoke of the Mexicans, and describes scenes *quorum pars magna fuit*. At the present moment, when all are watching with bated breath the results of the internecine war commencing between North and South, I believe that the volumes our author devotes to this subject will be read with special interest, for they impart much valuable information about the character of the combatants who will, to a great extent, form the nucleus of the confederated army. The North looks down on them with contempt, and calls them "Border ruffians;" but when the moment arrives, I entertain no doubt but that they will command respect by the brilliancy of their deeds.

Surprising though the events may be which are narrated in the present volume, they are surpassed by those that continue the series. The next volume, shortly to appear under the title of "The Freebooters," describes the progress of the insurrection till it attained the proportions of a revolution, while the third and last volume will be devoted to the establishment of order in that magnificent State of Texas, which has cast in its lot with the Secessionists, and will indubitably hold out to the very last, confident in the prowess of its sons, whose fathers Aimard has so admirably depicted in the present and the succeeding volumes of the new series.

L.W.

CHAPTER I
THE RUNAWAY

The immense virgin forests which once covered the soil of North America are more and more disappearing before the busy axes of the squatters and pioneers, whose insatiable activity removes the desert frontier further and further to the west.

Flourishing towns, well tilled and carefully-sown fields, now occupy regions where, scarce ten years ago, rose impenetrable forests, whose dense foliage hardly allowed the sunbeams to penetrate, and whose unexplored depths sheltered animals of every description, and served as a retreat for hordes of nomadic Indians, who, in their martial ardour, frequently caused these majestic domes of verdure to re-echo with their war-yell.

Now that the forests have fallen, their gloomy denizens, gradually repulsed by the civilization that incessantly pursues them, have fled step by step before it, and have sought far away other and safer retreats, to which they have borne the bones of their fathers with them, lest they might be dug up and desecrated by the inexorable ploughshare of the white men, as it traces its long and productive furrow over their old hunting-grounds.

Is this constant disafforesting and clearing of the American continent a misfortune? Certainly not: on the contrary, the progress which marches with a giant's step, and tends, before a century, to transform the soil of the New World, possesses all our sympathy; still we cannot refrain from a feeling of pained commiseration for that unfortunate race which is brutally placed beyond the pale of the law, and pitilessly tracked in all directions; which is daily diminishing, and is fatally condemned soon to disappear from that earth whose immense territory it covered less than four centuries ago with innumerable tribes.

Perhaps if the people chosen by God to effect the changes to which we allude had understood their mission, they might have converted a work of blood and carnage into one of peace and paternity, and arming themselves with the divine precepts of the Gospel, instead of seizing rifles, torches, and scalping-knives, they might, in a given time, have produced a fusion of the white and red races, and have attained a result more profitable to progress, civilization, and before all, to that great fraternity of nations which no one is permitted to despise, and for which those who forget its divine and sacred precepts will have a terrible account some day to render.

Men cannot become with impunity the murderers of an entire race, and constantly wade in blood; for that blood must at some time cry for vengeance, and the day of justice break, when the sword will be cast in the balance between conquerors and conquered.

At the period when our narrative commences, that is to say, about the close of 1812, the emigration had not yet assumed that immense extension which it was soon to acquire, for it was only beginning, as it were, and the immense forests that stretched out and covered an enormous space between the borders of the United States and Mexico, were only traversed by the furtive footsteps of traders and wood-rangers, or by the silent moccasins of the Redskins.

It is in the centre of one of the immense forests to which we have alluded that our story begins, at about three in the afternoon of October 27th, 1812.

The heat had been stifling under the covert, but at this moment the sunbeams growing more and more oblique, lengthened the tall shadows of the trees, and the evening breeze that was beginning to rise refreshed the atmosphere, and carried far away the clouds of mosquitoes which during the whole mid-day had buzzed over the marshes in the clearings.

We find ourselves on the bank of an unknown affluent of the Arkansas; the slightly inclined trees on either side the stream formed a thick canopy of verdure over the waters, which were scarce rippled by the inconstant breath of the breeze; here and there pink flamingos and white herons, perched on their tall legs, were fishing for their dinner, with that careless ease which generally characterizes the race of great aquatic birds; but suddenly they stopped, stretched out their necks as if listening to some unusual sound, then ran hurriedly along to catch the wind, and flew away with cries of alarm.

All at once the sound of a musket-shot was re-echoed through the forest, and two flamingos fell. At the same instant a light canoe doubled a little cape formed by some mangrove-trees jutting out into the bed of the stream, and darted in pursuit of the flamingos which had fallen in the water. One of them had been killed on the spot, and was drifting with the current; but the other, apparently but slightly wounded, was flying with extreme rapidity, and swimming vigorously.

The boat was an Indian canoe, made of birch bark removed from the tree by the aid of hot water, and there was only one man in it; his rifle lying in the bows and still smoking, shewed that it was he who had just fired. We will draw the portrait of this person, who is destined to play an important part in our narrative.

As far as could be judged from his position in the canoe, he was a man of great height; his small head was attached by a powerful neck to shoulders of more than ordinary breadth; muscles, hard as cords, stood out on his arms at each of his movements; in a word, the whole appearance of this individual denoted a vigour beyond the average.

His face, illumined by large blue eyes, sparkling with sense, had an expression of frankness and honesty which pleased at the first glance, and completed the *ensemble* of his regular features, and wide mouth, round which an unceasing smile of good humour played. He might be twenty-three, or twenty-four at the most, although his complexion, bronzed by the inclemency of the weather, and the dense light brown beard that covered the lower part of his face, made him appear older.

This man was dressed in the garb of a wood-ranger: a beaver-skin cap, whose tail fell down between his shoulders, hardly restrained the thick curls of his golden hair, which hung in disorder down his back; a hunting shirt of blue calico, fastened round his hips by a deerskin belt, fell a little below his muscular knees; *mitasses*, or a species of tight drawers, covered his legs, and his feet were protected against brambles and the stings of reptiles by Indian moccasins.

His game-bag, of tanned leather, hung over his shoulder, and, like all the bold pioneers of the virgin forest, his weapons consisted of a good Kentucky rifle, a straight-bladed knife, ten inches long and two wide, and a tomahawk that glistened like a mirror. These weapons, of course with the exception of the rifle, were passed through his belt, which also supported two buffalo horns filled with powder and bullets.

The appearance of the man thus equipped, and standing in the canoe amid the imposing scenery that surrounded him, had something grand about it which created an involuntary respect.

The wood-ranger, properly so termed, is one of those numerous types of the New World which must soon entirely disappear before the incessant progress of civilization.

The wood-rangers, those bold explorers of the deserts, in which their whole existence was spent, were men who, impelled by a spirit of independence and an unbridled desire for liberty, shook off all the trammels of society, and who, with no other object than that of living and dying unrestrained by any other will save their own, and in no way impelled by the hope of any sort of lucre, which they despised, abandoned the towns, and boldly buried themselves in the virgin forests, where they lived from day to day indifferent about the present, careless as to the future, convinced that God would not desert them in the hour of need, and thus placed themselves outside of that common law they misunderstood, on the extreme limit that separates barbarism from civilization.

Most of the celebrated wood-rangers were French Canadians; in truth, there is in the Norman character something daring and adventurous, which is well adapted to this mode of life, so full as it is of strange interludes and delicious sensations, whose intoxicating charms only those who have led it can understand.

The Canadians have never admitted in principle the change of nationality which the English tried to impose on them; they still regard themselves as Frenchmen, and their eyes are constantly fixed on that ungrateful mother-country which has abandoned them with such cruel indifference.

Even at the present day, after so many years, the Canadians have still remained French; their fusion with the Anglo-Saxon race is only apparent, and the slightest pretext would suffice to produce a definitive rupture between them and the English. The British government is well, aware of this fact, and hence displays toward the Canadian colonies a marked kindliness and deference.

At the earlier period of the conquest this repulsion (not to call it hatred) was so prominent between the two races, that the Canadians emigrated in a mass, sooner than endure the humiliating yoke which was attempted to be placed on them. Those of them who, too poor to leave their country definitively, were compelled to remain in a country henceforth sullied by a foreign occupation, chose the rude trade of wood-rangers, and preferred such an existence of misery and danger to the disgrace of enduring the laws of a detested conqueror. Shaking the dust over their shoes on the paternal roof, they threw their rifles over their shoulders, and stifling a sigh of regret, went away not to return, burying themselves in the impenetrable forests of Canada, and laying unconsciously the foundation of that generation of intrepid pioneers, to one of the finest specimens of whom we introduced the reader at the beginning of this chapter.

The hunter went on paddling vigorously; he soon reached the first flamingo, which he threw into the bottom of his canoe. But the second gave him more trouble. It was for a while a struggle of speed between the wounded bird and the hunter: still the former gradually lost its strength; its movements became uncertain, and it beat the water convulsively. A blow from the Canadian's paddle at length put an end to its agony, and it joined its mate in the bottom of the canoe.

So soon as he had secured his game, the hunter shipped his paddles, and prepared to reload his rifle, with the care which all devote to the operation who know that their life depends on a charge of powder. When his gun was in order again, the Canadian took an inquiring glance around.

"Why," he presently said, talking to himself, a habit which men who live in solitude very frequently acquire, "hang me! if I have not reached the meeting-place without suspecting it. I cannot be mistaken: over there are the two oaks fallen across each other, and that rock, which stands out over the water. But what's that?" he exclaimed, as he stooped, and cocked his rifle.

The furious barking of several dogs became suddenly audible in the centre of the forest; the bushes were parted eagerly, and a Negro appeared on the top of the rock, at which the Canadian was at this moment looking. This man, on reaching the extremity of the rock, stopped for an instant, and seemed to listen attentively, while displaying signs of the most extreme agitation. But this halt was short, for he had hardly rested there for a few seconds, ere, raising his eyes to heaven in despair, he leaped into the river, and swam vigorously to the opposite bank.

The sound of the Negro's fall into the water had hardly died away, when several dogs dashed on to the platform, and began a concert of horrible barking. These dogs were powerful animals; their tongues were pendant, their eyes infested with blood, and their hair standing on end, as if they had come a long distance.

The hunter shook his head several times while giving a glance of pity at the hapless Negro, who was swimming with that energy of despair which doubles the strength—and seizing his paddles, he turned the canoe toward him, with the evident intention of rendering him assistance. At this moment a hoarse voice was heard on the river-bank.

"Hilloh, there! silence, you demons incarnate! silence, I tell you!"

The dogs gave vent to a few whines of pain, and were suddenly silent. The individual who had reproved the animals then said, in a louder key—

"Hilloh, you fellow in the canoe there!—hilloh!"

The Canadian had just pulled to the opposite bank; he ran his canoe on the sand, and then carelessly turned to the person who addressed him.

This was a man of middle height, muscular, and dressed like the majority of rich farmers. His face was brutal, crafty, and four persons, apparently servants, stood by his side; it is needless to say that all were armed with guns.

The stream at this spot was rather wide, being about fifty yards, which, temporarily, at any rate, established a respectable barrier between the Negro and his pursuers. The Canadian leaned against a tree.

"Are you by chance speaking to me?" he asked, in a somewhat contemptuous tone.

"Who else do you suppose?" the first speaker continued, angrily: "so try and answer my questions!"

"And why should I answer them? Will you be good enough to tell me?" the Canadian continued, with a laugh.

"Because I order you to do so, you scoundrel!" the other said, brutally.

The hunter shrugged his shoulders disdainfully.

"Good-bye," he said, and made a movement as if to retire.

"Stop where you are!" the American shouted, "or so truly as my name is John Davis I will put a bullet through your skull!"

While uttering the threat he levelled his gun.

"Ah! ah!" the Canadian went on, with a laugh, "then you're John Davis, the famous slave-dealer?"

"Yes, I am," the other said, harshly.

"Pardon me; but I had hitherto only known you by reputation. By Jove! I am delighted to have seen you."

"Well, and now that you know me, are you disposed to answer my questions?"

"I must know their nature first, so you had better ask them."

"What has become of my slave?"

"Do you mean the man who leaped off the platform just before you reached it?"

"Yes. Where is he?"

"Here, by my side."

In fact, the Negro, his strength and courage quite exhausted from the desperate efforts he had made during the obstinate pursuit of which he had been the object, had dragged himself to the spot where the Canadian stood, and now lay in a half fainting condition at his feet.

On hearing the hunter reveal his presence so clearly, he clasped his hands with an effort, and raised toward him a face bathed in tears.

"Oh! master, master!" he cried, with an expression of agony impossible to render, "Save me! Save me!"

"Ah, ah!" John Davis shouted, with a grin, "I fancy we can come to an understanding, my fine fellow, and that you will not be sorry to gain the reward."

"In truth I should not be sorry to hear the price set on human flesh in what is called your free country. Is the reward large?"

"Twenty dollars for a runaway nigger."

"Pooh!" the Canadian said, thrusting out his lower lip in disgust, "that is a trifle!"

"Do you think so?"

"Indeed I do."

"Still, I only ask you to do a very simple matter in order to earn them."

"What is it?"

"Tie that nigger, put him in your canoe, and bring him to me."

"Very good. It is not difficult, I allow; and when he is in your power, supposing I do what you wish, what do you intend doing with him?"

"That is not your business."

"Granted: hence I only asked you for information."

"Come! Make up your mind; I have no time to waste in chattering. What is your decision?"

"This is what I have to say to you, Mr. John Davis, who hunt men with dogs less ferocious than yourself, which in obeying you only yield to their instincts—you are a villain! And if you only reckon on my help in regaining your Negro, you may consider him lost."

"Ah, that is it!" the American shouted, as he gnashed his teeth furiously, and turned to his servants; "fire at him! Fire! Fire!"

And joining example to precept, he quickly shouldered his gun and fired. His servants imitated him, and four shots were confounded in a single explosion, which the echoes of the forest mournfully repeated.

CHAPTER II
QUONIAM

The Canadian did not lose one of his adversaries' movements while he was speaking with them; hence, when the shots ordered by John Davis were fired, they proved ineffectual; he had rapidly hidden himself behind a tree, and the bullets whistled harmlessly past his ears.

The slave-dealer was furious at being thus foiled by the hunter; he gave him the most fearful threats, blasphemed, and stamped his foot in rage.

But threats and imprecations availed but little; unless they swam the river, which was impracticable, in the face of a man so resolute as the hunter seemed to be, there were no means of taking any vengeance on him, or recapturing the slave he had so deliberately taken under his protection.

While the American racked his brains in vain to find an expedient that would enable him to gain the advantage, a bullet dashed the rifle he held in his hand to pieces.

"Accursed dog!" he yelled in his fury, "do you wish to assassinate me?"

"I should have a right to do so," the Canadian replied, "for I am only defending myself fairly, after your attempt to kill me; but I prefer dealing amicably with you, although I feel convinced I should be doing a great service to humanity by lodging a couple of slugs in your brain."

And a second bullet at this moment smashed the rifle one of the servants was reloading.

"Come, enough of this," the American shouted, greatly exasperated; "what do you want?"

"I told you—treat amicably with you."

"But on what conditions? Tell me them at least."

"In a moment."

The rifle of the second servant was broken like that of the first: of the five men, three were now disarmed.

"Curses," the slave-dealer howled; "have you resolved to make a target of us in turn?"

"No, I only wish to equalise chances."

"But—"

"It is done now."

The fourth rifle was broken.

"And now," the Canadian said, as he showed himself "suppose we have a talk."

And, leaving his shelter, he walked to the river bank.

"Yes, talk, demon," the American shouted.

With a movement swift as thought, he seized the last rifle, and shouldered it; but, ere he could pull the trigger, he rolled on the platform, uttering a cry of pain.

The hunter's bullet had broken his arm.

"Wait for me, I am coming," the Canadian continued with perfect calmness.

He reloaded his rifle, leaped into the canoe, and with a few strokes of his paddle, found himself on the other side of the river.

"There," he said as he landed and walked up to the American, who was writhing like a serpent on the platform, howling and blaspheming; "I warned you: I only wished to equalise the chances, and you have no right to complain of what has happened to you, my dear sir: the fault rests entirely with yourself."

"Seize him! kill him!" the wretch shouted, a prey to indescribable fury.

"Come, come, calm yourself. Good gracious, you have only a broken arm, after all; remember, I could have easily killed you, had I pleased. Hang it, you are not reasonable."

"Oh! I will kill him," he yelled, as he gnashed his teeth.

"I hardly think so, at least not for the present; I will say nothing about by and by. But let that be: I will examine your wound, and dress it while we talk."

"Do not touch me! Do not come near me, or I know not to what extremities I may proceed."

The Canadian shrugged his shoulders.

"You must be mad," he said.

Incapable of enduring longer the state of exasperation in which he was, the dealer, who was also weakened by the loss of blood, made a vain effort to rise and rush on his foe; bat he fell back and fainted while muttering a final curse.

The servants stood startled, as much by the unparalleled skill of this strange man, as by the boldness with which, after disarming them all in turn, he had crossed the river, in order, as it were, to deliver himself into their hands; for, if they had no longer their rifles, their knives and pistols were left them.

"Come, gentlemen," the Canadian said with a frown, "have the goodness to shake out the priming of your pistols, or, by Heaven! We shall have a row."

The servants did not at all desire to begin a fight with him; moreover, the sympathy they felt for their master was not great, while, on the other hand, the Canadian, owing to the expeditious way in which he had acted, inspired them with a superstitious fear: hence they obeyed his orders with a species of eagerness, and even wished to hand him their knives.

"It is not necessary," he said; "now, let us see about dressing this worthy gentleman's wound: it would be a pity to deprive society of so estimable a person, who is one of its brightest ornaments."

He set to work at once, aided by the servants, who executed his orders with extraordinary rapidity and zeal, for they felt so thoroughly mastered by him.

Compelled by the mode of life they pass to do without any strange assistance, the wood-rangers all possess, to a certain extent, elementary notions of medicine, and especially of surgery, and can, in case of need, treat a fracture or wound of any nature as well as a professional man; and that, too, by simple means usually employed with the greatest success by the Indians.

The hunter proved by the skill and dexterity which he dressed the slave-dealer's wound, that, if he knew how to inflict wounds, he was equally clever in curing them.

The servants regarded with heightening admiration this extraordinary man, who seemed suddenly metamorphosed, and proceeded with a certainty of glance and lightness of hand which many a surgeon might have envied him. During the bandaging, the wounded man returned to consciousness, and opened his eyes, but remained silent; his fury had been calmed, and his brutal nature subdued by the energetic resistance the Canadian opposed to him. The first and piercing pain of the wound had been succeeded, as always happens when the bandaging is properly done, by an extraordinary feeling of relief: hence, recognising, in spite of himself, the comfort he had experienced, he had felt his hatred melting away in a feeling for which he could not yet account, but which now made him regard his enemy almost with a friendly air.

To render John Davis the justice due to him, we will say that he was neither better nor worse than any of his fellows who trafficked in human flesh. Accustomed to the sufferings of slaves, who to him were nothing but beings deprived of reason, or merchandize in a word, his heart had gradually grown callous to softer emotions: he only saw in a Negro the money he had expended, and what he expected to gain by him, and like a true tradesman, he was very fond of money: a runaway Negro seemed to him a wretched thing, against whom any means were permissible in order to prevent a loss.

Still, this man was not insensible to every good feeling; apart from his trade, he even enjoyed a certain reputation for kindness, and passed for a gentleman.

"There, that is all right," the Canadian said, as he gave a satisfied glance at the bandages; "in three weeks there will be nothing to be seen, if you take care of yourself; for, through a remarkable piece of good luck, the bone has not been touched, and the ball has only passed through the fleshy part of the arm. Now, my good friend, if you like to talk, I am ready."

"I have nothing to say, except to ask you to return the scoundrel who is the cause of the whole mishap."

"Hum! If we go on in that way, I am afraid we shall not come to an understanding. You know perfectly that the whole quarrel arose about the surrender of the scoundrel, as you term him."

"Still, I cannot lose my money."

"What money do you mean?"

"Well, my slave, if you prefer it; he represents a sum I do not at all care to lose; the less so, because things have been going very queerly with me lately, and I have suffered some heavy losses."

"That is annoying, and I pity you sincerely; still, I should like to settle the affair amicably as I began," the Canadian continued.

The American made a grimace.

"It is a deuced amicable way you have of settling matters," he said.

"It is your fault, my friend; if we did not come to an immediate arrangement, it was because you were a little too quick, as you will allow."

"Well, we will not say any more about that, for what's done cannot be undone."

"You are right, so let us return to business. Unluckily, I am poor; were not so, I would give you a few hundred dollars, and all would be settled."

The dealer scratched his head.

"Listen," he said. "I do not know why, but, in spite of all that has passed between us, perhaps in consequence of it, I should not like for us to separate on bad terms; the more so, because, to tell you the truth, I care very little for Quoniam."

"Who's Quoniam?"

"The nigger."

"Oh, very good, that's a funny name you have given him; however, no matter, you say you care very little for him?"

"Indeed I do."

"Then why did you begin the obstinate hunt with dogs and guns?"

"Through pride."

"Oh!" the Canadian said, with a start of dissatisfaction.

"Listen to me, I am a slave dealer."

"A very ugly trade, by the way," the hunter observed.

"Perhaps so, but I shall not discuss that point.

"About a month ago, a large sale was announced at Baton Rouge, of slaves of both sexes, belonging to a rich gentleman who had died suddenly, and I proceeded there. Among the slaves exposed for sale was Quoniam. The rascal is young, active, and vigorous; he has a bold and intelligent look; so he naturally pleased me at the first glance, and I felt desirous to buy him. I went up and questioned him; and the scamp answered me word for word as follows, which put me out of countenance for a moment, I confess.

"'Master, I do not advise you to buy me, for I have sworn to be free or die; whatever you may do to prevent me, I warn you that I shall escape. Now you can do as you please.'

"This clear and peremptory declaration piqued me, 'We shall see,' I said to him, and then went to find the auctioneer. The latter, who was a friend of mine, dissuaded me from buying Quoniam, giving me reasons, each better than the other, against doing so. But my mind was made up, and I stuck to it. Quoniam was knocked down to me for ninety dollars, an absurd price for a Negro of his age, and built as he is; but no one would have him at any price. I put irons on him, and took him away, not to my house, but to the prison, so that I might feel sure he would not escape. The next day, when I returned to the prison, Quoniam was gone; he had kept his word.

"At the end of two days he was caught again; the same evening he was off once more, and it was impossible for me to discover how he had foiled the plans I had formed to restrain him. This has been going on for a month; a week ago he escaped again, and since then I have been in search of him; despairing of being able to keep him, I got into a passion, and started after him, this time with my blood-hounds, resolved to finish, once for all, with this accursed Negro, who constantly slips through my fingers like a lizard."

"That is to say," the Canadian remarked, who had listened with interest to the dealer's story, "you would not have hesitated to kill him."

"That I should, for the confounded scamp is so crafty; he has so constantly taken me in, that I have grown to hate him."

"Listen in your turn, Mr. John Davis; I am not rich, but a long way from it. What do I need gold or silver, as a man of the desert to whom Heaven supplies daily food so liberally? This Quoniam, who is so eager for liberty and the open air, inspires me with a lively interest, and I wish to try and give him that freedom to which he so persistently aspires. This is what I propose; I have in my canoe three jaguar skins and twelve beaver skins, which, if sold at any town of the Union, will be worth from one hundred and fifty to two hundred dollars; take them, and let all be finished."

The dealer looked at him with a surprise mingled with a certain degree of kindliness.

"You are wrong," he said, presently; "the bargain you offer is too advantageous for me, and too little so for you. That is not the way to do business."

"How does that concern you? I have got it in my head that this man shall be free."

"You do not know the ungrateful nature of niggers," the other persisted; "this one will be in no way grateful to you for what you do for him; on the contrary, on the first opportunity he will probably give you cause to repent your good action."

"That is possible, but it is his business, for I do not ask gratitude of him; if he shows it, all the better for him; if not, the Lord's will be done! I act in accordance with my heart, and my reward is in my conscience."

"By the Lord, you are a fine fellow, I tell you," the dealer exclaimed, incapable of restraining himself longer. "It would be all the better if a fellow could meet with more of your sort. Well, I intend to prove to you that I am not so bad as you have a right to suppose, after what has passed between us. I will sign the assignment of Quoniam to you, and I will only accept in return one tiger skin in remembrance of our meeting, although," he added, with a grimace, as he pointed to his arm, "you have already given me another."

"Done," the Canadian exclaimed, eagerly; "but you must take two skins instead of one, as I intend to ask of you a rifle, an axe, and a knife, so that the poor devil we now set at liberty (for you are now halves in my good deed) may provide for his support."

"Be it so," the dealer said, good humouredly; "as the scoundrel insists on being at liberty, let him be, and he can go to the deuce."

At a sign from his master, one of the servants produced from his game bag ink, pens, and paper, and drew up on the spot, not a deed of sale, but a regular ticket of freedom, to which the dealer put his signature, and which the servants afterwards witnessed.

"On my word," John Davis exclaimed, "it is possible that from a business point of view I have done a foolish thing, but, you may believe me or not, as you like, I never yet felt so satisfied with myself."

"That is," the Canadian answered, seriously, "because you have to-day followed the impulses of your heart."

The Canadian then quitted the platform to go and fetch the skins. A moment after, he returned with two magnificent jaguar hides, perfectly intact, which he handed to the dealer. The latter, as was arranged, then delivered the weapons to him; but a scruple suddenly assailed the hunter.

"One moment," he said; "if you give me these weapons, how will you manage to return to town?"

"That need not trouble you," John Davis replied; "I left my horse and people scarce three leagues from here. Besides, we have our pistols, which we could use if necessary."

"That is true," the Canadian remarked, "you have therefore nothing to fear; still, as your wound will not allow you to go so far a-foot, I will help your servants to prepare you a litter."

And with that skill, of which he had already supplied so many proofs, the Canadian manufactured, with branches of trees he cut down with his hatchet, a litter, on which the two tiger skins were laid.

"And now," he said, "good bye; perhaps we shall never meet again. We part, I trust, on better terms than we came together: remember, there is no trade, however shameful, which an honest man cannot carry on honourably;

when your heart inspires you to do a good action, do not be deaf to it, but do it without regret, for God will have spoken to you."

"Thanks," the dealer said, with considerable emotion, "but grant me one word before we part."

"Say on."

"Tell me your name, so that if any day accident brought us together again, I might appeal to your recollections, as you could to mine."

"That is true, my name is Tranquil; the wood-rangers, my companions, have surnamed me the Panther killer."

And, ere the slave dealer had recovered from the astonishment caused by this sudden revelation of the name of a man whose renown was universal on the border, the hunter, after giving him a parting wave of the hand, bounded from the platform, unfastened his canoe, and paddled vigorously to the other bank.

"Tranquil, the Panther-killer," John Davis muttered when he was alone; "it was truly my good genius which inspired me to make a friend of that man."

He lay down on the litter which two of his men raised, and after giving a parting glance at the Canadian, who at this moment was landing on the opposite bank, he said:—

"Forward!"

The platform was soon deserted again, the dealer and his men had disappeared under the covert, and nothing was audible but the gradually departing growls of the bloodhounds, as they ran on ahead of the little party.

CHAPTER III
BLACK AND WHITE

In the meanwhile, as we have said, the Canadian hunter, whose name we at length know, had reached the bank of the river where he left the Negro concealed in the shrubs.

During the long absence of his defender, the slave could easily have fled, and that with the more reason, because he had almost the certainty of not being pursued before a lapse of time, which would have given him a considerable start on those who were so obstinately bent on capturing him.

He had not done so, however, either because the idea of flight did not appear to him realizable, or because he was too wearied, he had not stirred from the spot where he sought a refuge at the first moment, and had remained with his eyes obstinately fixed on the platform, following with anxious glance the movements of the persons collected on it.

John Davis had not at all flattered him in the portrait he had drawn of him to the hunter. Quoniam was really one of the most magnificent specimens of the African race: twenty-two years of age at the most, he was tall, well-proportioned and powerfully built; he had wide shoulders, powerfully developed chest, and well-hung limbs; it was plain that he combined unequalled strength with far from ordinary speed and lightness; his features were fine and expressive, his countenance breathed frankness, his widely opened eyes were intelligent—in short, although his skin was of the deepest black, and unfortunately, in America, the land of liberty, that colour is an indelible stigma of servitude, this man did not seem at all to have been created for slavery, for everything about him aspired to liberty and that free-will which God has given to his creatures, and men have tried in vain to tear from them.

When the Canadian re-entered the canoe, and the American quitted the platform, a sigh of satisfaction expanded the Negro's chest, for, without knowing positively what had passed between the hunter and his old master, as he was too far off to hear what was said, he understood that, temporarily at least, he had nothing to fear from the latter, and he awaited with feverish impatience the return of his generous defender, that he might learn from him what he had henceforth to hope or fear.

So soon as he reached land, the Canadian pulled his canoe on to the sand, and walked with a firm and deliberate step toward the spot where he expected to find the Negro.

He soon noticed him in a sitting posture, almost at the same spot where he had left him.

The hunter could not repress a smile of satisfaction.

"Ah, ah," he said to him, "there you are, then, friend Quoniam."

"Yes, master. Did John Davis tell you my name?"

"As you see; but what are you doing there? Why did you not escape during my absence?"

"Quoniam is no coward," he replied, "to escape while another is risking his life for him. I was waiting ready to surrender myself if the white hunter's life had been threatened."[1]

This was said with a simplicity full of grandeur, proving that such was really the Negro's intention.

"Good!" the hunter replied, kindly, "I thank you, for your intention was good; fortunately, your interference was unneeded; but, at any rate, you acted more wisely by remaining here."

"Whatever may happen to me, master, be assured that I shall feel ever grateful to you."

"All the better for you, Quoniam, for that will prove to me that you are not ungrateful, which is one of the worst vices humanity is afflicted by; but be good enough not to call me master again, for it grieves me; the word implies a degrading inferiority, and besides, I am not your master, but merely your companion."

"What other name can a poor slave give you?"

"My own, hang it. Call me Tranquil, as I call you Quoniam. Tranquil is not a difficult name to remember, I should think."

"Oh, not at all," the Negro said with a laugh.

[1] Nothing appears to us so ridiculous as that conventional jargon Which is placed in the mouth of Negroes; a jargon which, in the first place, impedes the story, and is moreover false; a double reason which urges us not to employ it here— all the worse for the local colouring.—G.A.

"Good! That is settled, then; now, let us go to something else, and, in the first place, take this."

The hunter drew a paper from his belt, which he handed to the Black.

"What is this?" the latter asked with a timid glance, for his ignorance prevented him deciphering it.

"That?" the hunter said with a smile; "it is a precious talisman, which makes of you a man like all the rest of us, and removes you from the animals among which you have been counted up to this day; in a word, it is a deed by which John Davis, native of South Carolina, slave dealer, from this day restores to Quoniam his full and entire liberty, to enjoy it as he thinks proper—or, if you prefer it, it is your deed of liberation written by your former master, and signed by competent witnesses, who will stand by you if necessary."

On hearing these words the Negro turned pale after the fashion of men of his colour; that is to say, his face assumed a tinge of dirty gray, his eyes were unnaturally dilated, and for a few seconds he remained motionless, crushed, incapable of uttering a word or making a movement.

At length he burst into a loud laugh, leaped up twice or thrice with the suppleness of a wild beast, and then broke suddenly into tears.

The hunter attentively watched the Negro's movement, feeling interested to the highest degree in what he saw, and evidencing each moment a greater sympathy with this man.

"Then," the Black at length said, "I am free—truly free?"

"As free as a man can be," Tranquil replied, with a smile.

"Now I can come, go, sleep, work, or rest, and no one can prevent me, and I need not fear the lash?"

"Quite so."

"I belong to myself, myself alone? I can act and think like other men? I am no longer a beast of burthen, which is loaded and harnessed? I am as good as any other man, white, yellow, or red?"

"Quite so," the hunter answered, amused and interested at the same time by these simple questions.

"Oh!" the Negro said, as he took his head in his hands, "I am free then—free at last!"

He uttered these words with a strange accent, which made the hunter quiver.

All at once he fell on his knees, clasped his hands, and raised his eyes to Heaven.

"My God!" he exclaimed, with an accent of ineffable happiness. "Thou who canst do all, thou to whom all men are equal, and who dost not regard their colour to protect and defend them. Thou, whose goodness is unbounded like thy power; thanks! Thanks! My God, for having drawn me from slavery, and restored my liberty!"

After giving vent to this prayer, which was the expression of the feelings that boiled in his heart, the Negro fell on the ground, and for some minutes remained plunged in earnest thought. The hunter respected his silence.

At length the Negro raised his head again.

"Listen, hunter," he said. "I have returned thanks to God for my deliverance, as was my duty; for it was He who inspired you with the thought of defending me. Now that I am beginning to grow a little calmer, and feel accustomed to my new condition, be good enough to tell me what passed between you and my master, that I may know the extent of the debt I owe you, and that I may regulate my future conduct by it. Speak, I am listening."

"What need to tell you a story which can interest you so slightly? You are free, that ought to be sufficient for you."

"No, that is not sufficient; I am free, that is true, but how have I become so? That is what I do not know, and I have the right to ask of you."

"The story, I say again, has nothing that can interest you at all; still, as it may cause you to form a better opinion of the man to whom you belonged, I will not longer refuse to tell it to you; so listen."

Tranquil, after this opening, told in all their details the events that happened between himself and the slave dealer, and when he had finished, added—

"Well, are you satisfied now?"

"Yes," the Negro replied, who had listened to him with the most sustained attention. "I know that, next to God, I owe everything to you, and I will remember it; never will you have to remind me of the debt, under whatever circumstances we may meet."

"You owe me nothing, now that you are free; it is your duty to employ that liberty in the way a man of upright and honest heart should do."

"I will try not to prove myself unworthy of what God and you have done for me; I also thank John Davis sincerely for the good feeling that urged him to listen to your remonstrances; perhaps I may be able to requite him some day; and, if the opportunity offers, I shall not neglect it."

"Good! I like to hear you speak so, for it proves to me that I was not mistaken about you; and now what do you intend to do?"

"What advice do you give me?"

"The question you ask me is a serious one, and I hardly know how to answer it; the choice of a profession is always a difficult affair, and must be reflected upon ripely before a decision is formed; in spite of my desire to be of service to you, I should not like to give you advice, which you would doubtless follow for my sake, and which might presently cause you regret. Besides, I am a man whose life since the age of seven has always been spent in the woods, and I am, consequently, far too unacquainted with what is called the world to venture to lead you on a path which I do not know myself."

"That reasoning seems to me perfectly correct. Still, I cannot remain here, and must make up my mind to something or other."

"Do one thing."

"What is it?"

"Here are a knife, gun, powder, and bullets; the desert is open before you, so go and try for a few days the free life of the great solitudes; during your long hours of hunting you will have leisure to reflect on the vocation you are desirous to embrace; you will weigh in your mind the advantages you expect to derive from it, and then, when your mind is quite made up, you can turn your back on the desert, go back to the towns, and, as you are an active, honest, and intelligent man, I am certain you will succeed in whatever calling you may choose."

The Negro nodded his head several times.

"Yes," he said, "in what you propose to me there is both good and bad; that is not exactly what I should wish."

"Explain yourself clearly, Quoniam; I can see you have something at the end of your tongue which you do not like to say."

"That is true; I have not been frank with you, Tranquil, and I was wrong, as I now see clearly. Instead of asking you hypocritically for advice, which I did not at all intend to follow, I ought to have told you honestly my way of thinking, and that would have been altogether better."

"Come," the hunter said, laughingly, "speak."

"Well, really I do not see why I should not tell you what I have on my heart. If there be a man in the world who takes an interest in me it is certainly you; and hence, the sooner I know what I have to depend on, the better: the only life that suits me is that of a wood-ranger. My instincts and feelings impel me to it; all my attempts at flight, when I was a slave, tended to that object. I am only a poor Negro, whom his narrow mind and intelligence would not guide properly in towns, where man is not valued for what he is worth, but for what he appears. What use would that liberty, of which I am so proud, appear to me, in a town where I should have to dispose of it to the first comer, in order to procure the food and clothing I need? I should only have regained my liberty to render myself a slave. Hence it is in the desert alone I can profit by the kindness I owe to you, without fear of ever being impelled by wretchedness to actions unworthy of a man conscious of his own worth. Hence it is in the desert I desire henceforth to live, only visiting the towns to exchange the skins of animals I have killed for powder, bullets, and clothing. I am young and strong, and the God who has hitherto protected me will not desert me."

"You are perhaps right, and I cannot blame you for wishing to follow my example, when the life I lead seems to me preferable to all others. Well, now that is all settled, my good Quoniam, we can part, and I wish you luck; perhaps we shall meet again, sometimes, on the Indian territory."

The Negro began laughing, and showed two rows of teeth white as snow, but made no reply.

Tranquil threw his rifle on his shoulder, gave him a last friendly sign of parting, and turned to go back to his canoe.

Quoniam seized the rifle the hunter had left him, passed the knife through his girdle, to which he also fastened the horns of powder and bullets, and then, after a final glance to see he had forgotten nothing, he followed the hunter, who had already gained a considerable start on him.

He caught Tranquil up at the moment he reached his canoe, and was about to thrust it into the water; at the sound of footsteps, the hunter turned round.

"Halloh," he said, "is that you again, Quoniam?"

"Yes," he answered.

"What brings you here?"

"Why," the Negro said, as he buried his fingers in his woolly hair, and scratched his head furiously, "you forgot something."

"What was it?"

"To take me with you."

"That is true," the hunter said, as he offered him his hand; "forgive me, brother."

"Then you consent?" he asked, with ill-restrained joy.

"Yes."

"We shall not part again?"

"It will depend on your will."

"Oh, then," he exclaimed, with a joyous outburst of laughter, "we shall be together a long time."

"Well, be it so," the Canadian went on. "Come; two men, when they have faith in each other, are very strong in the desert. Heaven, doubtless, willed that we should meet. Henceforth we shall be brothers."

Quoniam leaped into the canoe, and gaily caught up the paddles.

The poor slave had never been so happy; never had the air seemed to him purer, or nature more lovely—everything smiled on him, and made holiday for him, for that moment he was about to begin really living the life of other men, without any bitter afterthought; the past was no more than a dream. He had found in his defender what so many men seek in vain, throughout a lengthened existence—a friend, a brother, to whom he could trust entirely, and from whom he would have no secrets.

In a few minutes they reached the spot which the Canadian had noticed on his arrival; this spot, clearly indicated by the two oaks which had fallen in a cross, formed a species of small sandy promontory, favourable to the establishment of a night bivouac; for thence not only could the river be surveyed a long distance up and down, but it was also easy to watch both banks, and prevent a surprise.

"We will pass the night here," Tranquil said; "let us carry up the canoe, so as to shelter our fire."

Quoniam seized the light skiff, raised it, and placing it on his muscular shoulders, carried it to the spot his comrade had pointed out.

In the meanwhile, a considerable period had elapsed since the Canadian and the Negro met so miraculously. The sun, which had been low when the hunter doubled the promontory and chased the herons, was now on the point of disappearing; night was falling rapidly, and the background of the landscape was beginning to be confused in the shades of night, which grew momentarily denser.

The desert was awakening, the hoarse roar of the wild beasts was heard at intervals, mingled with the miawling of the carcajou, and the sharp snapping bark of the prairie wolves.

The hunter chose the driest wood he could find to kindle the fire, in order that there might be no smoke, and the flame might light up the vicinity, so as to reveal at once the approach of the dangerous neighbours whose cries they could hear, and whom thirst would not fail soon to bring toward them.

The roasted birds and a few handfuls of pemmican composed the rangers' supper; a very sober meal, only washed down with water from the river, but which they ate with good appetite, like men who knew how to appreciate the value of any food Providence places at their disposal.

When the last mouthful was swallowed, the Canadian paternally shared his stock of tobacco with his new comrade, and lit his Indian pipe, in which he was scrupulously imitated by Quoniam.

"Now," said Tranquil, "it is as well you should know that an old friend of mine gave me the meeting at this spot about three months ago; he will arrive at daybreak to-morrow. He is an Indian Chief, and, although still very young, enjoys a great reputation in his tribe. I love him as a brother, and we were, I may say, brought up together. I shall be glad to see you gain his favour, for he is a wise and experienced man, for whom desert life possesses no secrets. The friendship of an Indian Chief is a precious thing to a wood-ranger; remember that. However, I feel certain you will be good friends at once."

"I will do all that is required for that. It is sufficient that the Chief is your friend, for me to desire that he should become mine. Up to the present, though I have wandered about the woods a long time as a runaway slave, I have never seen an independent Indian; hence it is possible that I may commit some awkwardness without my knowledge. But be assured that it will not happen through any fault of mine."

"I am convinced of it, so be easy on that head. I will warn the Chief, who, I fancy, will be as surprised as yourself, for I expect you will be the first person of your colour he has ever met. But night has now quite set in; you must be fatigued by the obstinate pursuit you experienced the whole day, and the powerful emotion you endured: sleep, while I watch for both, especially as I expect we shall make a long march to-morrow, and you must be prepared for it."

The Negro understood the correctness of his friend's remarks, the more so as he was literally exhausted with fatigue; he had been hunted so closely by his ex-master's blood-hounds, that for four days he had not closed his eyes. Hence, laying aside any false shame, he stretched out his feet to the fire, and slept almost immediately.

Tranquil remained seated on the canoe with his rifle between his legs, to be prepared for the slightest alarm, and plunged into deep thought, while attentively watching the neighbourhood, and pricking his ear at the slightest noise.

CHAPTER IV
THE MANADA

The night was splendid, the dark blue sky was studded with millions of stars which shed a gentle and mysterious light.

The silence of the desert was traversed by thousands of melodious and animated whispers; gleams, flashing through the shadows, ran over the grass like will-o'-the-wisps. On the opposite bank of the river the old moss-clad oaks stood out like phantoms, and waved in the breeze their long branches covered with lichens and lianas; vague sounds ran through the air, nameless cries emerged from the forest lairs, the gentle sighing of the wind in the foliage was heard, and the murmur of the water on the pebbles, and last that inexplicable and unexplained sound of buzzing life which comes from God, and which the majestic solitude of the American savannahs renders more imposing.

The hunter yielded involuntarily to all the puissant influences of the primitive nature that surrounded him. He felt strengthened and cheered by it; his being was identified with the sublime scene he surveyed; a gentle and pensive melancholy fell upon him; so far from men and their stunted civilization, he felt himself nearer to God, and his simple faith was heightened by the admiration aroused in him by these secrets of nature, which were partly unveiled in his presence.

The soul is expanded, thought enlarged, by contact with this nomadic life, in which each minute that passes produces new and unexpected incidents; where at each step man sees the finger of God imprinted in an indelible manner on the abrupt and grand scenery that surrounds him.

Hence this existence of danger and privation possesses, for those who have once essayed it, a nameless charm and intoxication, incomprehensible joys, which cause it ever to be regretted; for it is only in the desert man feels that he lives, takes the measure of his strength, and the secret of his power is revealed to him.

The hours passed thus rapidly with the hunter, though slumber did not once close his eyelids. Already the cold morning breeze was curling the tops of the trees, and rippling the surface of the stream, whose silvery waters reflected the shadows of its irregular banks; on the horizon broad pink stripes revealed the speedy dawn of day. The owl, hidden beneath the foliage, had twice saluted the return of light, with its melancholy toowhit—it was about three o'clock in the morning.

Tranquil left the rustic seat on which he had hitherto remained, shook off the stiffening feeling which had seized on him, and walked a few paces up and down the sand to restore the circulation in his limbs.

When a man, we will not say awakes—for the worthy Canadian had not closed his eyes once during the whole of this long watch—but shakes off the torpor into which the silence, darkness, and, above all, the piercing cold of night have plunged him, he requires a few minutes to regain possession of his faculties, and restore perfect lucidity of mind. This was what happened to the hunter; still, long habituated as he had been to desert life, the time was shorter to him than to another, and he was soon as acute and watchful as he had been on the previous evening; he therefore prepared to arouse his comrade, who was still enjoying that good and refreshing sleep which is only shared here below by children and men whose conscience is void of any evil thought—when he suddenly stopped, and began listening anxiously.

From the remote depths of the forest, which formed a thick curtain behind his camping-place, the Canadian had heard an inexplicable rumour rise, which increased with every moment, and soon assumed the proportions of hoarsely-rolling thunder.

This noise approached nearer; it seemed like sharp and hurried stamping of hoofs, rustling of trees and branches, hoarse bellowing, which had nothing human about it; in short, it was a frightful, inexplicable sound, momentarily growing louder and louder, and yet more confused.

Quoniam, startled by the strange noise, was standing, rifle in hand, with his eye fixed on the hunter, ready to act at the first sign, though unable to account for what was occurring, a prey to that instinctive terror which assails the bravest man when he feels himself menaced by a terrible and unknown danger.

Several minutes passed thus.

"What is to be done?" Tranquil murmured, hesitatingly, as he tried in vain to explore the depths of the forest, and account for what was occurring.

All at once a shrill whistle was audible a short distance off.

"Ah," Tranquil exclaimed, with a start of joy as he threw up his head, "now I shall know what I have to depend on."

And, placing his fingers in his mouth, he imitated the cry of the heron; at the same moment a man bounded from the forest, and with two tiger-like leaps was by the hunter's side.

"Wah!" he exclaimed, "What is my brother doing here?"

It was Black-deer, the Indian Chief.

"I am awaiting you, Chief," the Canadian answered.

The Redskin was a man of twenty-six to twenty-seven years of age, of middle height, but admirably proportioned. He wore the great war-garb of his nation, and was painted and armed as if on the war-trail; his face was handsome, his features intelligent, and his whole countenance indicated bravery and kindness.

At this moment he seemed suffering from an agitation, the more extraordinary because the Redskins make it a point of honour never to appear affected by any event, however terrible in its nature; his eyes flashed fire, his words were quick and harsh, and his voice had a metallic accent.

"Quick," he said, "we have lost too much time already."

"What is the matter?" Tranquil asked.

"The buffaloes!" said the Chief.

"Oh! oh!" Tranquil exclaimed, in alarm.

He understood all; the noise he had heard for some time past was occasioned by a *manada* of buffaloes, coming from the east, and probably proceeding to the higher western prairies.

What the hunter so quickly comprehended requires to be briefly explained to the reader, in order that he may understand to what a terrible danger our characters were suddenly exposed.

Manada is the name given in the old Spanish possessions to an assemblage of several thousand wild animals. Buffaloes, in their periodical migrations during the pairing season, collect at times in manadas of fifteen and twenty thousand animals, forming a compact herd; and travelling together, they go straight onwards, closely packed together, leaping over everything, and overthrowing every obstacle that opposes their passage. Woe to the rash man who would attempt to check or change the direction of their mad course, for he would be trampled like a wisp of straw beneath the feet of these stupid animals, which would pass over him without even noticing him.

The position of the three hunters was consequently extremely critical, for hazard had placed them exactly in front of a manada, which was coming towards them at lightning speed.

Flight was impossible, and could not be thought of, while resistance was more impossible still.

The noise approached with fearful rapidity; already the savage bellowing of the buffaloes could be distinctly heard, mingled with the barking of the prairie wolves; and the shrill miauls of the jaguars which dashed along on the flanks of the manada, chasing the laggards or those that imprudently turned to the right or left.

Within a quarter of an hour all would be over; the hideous avalanche already appeared, sweeping away all in its passage with that irresistible brute force which nothing can overcome.

We repeat it, the position was critical.

Black-deer was proceeding to the meeting place; he had himself indicated to the Canadian hunter, and was not more than three or four leagues from the spot where he expected to find him, when his practised ear caught the sound of the mad chase of the buffaloes. Five minutes had sufficed for him to recognize the imminence of the danger his friend incurred; with that rapidity of decision which characterizes Redskins in extreme cases, he had resolved to warn his friend, and to save or perish with him. He had then rushed forward, leaping with headlong speed over the space that separated him from the place of meeting, having only one thought, that of distancing the manada, so that the hunter might escape. Unhappily, however quickly he went—and the Indians are remarkable for their fabulous agility—he had not been able to arrive soon enough to save his friend.

"When the Chief, after warning the hunter, recognized the futility of his efforts, a sudden change took place in him. His features reassumed their old stoicism; a sad smile played round his mocking lips, and he sank to the ground, muttering, in a hollow voice—

"The Wacondah would not permit it."

But Tranquil did not accept the position with the same resignation and fatalism, for he belonged to that race of energetic men whose powerful character causes them to struggle to their dying breath.

When he saw that the Redskin, with the fatalism peculiar to his race, gave up the contest for life, he resolved to make a supreme effort, and attempt impossibilities.

About twenty yards in front of the spot where the hunter had established his bivouac, were several trees lying on the ground, dead, and, as it were, piled on each other; then, behind this species of breastwork a clump of five or six oaks grew, isolated from all the rest, and formed a sort of oasis in the midst of the sand on the river bank.

"Quick!" the hunter shouted. "Quoniam, pick up as much dead wood as you can find, and come here. Chief, do the same."

The two men obeyed without comprehending, but reassured by their comrade's coolness.

In a few minutes a considerable pile of dead wood was piled over the fallen oaks.

"Good!" the hunter exclaimed; "By Heaven! All is not lost yet—take courage!"

Then, carrying to this improvised bonfire the remains of the fire he had lit at his bivouac, to defeat the night cold, he enlarged the flames with resinous matters, and in less than five minutes a large column rose whirling to the clouds, and soon formed a dense curtain more than ten yards in width.

"Back! back!" the hunter then shouted,—"follow me."

Black-deer and Quoniam dashed after him.

The Canadian did not go far; on reaching the clump of trees we have alluded to, he clambered up the largest with unparalleled skill and agility, and soon he and his comrades found themselves perched a height of fifty feet in the air, comfortably lodged on strong branches, and completely concealed by the foliage.

"There," the Canadian said, with the utmost coolness, "this is our last resource; so soon as the column appears, fire at the leaders; if the flash startles the buffaloes, we are saved; if not, we shall only have death to await. But, at any rate, we shall have done all that was humanly possible to save our lives."

The fire kindled by the hunter had assumed gigantic proportions; it had extended from tree to tree, lighting up the grass and shrubs, and though too remote from the forest to kindle it, it soon formed a curtain of flames nearly a quarter of a mile in length, whose reddish gleam tinged the sky for a long distance, and gave the landscape a character of striking and savage grandeur.

From the spots where the hunters had sought shelter they commanded this ocean of flame, which could not reach them, and completely hovered over its furnace.

All at once a terrible crash was heard, and the vanguard of the manada appeared on the skirt of the forest.

"Look out!" the hunter shouted, as he shouldered his rifle.

The buffaloes, startled by the sight of this wall of flame that rose suddenly before them, dazzled by the glare, and at the same time burned by its extreme heat, hesitated for an instant, as if consulting, but then rushed forward with blind fury, and uttering snorts of fury.

Three shots were fired.

The three leading buffaloes fell and rolled in the agonies of death.

"We are lost!" Tranquil said, coldly.

The buffaloes still advanced.

But soon the heat became insupportable; the smoke, driven in the direction of the manada by the wind, blinded the animals; then a reaction was effected; there was a delay, soon followed by a recoil.

The hunters, with panting breasts, followed anxiously the strange interludes of this terrible scene. A question of life or death for them was being decided at this moment, and their existence only hung on a thread.

In the meanwhile the mass still pushed onward. The animals that led the manada could not resist the pressure of those that followed them; they were thrown down and trampled underfoot by the rear, but the latter, assailed in their turn by the heat, also tried to turn back. At this moment some of the buffaloes diverged to the right and left; this was enough, the others followed them: two currents were established on either side the fire, and the manada cut in two, overflowed like a torrent that has burst its dykes, rejoining on the bank, and crossing the stream in close column.

Terrible was the spectacle presented by this manada flying in horror, pursued by wild beasts, and enclosing, amid its ranks, the fire kindled by the hunter, and which seemed like a gloomy lighthouse intended to indicate the track.

They soon plunged into the stream, which they crossed in a straight line, and their long serried columns glided up the other bank, where the head of the manada speedily disappeared.

The hunters were saved by the coolness and presence of mind of the Canadian; still, for nearly two hours longer, they remained Concealed among the branches that sheltered them.

The buffaloes continued to pass on their right and left. The fire had gone out through lack of nourishment, but the direction had been given, and, on reaching the fire, which was now but a pile of ashes, the column separated of its own accord into two parts.

At length, the rearguard made its appearance, harassed by the jaguars that leaped on their back and flank, and then all was over. The desert, whose silence had been temporarily disturbed, fell back into its usual calmness, and merely a wide track made through the heart of the forest, and covered with fallen trees, testified to the furious passage of this disorderly herd.

The hunters breathed again; now they could without danger leave their airy fortress, and go back again to earth.

CHAPTER V
BLACK-DEER

So soon as the three rangers descended, they collected the scattered logs, in order to rekindle the fire over which they would cook their breakfast.

As there was no lack of provisions, they had no occasion to draw on their own private resources; several buffaloes that lay lifeless on the ground offered them the most succulent meal known in the desert.

While Tranquil was engaged in getting a buffalo hump ready, the Black and Redskin examined each other with a curiosity revealed in exclamations of surprise from both sides.

The Negro laughed like a maniac on remarking the strange appearance of the Indian warrior, whose face was painted of four different colours, and who wore a costume so strange in the eyes of Quoniam; for that worthy, as he himself said, had never before come in contact with Indians.

The other manifested his astonishment in a different way: after standing for a long time motionless, and watching the Negro, he walked up to him, and not uttering a word, seized Quoniam's arm, and began rubbing it with all his strength with the skirt of his buffalo robe.

The Negro, who at the outset readily indulged the Indian's whims, soon began to grow impatient; he tried at first to liberate himself, but was unable to succeed, for the Chief held him firmly, and conscientiously went on with his singular operation. In the meanwhile, the Negro, whom this continued rubbing was beginning not merely to annoy, but cause terrible suffering, began uttering frequent yells, while making the most tremendous efforts to escape from his pitiless torturer.

Tranquil's attention was aroused by Quoniam's cries; he threw up his head smartly, and ran up at full speed to deliver the Negro, who was rolling his eyes in terror, leaping from one side to the other, and yelling like a condemned man.

"Why does my brother torture that man so?" the Canadian asked as he interposed.

"I?" the Chief asked in surprise, "I am not torturing him; his disguise is not necessary, so I am removing it."

"What! My disguise?" Quoniam shouted.

Tranquil made him a sign to be silent.

"This man is not disguised," he continued.

"Why, then, has he painted all his body in this way?" the Chief asked obstinately, "Warriors only paint their face."

The hunter could not repress a burst of laughter.

"My brother is mistaken," he said, so soon as he recovered his seriousness; "this man belongs to a separate race; the Wacondah has given him a black skin, in the same way as he made my brother's red, and mine white; all the brothers of this man are of his colour; the great Spirit has willed it so, in order that they may not be confused with the Redskin nations and the Palefaces; if my brother look at his buffalo robe, he will see that not the least bit of black has come off on it." "Wah!" the Indian said, letting his head sink, like a man placed before an insoluble problem; "the Wacondah can do everything!"

And he mechanically obeyed the hunter by taking a peep at the tail of his robe, which he had not yet thought of letting go.

"Now," Tranquil went on, "be kind enough to regard this man as a friend, and do for him what you would do, if wanted, for me, and I shall feel under the greatest obligations to you."

The Chief bowed gracefully, and held out his hand to the Negro.

"The words of my brother the hunter warble in my ears with the sweetness of the song of the *centzontle*," he said. "Black-deer is a Sachem of his nation, his tongue is not forked, and the words his chest breathes are clear, for they come from his heart; Black-face will have his place at the Council fire of the Pawnees, for from this moment he is the friend of a Chief."

Quoniam bowed to the Indian, and warmly returned the pressure of his hand.

"I am only a poor black," he said, "but my heart is pure, and the blood is as red in my veins as if I were Indian or white; both of you have a right to ask my life of me, and I will give it you joyfully."

After this mutual exchange of assurances of friendship, the three men sat down on the ground, and began their breakfast.

Owing to the excitement of the morning, the three adventurers had a ferocious appetite; they did honour to the buffalo hump, which disappeared almost entirely before their repeated attacks, and which they washed down with a few horns of water mixed with rum, of which liquor Tranquil had a small stock in a gourd, hanging from his waist belt.

When the meal was ended, pipes were lighted, and each began smoking, silently, with the gravity peculiar to men who live in the woods.

When the Chief's pipe was ended, he shook out the ashes on his left thumbnail, passed the stem through his belt, and turned to Tranquil,

"Will my brothers hold a council?" he asked.

"Yes," the Canadian answered: "when I left you on the Upper Missouri, at the end of the Moon of the burned fruit (July), you gave me the meeting at the creek of the dead oaks of the Elk River, on the tenth day of the Moon of the falling leaves (September), two hours before sunrise: both of us were punctual, and I am now waiting till it please you to explain to me, Chief, why you gave me this meeting."

"My brother is correct, Black-deer will speak."

After uttering these words, the Indian's face seemed to grow dark, and he fell into a profound reverie, which his comrades respected by patiently waiting till he spoke again.

At length, after about a quarter of an hour, the Indian Chief passed his hand over his brow several times, raised his head, took a searching glance around, and made up his mind to speak, though in a low and restrained voice, as if, even on the desert, he feared lest his words might fall on hostile ears.

"My brother the hunter has known me since child-hood," he said, "for he was brought up by the Sachems of my nation: hence I will say nothing of myself. The great Paleface hunter has an Indian heart in his breast; Black-deer will speak to him as a brother to a brother. Three moons ago, the Chief was following with his friend the elks and the deer on the prairies of the Missouri, when a Pawnee warrior arrived at full speed, took the Chief aside, and spoke with him privately for long hours; does my brother remember this?"

"Perfectly, Chief; I remember that after the conversation Blue Fox, for that was the name of the Chief, set off as rapidly as he had come, and my brother, who till then had been gay and cheerful, became suddenly sad. In spite of the questions I addressed to my brother he could not tell me the cause of this sudden grief, and on the morrow, at sunrise, he left me, giving me the meeting here for this day."

"Yes," the Indian said, "that is exact. Things happened so; but what I could not then tell, I will now impart to my brother."

"My ears are open," the hunter replied, with a bow. "I fear that, unfortunately, my brother has only bad news to tell me."

"My brother shall judge," he said. "This is what Blue Fox came to tell me. One day a Paleface of the Long Knives of the West arrived on the banks of Elk River, where stood the village of the Snake Pawnees, followed by some thirty warriors of the Palefaces, several women, and large medicine lodges, drawn by buffaloes without humps or manes. This Paleface halted two arrow shots' lengths from the village of my nation, on the opposite bank, lit his fires, and camped. My father, as my brother knows, was the first sachem of the tribe. He mounted his horse and, followed by several warriors, crossed the river and presented himself to the stranger, in order to bid him welcome on the hunting grounds of our nation, and offer him the refreshments he might have need of.

"This Paleface was a man of lofty stature, with harsh and marked features. The snow of several winters had whitened his scalp. He began laughing at my father's words, and replied to him—'Are you the chief of the Redskins of this village?' 'Yes,' said my father. Then the Paleface took from his clothes a great necklace, on which strange figures were drawn, and showing it to my father, said, 'Your Pale Grandfather of the United States has given me the property in all the land stretching from Antelope's Fall to Buffalo Lake. This,' he added, as he struck the necklace with the back of his hand, 'proves my title.'

"My father and the warriors who accompanied him burst into a laugh.

"'Our Pale Grandfather,' he answered, 'cannot give what does not belong to him. The land of which you speak has been the hunting ground of my nation ever since the great tortoise came out of the sea to support the world on its shell.'

"'I do not understand what you say to me,' the Paleface continued. 'I only know that this land has been given to me; and that, if you do not consent to withdraw and leave me to the full enjoyment of it, I possess the means to compel you.'"

"Yes," Tranquil interrupted, "such is the system of those men—murder and rapine."

"My father retired," the Indian continued, "under the blow of this threat. The warriors immediately took up arms, the women were hidden in a cave, and the tribe prepared for resistance. The next morning, at daybreak, the Palefaces crossed the river and attacked the village. The fight was long and obstinate. It lasted the whole period contained between two suns. But what could poor Indians do against Palefaces armed with rifles? They were conquered and forced to take to flight. Two hours later, their village was reduced to ashes, and the bones of their ancestors cast to the four winds. My father was killed in the battle."

"Oh!" the Canadian exclaimed, sadly.

"That is not all," the Chief went on. "The Palefaces discovered the cave where the women of my tribe were sheltered; and nearly all—for about a dozen contrived to escape with their papooses—were coldly massacred, with all the refinements of the most horrible barbarity."

After uttering these words, the Chief hid his head on his buffalo robe, and his comrades heard the sobs he tried in vain to stifle.

"Such," he went on a moment later, "was the news Blue Fox communicated to me. 'My father died in his arms, leaving his vengeance as my inheritance. My brothers, pursued like wild beasts by their ferocious enemies, and compelled to hide themselves in the most impenetrable forests, had elected me as Chief. I accepted, making the warriors of my nation swear to avenge themselves on the Palefaces, who had seized our village and massacred our brothers. Since our parting, I have not lost a moment in collecting all the means of revenge. To-day all is ready. The Palefaces have gone to sleep in a deceitful security, and their awakening shall be terrible. Will my brother follow me?'"

"Yes, by Heaven! I will follow you, Chief, and help you with all my ability," Tranquil answered, resolutely, "for your cause is just; but on one condition."

"My brother can speak."

"The law of the desert says, 'Eye for eye and tooth for tooth,' it is true; but you can avenge yourself without dishonouring your victory by useless barbarity. Do not follow the example given you, but be humane, Chief; and the Great Spirit will smile on your efforts and be favourable to you."

"Black-deer is not cruel," the Chief answered. "He leaves that to the Palefaces. He only wishes to be just."

"What you say is noble, Chief; and I am happy to hear you speak thus; but are your measures well taken? Is your force large enough to ensure success? You know that the Palefaces are numerous, and never allow one aggressor to pass unpunished. Whatever may happen, you have to expect terrible reprisals."

The Indian smiled disdainfully. "The Long Knives of the West are cowardly dogs and rabbits. The squaws of the Pawnees will make them petticoats," he answered. "Black-deer will go with his tribe to settle on the great prairies of the Comanches, who will receive them as brothers, and the Palefaces of the West will not know where to find them."

"That is a good idea, Chief; but, since you have been driven from your village, have you not kept spies round the Americans, in order to be informed of their actions? that was important for the success of your further plans."

Black-deer smiled, but made no other answer, whence the Canadian concluded that the Redskin had, with the sagacity and prudence which characterize his race, taken all the necessary precautions to insure the success of the blow he was about to deal at the new clearing.

Tranquil, owing to his semi-Indian education, and the hereditary hatred which, as a true Canadian, he bore to the Anglo-Saxon race, was perfectly well inclined to help the Pawnee Chief in taking an exemplary vengeance on the Americans for the insults he had received at their hands; but with that correctness of judgment which formed the basis of his character, he did not wish to let the Indians indulge in those atrocious cruelties, to which they only too often yield in the first intoxication of victory. Hence the determination he formed had a double object—in the first place, to insure as far as he could the success of his friends, and, secondly, to employ all the influence he possessed over them, to restrain them after the battle, and prevent them satiating their vengeance on the conquered, and, above all, on the women and children.

As we have seen, he did not attempt to conceal his object from Black-deer, and laid down as the first condition of his co-operation, which the Indians would be delighted to receive, that no unnecessary cruelty should be committed.

Quoniam, for his part, did not make any stipulation; a natural enemy of the Whites, and specially of the North Americans, he eagerly seized the occasion of dealing them as much injury as possible, and avenging himself for the ill treatment he had experienced, without taking the trouble to reflect that the people he was about to fight were innocent in the matter of his wrong; these individuals were North Americans, and that reason was more than sufficient to justify, in the sight of the vindictive Negro, the conduct he proposed to carry out when the moment arrived.

After a few minutes the Canadian spoke again.

"Where are your warriors?" he asked the Chief.

"I left them three suns' march from the spot where we now are; if my brother has nothing to keep him longer here, we will set out immediately, in order to join them as soon as possible, for my return is impatiently expected by the warriors."

"Let us go," the Canadian said; "the day is not yet far advanced, and it is needless for us to waste our time in chattering like curious old women."

The three men rose, drew on their belts, walked hastily along the path formed by the manada through the forest, and soon disappeared under its covert.

CHAPTER VI
THE CLAIM

We will now leave our three travellers for a while, and employing our privilege of narrator, transfer the scene of our story a few hundred miles away, to a rich and verdant valley of the Upper Missouri, that majestic river, with its bright and limpid waters, on the banks of which now stand so many flourishing towns and villages, and which magnificent steamboats furrow in every direction, but which, at the period when our story opens, was almost unknown, and only reflected in the mirror of its waters the lofty and thick frondage of the gloomy and mysterious virgin forests that covered its banks.

At the extremity of a fork, formed by two rather large affluents of the Missouri, stretches out a vast valley, bordered on one side by abrupt mountains, and on the other by a long line of wooded hills.

This valley, almost entirely covered with thick forests, full of game of every description, was a favourite gathering-place of the Pawnee Indians, a numerous tribe of whom, the Snakes, had established their abode in the angle of the fork, in order to be nearer their hunting-grounds. The Indian village was rather large, for it counted nearly three hundred and fifty fires, which is enormous for Redskins, who usually do not like to collect in any considerable number, through fear of suffering from famine. But the position of the village was so well chosen, that in this instance the Indians had gone out of their usual course; in fact, on one side the forest supplied them with more game than they could consume; on the other, the river abounded with deliciously tasted fish of every description; while the surrounding prairies were covered throughout the year with a tall close grass, that supplied excellent pasturage for their horses.

For several centuries the Snake Pawnees had been settled in this happy valley, which, owing to its sheltered position on all sides, enjoyed a soft climate, exempt from those great atmospheric perturbations which so frequently disturb the high American latitudes. The Indians lived there quiet and unknown, occupying themselves with hunting and fishing, and sending annually small bodies of their young men to follow the war-trail, under the most renowned chiefs of the nation.

All at once this peaceful existence was hopelessly disturbed; murder and arson spread like a sinister winding-sheet over the valley; the village was utterly destroyed, and the inhabitants were pitilessly massacred.

The North Americans had at length gained knowledge of this unknown Eden, and, in their usual way announced their presence on this remote nook of earth, and their taking possession of it by theft, rapine, and assassination.

We will not repeat here the story Black-deer told the Canadian, but confine ourselves to the assertion that it was in every point true, and that the Chief, in telling it, far from rendering it more gloomy by emphatic exaggeration, had, on the contrary, toned it down with uncommon justice and impartiality.

We will enter this valley three months after the arrival of the Americans which proved so fatal to the Redskins, and describe, in a few words, the way in which they formerly had established themselves on the territory from which they so cruelly expelled the legitimate owners.

Hardly had they become uncontested owners of the soil, than they commenced what is called a clearing.

The government of the United States had, about forty years ago, and probably still has, a habit of requiting the services of old officers, by making them concessions of land on those frontiers of the Republic most threatened by the Indians. This custom had the double advantage of gradually extending the limits of the American territory by driving back the Indians into the desert, and of not abandoning in their old days soldiers who during the greater portion of their life had shed their blood nobly for their country.

Captain James Watt was the son of an officer who distinguished himself in the war of Independence. Colonel Lionel Watt, aide-de-camp to Washington, had fought by the side of that celebrated founder of the Republic in all the battles against the English. Seriously wounded at the siege of Boston, he had been, to his great regret, compelled to retire into private life; but, faithful to his principles, so soon as his son James reached his twentieth year, he made him take his place under the flag.

At the period when we bring him on the scene, James Watt was a man of about five-and-forty, although he appeared at least ten years older, owing to the incessant fatigue of the exacting profession in which his youth had been passed.

He was a man of five feet eight, powerfully built, with broad shoulders, dry, muscular, and endowed with an iron health; his face, whose lines were extremely rigid, was imprinted with that expression of energetic will, blended with carelessness, which is peculiar to those men whose existence has been only one continual succession of dangers surmounted. His short grey hair, his bronzed complexion, black and piercing eyes, his well-chiselled mouth, gave his face an expression of inflexible severity, which was not deficient in grandeur.

Captain Watt, who had been married for two years past to a charming young lady he adored, was father of two children, a son and daughter.

His wife, Fanny by name, was a distant relation of his. She was a brunette, with exquisite blue eyes, and was most gentle and modest. Although much younger than her husband, for she was not yet two-and-twenty, Fanny felt for him the deepest and sincerest affection.

When the old soldier found himself a father, and began to experience the intimate joys of a family life, a revolution was effected in him; he suddenly took a disgust to his profession, and only desired the tranquil joys of home.

James Watt was one of those men with whom it is only one step from the conception to the execution of a plan. Hence, no sooner had the idea of retiring from the service occurred to him than he at once carried it out, resisting all the objections and remonstrances his friends raised.

Still, although the Captain was inclined to retire into private life, he did not mean to put off military harness and assume a citizen's coat. The monotonous life of Union towns had nothing very seductive for an old soldier, for whom excitement and movement had been the normal condition almost from his birth.

Consequently, after ripe reflection, he stopped half way, which, in his opinion, would remedy the excessive simplicity and peace a citizen life might have for him.

This was to be effected by asking for a claim on the Indian border, clearing it with the help of his servants, and living there happy and busy, like a mediæval lord among his vassals.

This idea pleased the Captain the more, because he fancied that in this way he should still be serving his country, as he would lay the foundation of future prosperity, and develop the first traces of civilization in a district still given up to all the horrors of barbarity.

The Captain had long been engaged with his company in defending the frontier of the Union against the incessant depredations of the Redskins, and preventing their incursions; hence he had a knowledge—superficial it is true, but sufficient—of Indian manners, and the means he must employ not to be disturbed by these restless neighbours.

During the course of the numerous expeditions which the service had compelled him to make, the Captain had visited many fertile valleys, and many territories, the appearance of which had pleased him; but there was one above all, the memory of which had been obstinately engraved on his mind—a delicious valley he had seen one day as in a dream, after a hunting expedition, made in company of a wood-ranger—an excursion which lasted three weeks, and had insensibly taken him further into the desert than ever civilized man had gone before.

Though he had not seen this valley again for more than twenty years, he remembered it as if he had seen it but yesterday—recalling it, as it were, in its minutest details. And this obstinacy of his memory in constantly bringing before him this nook of earth, had ended by affecting the Captain's imagination to such a degree, that when he resolved to leave the service and ask for a claim, it was to this place and no other that he was determined to go.

James Watt had numerous friends in the offices of the Presidency; besides, the services of his father and himself spoke loudly in his favour: hence he experienced no difficulty in obtaining the claim he requested.

Several plans were shewn him, drawn up by order of government, and he was invited to select the territory that suited him best.

But the Captain had chosen the one he wanted long before; he rejected the plans shewn him, produced from his pocket a wide slip of tanned elk hide, unrolled it, and shewed it to the Commissioner of Claims, telling him he wanted this, and no other.

The Commissioner was a friend of the Captain, and could not refrain from a start of terror on hearing his request.

This claim was situated in the heart of the Indian territory, more than four hundred miles from the American border. The Captain wished to commit an act of madness, of suicide; it would be impossible for him to hold his ground among the warlike tribes that would surround him on all sides; a month would not elapse ere he would be piteously massacred, as must be his family and those servants who were mad enough to follow him.

To all these objections, which his friend piled up one atop of the other, in order to make him change his opinion, the Captain only replied by a shake of the head, accompanied by a smile, which proved that his mind was irrevocably made up.

At length, the Commissioner being driven into his last intrenchments, told him point-blank that it was impossible to grant him this claim, as the territory belonged to the Indians, and, moreover, a tribe had built its village there since time immemorial.

The Commissioner had kept this argument to the last, feeling convinced that the Captain could find no answer, and would be compelled to change, or, at least, modify his plans.

He was mistaken; the worthy Commissioner was not so well acquainted with his friend's character as he might fancy.

The latter, not at all affected by the triumphant gesture with which the Commissioner concluded his speech, coolly drew from another pocket a second slip of tanned deer-hide, which he handed his friend, without saying a word.

The latter took it with an inquiring glance, but the Captain merely nodded to him to look at it.

The Commissioner unrolled it with marked hesitation; from the old soldier's behaviour he suspected that this document contained a peremptory answer.

In fact, he had scarce looked at it, ere he threw it on the table with a violent movement of ill humour.

This slip of deer-skin contained the sale of the valley and the surrounding territory made by Itsichaichè or Monkey-face, one of the principal sachems of the Snake Pawnees, in his name and that of the other chiefs of the nation, in exchange for fifty muskets, fourteen dozen scalping-knives, sixty pounds of gunpowder, sixty pounds of bullets, two barrels of whisky, and twenty-three complete militia uniforms.

Each of the chiefs had placed his hieroglyphic at the foot of the deed, beneath that of Monkey-face.

We will say at once that this deed was false, and the Captain in the affair was the perfect dupe of Monkey-face.

This chief, who had been expelled from the tribe of Snake Pawnees for various causes, as we shall reveal at the proper moment, had forged the deed, first to rob the Captain, and next to avenge himself on his countrymen; for he knew perfectly well that if the Captain received authority from his government he would seize the valley, whatever the consequences of this spoliation might be. The only condition the Captain made was, that the Redskin should act as his guide, which he consented to do without any hesitation.

When the deed of sale was laid before him, the Commissioner was forced to confess himself beaten, and *nolens volens* grant the authority so obstinately solicited by the Captain.

When all the documents were duly registered, signed, and sealed, the Captain began his preparations for departure without further delay.

Mrs. Watts loved her husband too well to offer any objections to the execution of his plans. Brought up herself on a clearing at no great distance from the Indian border, she had become familiarized with the savages, whom the habit of constantly seeing caused her no longer to fear them; besides, she cared little where she lived, so long as she had her husband by her side.

Quite calm as regarded his wife, the Captain therefore set to work with all that feverish activity which distinguished him.

America is a land of prodigies; it is, perhaps, the only country in the world where it is possible to find between to-day and the morrow the men and things indispensable for carrying out the maddest and most eccentric projects.

The Captain did not deceive himself in the slightest as to the probable consequences of the resolution he had formed; hence he wished, as far as was possible, to guard against any eventualities, and ensure the security of the persons who would accompany him to his claim, the first among these being his wife and children.

His selection, however, did not take him long: among his old comrades many wished for nothing better than to follow him, at the head of them being an old sergeant of the name of Walter Bothrel, who had served under him for more than fifteen years, and who, at the first news of his Chief's retirement, went to him and said that as his Captain was leaving the service, he did not care to remain in it, and the only favour he asked was leave to accompany him wherever he went.

Bothrel's offer was gladly accepted by the Captain, for he knew the value of the sergeant, who was a sort of bull-dog for fidelity, a man of tried courage, and one on whom he could entirely count.

To the sergeant Captain Watt entrusted the duty of enrolling the detachment of hunters he intended to take with him, in order to defend the new colony, if the Redskins took it into their head to attack it.

Bothrel carried out his instructions with the intelligent consciousness he displayed in all matters, and he soon found in the Captain's own company thirty resolute and devoted men, only too glad to follow the fortunes of their ex-Chief, and attach themselves to him.

On his side, the Captain had engaged some fifteen workmen of every description, blacksmiths, carpenters, &c., who signed an undertaking to serve him five years, after which they would become tenants at a small rental of farms the Captain would give them, and which would become their own property on the expiration of a further term of years.

All the preparations being at length terminated, the colonists, amounting to fifty men, and about a dozen females, at length set out for the claim in the middle of May, taking with them a long pile of waggons loaded with stores of every description, and a large herd of cattle, intended to provision the colony, as well as for breeding purposes.

Monkey-face acted as guide, as had been arranged. To do the Indian the justice due to him, we will say that he conscientiously performed the duty he undertook; and that during a journey of nearly three months across a desert infested by wild beasts and traversed in every direction by Indian hordes, he managed to save those he led from the majority of the dangers that menaced them at each step.

CHAPTER VII
MONKEY-FACE

We have seen in what summary manner the Captain seized on the territory conceded to him. We will now explain how he established himself there, and the precautions he took not to be disturbed by the Indians he had so brutally dispossessed, and who, he judged from his knowledge of their vindictive character, would probably not yet consider themselves beaten, but might begin at any moment the attempt to take a sanguinary and terrible vengeance for the insults put upon them.

The fight with the Indians had been rude and obstinate, but, thanks to Monkey-face, who revealed to the Captain the weakest points of the village, and especially the superiority of the American fire-arms, the Indians were at length compelled to take to flight, and abandon all they possessed to the conquerors.

It was a wretched booty, consisting only of animal skins, and a few vessels made of coarse clay.

The Captain, no sooner master of the place, began his work, and laid the foundation stone of the new colony; for he understood the necessity of protecting himself as quickly as possible against a *coup-de-main*.

The site of the village was completely freed from the ruins that encumbered it; the labourers then began levelling the ground, and digging a ditch six yards wide, and four deep, which was connected on one side by means of a drain with the affluent of the Missouri, on the other with the river itself; behind this ditch, and on the wall formed of the earth dug out of it, a line of stakes was planted, twelve feet high, and fastened together by iron bands, almost invisible interstices being left, through which a rifle barrel could be thrust and discharged under covert. In this entrenchment a gate was made large enough for a waggon to pass, and which communicated with the exterior by a drawbridge, which was pulled up at sunset.

These preliminary precautions taken, an extent of about four thousand square yards was thus surrounded by water, and defended by palisades on all sides, excepting on the face turned to the Missouri, for the width and depth of that river offered a sufficient guarantee of security.

It was in the free space to which we have just alluded, that the Captain began building the houses and offices for the colony.

At the outset these buildings were to be made of wood, as is usually the case in all clearings, that is to say, of trees with the bark left on them; and there was no lack of wood, for the forest was scarce a hundred yards from the colony.

The works were pushed on with such activity, that two months after the Captain's arrival at the spot all the buildings were finished, and the interior arrangements almost completed.

In the centre of the colony, on an elevation made for the purpose, a species of octagonal tower, about seventy feet in height, was erected, of which the roof was flat, and which was divided into three storeys. At the bottom were the kitchen and offices, while the upper rooms were allotted to the members of the family, that is to say, the Captain and his lady, the two nursemaids, young and hearty Kentuckians, with rosy and plump cheeks, called Betsy and Emma; Mistress Margaret, the cook, a respectable matron entering on her ninth lustre, though she only confessed to five-and-thirty, and still had some pretence to beauty, and, lastly, to Sergeant Bothrel. This tower was closed with a stout iron-lined door, and in the centre was a wicket to reconnoitre visitors.

About ten yards from the tower, and communicating with it by a subterraneous passage, were the log huts of the hunters, the workmen, the neatherds, and labourers.

After these, again came the stables and cow houses.

In addition, scattered here and there, were large barns and granaries intended to receive the produce of the colony.

But all these different buildings were arranged so as to be isolated, and so far from each other, that in the event of fire, the loss of one building need not absolutely entail that of the rest; several wells were also dug at regular distances, so as to have abundance of water, without the necessity of fetching it from the river.

In a word, we may say that the Captain, as an old experienced soldier, accustomed to all the tricks of border warfare, had taken the minutest precautions to avoid not merely an attack, but a surprise.

Three months had elapsed since the settlement of the Americans; this valley, hitherto uncultivated, and covered with forests, was now in great part ploughed up; clearings effected on a large scale had removed the forest more than a mile from the colony; all offered the image of prosperity and comfort at a spot where, so shortly before, the carelessness of the Redskins allowed nature to produce at liberty the small stock of fodder needed for their beasts.

Inside the colony, all offered the most lively and busy sight; while outside, the cattle pastured under the care of mounted and well-armed herds, and the trees fell beneath the blows of the axemen; inside, all the workshops were in full activity, long columns of smoke rose from the forges, the noise of hammers was mingled with the whirring of the saw; on the river bank, enormous piles of planks stood near others composed of fire-wood; several boats were tied up, and from time to time the shots of the hunters could be heard, who were carrying out a battue in the woods in order to stock the colony with deer-meat.

It was about four in the afternoon, and the Captain, mounted on a magnificent black horse, with four white stockings, was ambling across a freshly-cleared prairie.

A smile of quiet satisfaction played over the old soldier's stern face at the sight of the prodigious change his will and feverish activity had effected in so short a time on this unknown corner of earth, which must, however, in no remote future, acquire a great commercial importance, owing to its position; he was approaching the colony, when a man, hitherto hidden behind a pile of roots and bushes heaped up to dry, suddenly appeared at his side.

The Captain repressed a start of anger on perceiving this man, in whom he recognised Monkey-face.

We will say here a few words about this man, who is destined to play a rather important part in the course of our narrative.

Itsichaichè was a man of forty, tall, and well proportioned; he had a crafty face, lit up by two little gimlet eyes; his vulture-beaked nose, his wide mouth, with its thin and retiring lips, gave him a cunning and ugly look, which, in spite of the cautious and cat-like obsequiousness of his manner, and the calculated gentleness of his voice, inspired those whom accident brought in contact with him with an impulsive repugnance which nothing could overcome.

Contrary to the usual state of things, the habit of seeing him, instead of diminishing, and causing this unpleasant feeling to disappear, only increased it.

He had conscientiously and honestly performed his contract in leading the Americans, without any obstacle, to the spot they wished to reach; but, since that period, he had remained with them, and had, so to speak, foisted himself on the colony, when he came and went as he pleased, and no one paid any attention to his actions.

At times, without saying anything, he would disappear for several days, then suddenly return, and it was impossible to obtain any information from him as to where he had been and what he had been doing during his absence.

Still, there was one person to whom the Indian's gloomy face constantly caused a vague terror, and who had been unable to overcome the repulsion with which he inspired her, although she could give no explanation of the feeling: this person was Mrs. Watt. Maternal love produces clearsightedness: the young lady adored her children, and when at times the Redskin by chance let a careless glance fall on the innocent creatures, the poor mother shivered in all her limbs, and she hastily withdrew from the sight of the man the two beings who were all in all to her.

At times she tried to make her husband share her fears, but to all her remarks the Captain merely replied by a significant shrug of his shoulders, supposing that with time this feeling would wear off and disappear. Still, as Mrs. Watt constantly returned to the charge with the obstinacy and perseverance of a person whose ideas are positively formed and cannot change, the Captain, who had no cause or plausible reason to defend against the wife he loved and respected, a man for whom he did not profess the slightest esteem, at length promised to get rid of him. As, moreover, the Indian had been absent from the colony for several days, he determined immediately on his return to ask for an explanation of his mysterious conduct, and if the other did not reply in a plain and satisfactory manner, to tell him that he would not have him any longer about the settlement, and the sooner he took himself off the better for all parties.

Such was the state of the Captain's feelings toward Monkey-face, when accident brought him across his path at the moment he least expected him.

On seeing the Indian, the Captain checked his horse.

"Is my father visiting the valley?" the Pawnee asked.

"Yes," was the answer.

"Oh!" the Indian went on as he looked around him, "All has greatly changed since the beasts of the Long Knives of the West have been grazing peacefully on the territories of which they dispossessed the Snake Pawnees."

The Indian uttered these words in a sad and melancholy voice, which caused the Captain some mental anxiety.

"Is that a regret you are giving vent to, Chief?" he asked him. "If so, it seems to me very unsuitable from your lips, since it was you who sold me the territory I occupy."

"That is true," the Indian said with a shake of his head. "Monkey-face has no right to complain, for it was he who sold to the Palefaces of the West the ground where his fathers repose, and where he and his brothers so often hunted the elk and the jaguar."

"Hum, Chief, I find you very sad to-day; what is the matter with you? Did you, on waking this morning find yourself lying on your left side?" he said, alluding to one of the most accredited superstitions among the Indians.

"No," he continued, "the sleep of Monkey-face was exempt from evil omens, nothing arrived to alter the calmness of his mind."

"I congratulate you, Chief."

"My father will give tobacco to his son, in order that he may smoke the calumet of friendship on his return."

"Perhaps so, but first I have a question to ask of you."

"My father can speak, his son's ears are open."

"It is now a long time, Chief," the Captain continued, "since we have been established here."

"Yes, the fourth moon is beginning."

"Since our arrival, you have left us a great many times without warning us."

"Why should I do so? Air and space do not belong to the Palefaces, I suppose; the Pawnee warrior is at liberty to go where he thinks proper; he was a renowned Chief in his tribe."

"All that may be true, Chief, and I do not care about it; but what I do care about is the safety of my family and the men who accompanied me here."

"Well," the Redskin said, "in what way can Monkey-face injure that safety?'

"I will tell you, Chief; listen to me attentively, for what you have to hear is serious."

"Monkey-face is only a poor Indian," the Redskin answered, ironically; "the Great Spirit has not given him the clear and subtle mind of the Palefaces, still he will try to understand my father."

"You are not so simple as you choose to appear at this moment, Chief; I am certain you will perfectly understand me, if you only take the trouble."

"The Chief will try."

The Captain repressed a movement of impatience.

"We are not here in one of the great cities of the American Union, where the law protects the citizens and guarantees their safety; we are, on the contrary, on the Redskin territory, far from any other protection than our own; we have no help to expect from anyone, and are surrounded by vigilant enemies watching a favourable moment to attack us and massacre us if they can; it is therefore our duty to watch over our own safety with the utmost vigilance, for the slightest imprudence would gravely compromise us. Do you understand me, Chief?"

"Yes, my father has spoken well; his head is grey; his wisdom is great."

"I must therefore carefully watch," the Captain continued, "the movements of all the persons who belong nearly or remotely to the colony; and when their movements appear to me suspicious, to ask those explanations which they have no right to refuse me. Now, I am compelled to confess to you, Chief, with extreme regret, that the life you have been leading for some time past seems to me more than suspicious. It has, therefore, attracted my attention, and I expect a satisfactory answer from you."

The Redskin had stood unmoved; not a muscle of his face moved; and the Captain, who watched him closely, could not notice the slightest trace of emotion on his features. The Indian had expected the question asked him, and was prepared to answer it.

"Monkey-face led my father and his children from the great stone villages of the Long-knives of the West to the spot. Has my father had any cause to reproach the Chief?"

"None, I am bound to allow," the Captain answered, frankly; "you did your duty honestly."

"Why, then, does a skin now cover my father's heart? and why has suspicion crept into his mind about a man against whom, as he says himself, he has not the slightest reproach to bring? Is that the justice of the Palefaces?"

"Let us not drift from the question, Chief, or change it, if you please. I could not follow you through all your Indian circumlocution; I will, therefore, confine myself to saying that, unless you consent to tell me frankly the cause of your repeated absences, and give me assured proof of your innocence, I will have you turned out of the colony, and you shall never set foot again on the territory I occupy."

A gleam of hatred flashed from the Redskin's eye; but, immediately recalling it, he replied, in his softest voice—

"Monkey-face is a poor Indian; his brothers have rejected him on account of his friendship with the Palefaces. He hoped to find among the Long-knives of the west, in the absence of friendship, gratitude for service rendered. He is mistaken."

"That is not the question," the Captain continued impatiently; "will you answer Yes or No?"

The Indian drew himself in, and walked up to the speaker close enough to touch him.

"And if I refuse?" he said, as he gave him a glance of defiance and fury.

"If you refuse, scoundrel! I forbid you ever appearing again before me; and if you disobey me, I will chastise you with my dog-whip!"

The Captain had hardly uttered these insulting words ere he repented of them. He was alone, and unarmed, with a man whom he had mortally insulted; hence he tried to arrange matters.

"But Monkey-face," he went on, "is a chief; he is wise; he will answer me—for he knows that I love him."

"You lie, dog of the Palefaces!" the Indian yelled, as he ground his teeth in fury; "you hate me almost as much as I hate you!"

The Captain, in his exasperation, raised the switch he carried in his hand; but, at the same moment, the Indian, with a panther-leap, bounded on to his horse's croup, dragged the Captain out of his stirrups, and rudely hurled him to the ground.

"The Palefaces are cowardly old women," he said; "the Pawnee warriors despise them, and will send them petticoats."

After uttering these words with a sarcastic accent impossible to describe, the Indian bent over the horse's neck, let loose the rein, uttered a fierce yell, and started at full speed, not troubling himself further about the Captain, whom he left severely bruised by his fall.

James Watt was not the man to endure such treatment without trying to revenge himself; he got up as quickly as he could, and shouted, in order to get together the hunters and wood-cutters scattered over the plain.

Some of them had seen what had happened, and started at full speed to help their Captain; but before they reached him, and he could give them his orders to pursue the fugitive, the latter had disappeared in the heart of the forest, toward which he had directed his rapid course.

The hunters, however, at the head of them being Sergeant Bothrel, rushed in pursuit of the Indian, swearing they would bring him in either dead or alive.

The Captain looked after them till he saw them disappear one after the other in the forest, and then returned slowly to the colony, reflecting on what had taken place between himself and the Redskin, and his heart contracted by a gloomy presentiment.

Something whispered to him that, for Monkey-face, generally so prudent and circumspect, to have acted as he had done, he must have fancied himself very strong, and quite certain of impunity.

CHAPTER VIII
THE DECLARATION OF WAR

There is an incomprehensible fact, which we were many times in a position to appreciate, during the adventurous course of our lengthened wanderings in America—that a man will at times feel the approach of a misfortune, though unable to account for the feeling he suffers from; he knows that he is menaced, though unable to tell when the peril will come, or in what way it will arrive; the day seems to grow more gloomy, the sunbeams lose their brilliancy, external objects assume a mournful appearance; there are strange murmurs in the air; all, in a word, seems to feel the impression of a vague and undefined restlessness.

Though nothing occurred to justify the Captain's fears after his altercation with the Pawnee, not only he, but the whole population of the colony felt under the weight of dull terror on the evening of this day.

At six o'clock, as usual, the bell was rung to recall the wood-cutters and herds; all had returned, the beasts were shut up in their respective stalls, and, apparently, at any rate nothing out of the common troubled the calm existence of the colonists.

Sergeant Bothrel and his comrades, who had pursued Monkey-face for several hours, had only found the horse the Indian so audaciously carried off, and which he probably abandoned, in order to hide his trail more effectually.

Although no Indian sign was visible in the vicinity of the colony, the Captain, more anxious than he wished to appear, had doubled the sentries intended to watch over the common safety, and ordered the Sergeant to patrol round the entrenchments every two hours.

When all these precautions had been taken, the family and servants assembled on the ground floor of the tower to spend the evening, as had been their wont ever since the beginning of the settlement.

The Captain, sitting in an easy chair by the fire, for the nights were beginning to become fresh, was reading an old work on Military Tactics, while Mrs. Watt, with the servants, was engaged in mending the household linen.

This evening, however, the Captain, instead of reading, seemed to be thinking profoundly, with his arms crossed on his chest, and his eyes fixed on the fire.

At last he raised his head, and turned to his wife—

"Do you not hear the children crying?" he said.

"I really do not know what is the matter with them to-day," she answered, "for we cannot quiet them; Betsy has been with them for more than an hour, and has not been able to get them to sleep."

"You should go yourself, my dear, that would be more proper than leaving these things to the care of a servant."

Mrs. Watt went out without answering, and her voice could soon be heard on the upper floor, where was the children's room.

"So, Sergeant," the Captain went on, addressing the old soldier, who was busy in a corner mending a yoke, "you found it impossible to catch up that accursed heathen, who threw me so roughly this morning?"

"We could not even see him, Captain," the Sergeant replied: "these Indians are like lizards, they slip through anywhere. Luckily I found Boston again; the poor brute seemed delighted at seeing me again."

"Yes, yes. Boston is a noble brute, I should have been vexed to lose him. The heathen has not wounded him, I hope, for you know that these demons are accustomed to treat horses badly."

"There is nothing the matter with him as far as I can see; the Indian was probably compelled to leap off his back in a hurry upon finding us so close at his heels."

"It must be so, Sergeant. Have you examined the neighbourhood carefully?"

"With the greatest attention, Captain, but I noticed nothing suspicious. The Redskins will look twice before attacking us: we gave them too rude a shaking for them to forget it."

"I am not of your opinion, Sergeant; the pagans are vindictive; I am convinced that they would like to avenge themselves on us, and that some day, before long perhaps, we shall hear them utter their war-yell in the valley."

"I do not desire it, it is true; but I believe, if they attempted it, they would sing small."

"I think so too; but they would give us a sorrowful surprise, especially now that, through our labours and our care, we are on the point of receiving the price of our fatigues, and beginning to see the end of our troubles."

"That is true, it would be vexatious, for the losses an attack from these bandits would entail on us are incalculable."

"Unluckily, we can only keep on our guard, and it will be impossible for us to foil the plans which these Red demons are doubtless ruminating against us. Have you placed the sentinels as I recommended, Sergeant?"

"Yes, Captain, and I ordered them to display the utmost watchfulness; I do not believe that the Pawnees can surprise us, however clever they may be."

"We cannot take our oath of anything, Sergeant," the Captain answered, as he shook his head with a doubtful air.

At this moment, and as if accident wished to confirm his views, the bell hung outside, and which was used to tell the colonists someone desired to come in, was rung violently.

"What does that mean?" the Captain exclaimed, as he looked at a clock on the wall in front of him; "it is nearly eight o'clock, who can come so late? Have not all our men returned?"

"All, Captain, there is no one outside the palisades." James Watt rose, seized his rifle, and making the Sergeant a sign to follow him, prepared to go out.

"Where are you going, my love?" a gentle, anxious voice asked him.

The Captain turned; his wife had re-entered the keeping room unnoticed by him.

"Did you not hear the bell?" he asked her; "someone wishes to come in."

"Yes, I heard it, dear," she replied; "but do you intend to open the gate at this hour?"

"I am the head of this colony, madam," the Captain answered, coldly but firmly; "and at such an hour as this it is my duty to open the gate, for there may be danger in doing it, and I must give to all an example of courage and accomplishment of duty."

At this moment the bell pealed a second time.

"Let us go," the Captain added, turning to the Sergeant.

His wife made no reply. She fell into a chair, pale and trembling with anxiety.

In the meanwhile the Captain had gone out, followed by Bothrel and four hunters, all armed with rifles.

The night was dark. There was not a star in the heavens, which were black as ink. Two paces ahead it was impossible to distinguish objects, and a cold breeze whistled fitfully. Bothrel had taken down a lanthorn to guide him through the room.

"How is it," the Captain said, "that the sentry at the drawbridge has not challenged?"

"Perhaps he is afraid of giving an alarm, knowing, as he did, that we should hear the bell from the tower."

"Hum!" the Captain muttered between his teeth.

They walked onward. Presently they heard a sound of voices, to which they listened. It was the sentry speaking.

"Patience!" he said. "Someone is coming. I see a lanthorn shining. You will only have a few moments longer to wait, though for your own sake I recommend you not to stir, or I shall put a bullet into you."

"Hang it!" a sarcastic voice replied outside, "you have a curious idea of hospitality in there. No matter, I will wait; so you can raise your barrel, for I have no idea of carrying your works by myself."

The Captain reached the intrenchments at this moment.

"What is it, Bob?" he asked the sentry.

"I really don't know, Captain," he answered. "There is a man on the edge of the ditch who insists on coming in."

"Who are you? What do you want?" the Captain shouted.

"And pray who may you be?" the stranger replied.

"I am Captain James Watt, and I warn you that unknown vagabonds are not allowed to enter here at such an hour. Return at sunrise, and then I may possibly allow you to come in."

"Take care what you are about," the stranger said. "Your obstinacy in causing me to shiver on the brink of this ditch may cost you dearly."

"Take care yourself," the Captain answered, impatiently. "I am not in the mood to listen to threats."

"I do not threaten: I warn you. You have already committed a grave fault to-day. Do not commit a grave one to-night, by obstinately refusing to let me come in."

This answer struck the Captain, and made him reflect.

"Supposing," he said presently, "I allow you to enter, who guarantees that you will not betray me? The night is dark, and you may have a large band with you, which I am unable to see."

"I have only one companion with me, for whom I answer with my head."

"Hum!" the Captain remarked, more undecided than ever, "and who will answer for you?"

"Myself."

"Who are you, as you speak our language with such correctness that you might almost be taken for one of our countrymen?"

"Well, I am nearly one; for I am a Canadian, and my name is Tranquil."

"Tranquil!" the Captain exclaimed. "Are you, then, the celebrated wood-ranger, surnamed the Panther-killer?"

"I do not know whether I am celebrated, Captain. All I am certain of is, that I am the man you refer to."

"If you are really Tranquil, I will allow you to enter; but who is the man that accompanies you, and for whom you answer?"

"Black-deer, the first Sachem of the Snake Pawnees."

"Oh! Oh!" the Captain muttered, "What does he want here?"

"Let us in, and you will know,"

"Well, be it so," the Captain shouted; "but I warn you that, at the slightest appearance of treachery, you and your comrade will be mercilessly killed."

"And you will be justified in doing it, if I break my word."

The Captain, after recommending his hunters to hold themselves in readiness for any event, ordered the drawbridge to be lowered.

Tranquil and Black-deer entered.

Both were unarmed, or, at any rate, seemed so. In the presence of such a proof of confidence, the Captain felt ashamed of his suspicions; and after the bridge had been raised again, he dismissed his escort, and only kept Bothrel with him.

"Follow me," he said to the strangers.

The latter bowed without further reply, and walked at his side.

They reached the tower without exchanging a syllable.

The Captain introduced them into the keeper's room, where Mrs. Watt was alone, a prey to the most lively anxiety.

By a sign her husband ordered her to retire. She gave him a suppliant glance, which he understood, for he did not insist, and she remained silent in her chair.

Tranquil had the same calm and open countenance as of yore. Nothing in his manner seemed to evidence that he had any hostile intentions towards the colonists.

Black-deer, on the contrary, was gloomy and stern. The Captain offered his guests seats by the fire.

"Be seated, gentlemen," he said. "You must feel the need of warmth. Have you come to me as friends or foes?"

"It is more easy to ask that question than answer it," the hunter said, honestly; "up to the present our intentions are kindly; you will decide yourself, Captain, as to the terms on which we shall leave you."

"In any case, you will not refuse some slight refreshment?"

"For the present, I must ask you to excuse us," Tranquil replied, who appeared to be spokesman for himself and friend; "it is better, I think, to settle at once the point that brings us here."

"Hum!" the Captain muttered, annoyed in his heart at this refusal, which foreboded nothing good; "in that case speak, and an amicable interview will not depend on me."

"I, wish it with all my heart, Captain; the more so, because if I am here it is with the object of avoiding the consequences either of a mistake or a moment of passion."

The Captain bowed his thanks, and the Canadian went on.

"You are an old soldier, sir," he said, "and the shorter the speech the better you will like it; in two words, then, this is what brings us: the Snake Pawnees accuse you of having seized their village by treachery, and massacred the greater part of their relations and friends. Is that true?"

"It is true that I seized their village, but I had the right to do so, since the Redskins refused to surrender it to me; but I deny that I acted treacherously: on the contrary, the Pawnees behaved in that way to me."

"Oh!" Black-deer exclaimed, as he rose quickly, "the Paleface has a lying tongue in his mouth."

"Peace!" Tranquil cried, as he forced him to take his seat again, "leave me to disentangle this skein, which seems to me very troublesome. Forgive me for insisting," he went on, addressing the Captain, "but the question is a grave one, and the truth must out. Were you not received, on your arrival, by the Chiefs of the tribe, in the light of a friend?"

"Yes; our first relations were amicable."

"Why, then, did they become hostile?"

"I have told you; because, contrary to sworn faith and pledged word, they refused to give up the land."

"What do you say?"

"Certainly, because they had sold me the territory they occupied."

"Oh, oh, Captain! This requires an explanation."

"It is very easy to give, and to prove my good faith in the matter, I will show you the deed of sale."

The hunter and the Chief exchanged a glance of surprise.

"I am quite out of my reckoning," said Tranquil.

"Wait a moment," the Captain went on, "I will fetch the deed and show it to you."

And he went out.

"Oh, sir!" the young lady exclaimed, as she clasped her hands entreatingly, "try to prevent a quarrel."

"Alas, madam!" the hunter said sadly, "that will be very difficult, after the turn matters have taken."

"Here, look," the Captain said, as he came in and showed them the deed.

The two men required but a glance to detect the trick.

"That deed is false," said Tranquil.

"False! That is impossible!" the Captain went on in stupor; "If it be, I am odiously deceived."

"Unfortunately that has happened."

"What is to be done?" the Captain muttered, mechanically.

Black-deer rose.

"Let the Palefaces listen," he said, majestically; "a Sachem is about to speak."

The Canadian tried to interpose, but the Chief sternly imposed silence on him.

"My father has been deceived; he is a just warrior, his head is grey; the Wacondah has given him wisdom; the Snake Pawnees are also just; they wish to live in peace with my father, because he is innocent of the fault with which he is reproached, and for which another must be rendered responsible."

The commencement of this speech greatly surprised the Chief's hearers; the young mother especially, on hearing the words, felt her anxiety disappear, and joy well up in her heart again.

"The Snake Pawnees," the Sachem continued, "will restore to my father all the merchandize he extorted from him; he, for his part, will pledge himself to abandon the hunting-grounds of the Pawnees, and retire with the Palefaces who came with him; the Pawnees will give up the vengeance they wished to take for the murder of their brothers, and the war hatchet will be buried between the Redskins and the Palefaces of the West. I have spoken."

After these words there was a silence.

His hearers were struck with stupor: if the conditions were unacceptable, war became inevitable.

"What does my father answer?" the Chief asked presently.

"Unhappily, Chief," the Captain answered sadly, "I cannot consent to such conditions, that is impossible; all I can do is to double the price I paid previously."

The Chief shrugged his shoulders in contempt.

"Black-deer was mistaken," he said, with a crushing smile of sarcasm; "the Palefaces have really a forked tongue."

It was impossible to make the Sachem understand the real state of the case; with that blind obstinacy characteristic of his race, he would listen to nothing; the more they tried to prove to him that he was wrong, the more convinced he felt he was right.

At a late hour of the night the Canadian and Black-deer withdrew, accompanied, as far as the entrenchments, by the Captain.

So soon as they had gone, James Watt returned thoughtfully to the tower; on the threshold he stumbled against a rather large object, and stooped down to see what it was.

"Oh!" he exclaimed as he rose again, "then they really mean fighting! By Heaven! They shall have it to their heart's content!"

The object against which the Captain had stumbled was a bundle of arrows fastened by a serpent skin; the two ends of this skin and the points of the arrows were blood stained.

Black-deer, on retiring, had let the declaration of war fall behind him.

All hope of peace had vanished, and preparation for fighting must be made.

After the first moment of stupor the Captain regained his coolness; and although day had not yet broken, he aroused the colonists and assembled them in front of the town, to hold a council and consult as to the means for neutralizing the peril that menaced them.

CHAPTER IX
THE SNAKE PAWNEES

We will now clear up a few points in this story which may appear obscure to the reader.

The Redskins, however great their other faults may be, have a fanatic love for the country where they are born, and nothing can take its place.

Monkey-face did not speak falsely when he told Captain Watt that he was one of the principal Chiefs of his tribe; but he had been careful not to reveal for what reason he had been expelled from his tribe.

This reason the time has now arrived for us to make known.

Monkey-face was not only a man of unbridled ambition, but also, an extraordinary thing for an Indian, he had no religious faith, and was completely exempt from those weaknesses and that superstitious credulity to which his fellows are so amenable: in addition, he was faithless, dishonourable, and of more than depraved manners.

Having been taken, when young, to the towns of the American Union, he had been in a position to see closely the eccentric civilization of the United States. Unable to comprehend the good and bad sides of this civilization, and steer between them, he had, as generally happens in such cases, been seduced by that which most flattered his tastes and instincts, and had only taken from the customs of the whites whatever completed and furnished his precocious depravity.

Hence, when he returned to his tribe, his language and manners were so discordant with what was done and said around him, that he speedily excited the contempt and hatred of his countrymen.

His most violent enemies were naturally the priests, or, at least, the sorcerers, whom he had tried several times to turn into ridicule.

So soon as Monkey-face had put on his back the omnipotent party of the sorcerers, it was all over with his ambitious plans: all his manoeuvres failed, a dull opposition constantly overthrew his schemes at the very moment when he expected to see them succeed.

For a long time, the Chief, not knowing how to act, kept prudently on the defensive, while actively watching the movements of his enemies; awaiting, with that feline patience which formed the basis of his character, for chance to reveal to him the name of the man on whom his vengeance should fall. As all his measures were taken, he soon discovered that the man to whom he owed his continual checks was no other than the principal sorcerer of the tribe.

This was an aged man, respected and beloved by all on account of his wisdom and goodness. Monkey-face hid his hatred for a season; but one day, in full council, after a lively discussion, he allowed his rage to carry him away, and, rushing on the unhappy old man, he stabbed him in the sight of all the elders of the tribe, before those present could prevent the execution of his design.

The murder of the sorcerer put the climax on the horror this villain inspired. On the spot, the Chief drove him from the territory of the nation, refusing him fire and water, and threatening him with the heaviest punishment if he dared to appear before them again.

Monkey-face, too weak to resist the execution of this sentence, retired with rage in his heart, and uttering the most horrible threats.

We have seen in what way he revenged himself by selling the territory of his tribe to the Americans, and thus causing the ruin of those who banished him. But he had scarce obtained the vengeance he had so long pursued, when a strange revolution took place in this man's heart. The sight of the land where he was born, and where the ashes of his father reposed, aroused in him with extreme force that love of his country which he thought dead, but was only asleep in his heart.

The shame at the odious action he had committed by surrendering to the enemies of his race the hunting grounds which he had himself so long freely traversed, the obstinacy with which the Americans set to work changing the face of the country, and destroying their aged trees, whose shadows had so long protected the councils of his nation—all these causes combined had caused him to reflect, and, rendered desperate by the sacrilege which hatred impelled him to commit, he tried to rejoin his comrades, in order to assist them in recovering what they had lost through his fault.

That is to say, he resolved to betray his new friends to the profit of his old friends.

This man was unhappily engaged in a fatal path where each step he took must be marked for a crime.

It was easier than he at first supposed for him to rejoin his countrymen, for they were scattered and wandering in despair through the forests round the colony.

Monkey-face presented himself boldly to them, and was very careful not to tell them that he alone was the cause of the misfortunes that overwhelmed them. On the other hand, he made a secret of his return, telling them that the news of the calamities which had suddenly fallen on them was the sole cause of his coming; that, had they continued to be happy, they would never have seen him again; but that, in the presence of such a frightful catastrophe as that which had crushed them, every feeling of hatred must disappear before the common vengeance to be taken on the Pale-faces, those eternal and implacable enemies of the Red race.

In a word, he displayed such noble sentiments, and put the step he was taking in such a brilliant light, that he completely succeeded in deceiving the Indians, and persuading them of the purity of his intentions, and his good faith.

After this, with the diabolical intelligence he possessed, he formed a vast plot against the Americans, a plot into which he had the cleverness to draw the other Indian people allied to his tribe; and, while ostensibly remaining the friend of the colonists, he silently prepared and organized their utter ruin.

The influence he succeeded in obtaining over his tribe within a short time was immense: three men alone entertained an instinctive distrust of him, and carefully watched his movements; they were Tranquil, the Canadian hunter, Black-deer, and Blue-fox.

Tranquil could not understand the conduct of the Chief; it seemed to him extraordinary that this man had thus become a friend of the Americans. Several times he asked him explanations on this head, but Monkey-face had always answered in an ambiguous way, or evaded his questions.

Tranquil, whose suspicions daily grew, and who was determined to know positively what opinion to have of a man whose manoeuvres appeared to him daily more suspicious, succeeded in getting himself chosen with Black-deer, by the Great Council of the Nation, to bear the declaration of war to Captain Watt.

Monkey-face was vexed at the choice of the envoys whom he knew to be secretly his enemies; but he concealed his resentment; the more so, because matters were too far advanced to withdraw, and everything was in readiness for the expedition.

Tranquil and Black-deer consequently set out with orders to declare war on the Palefaces.

"If I am not greatly mistaken," the Canadian said to his friend as they rode along, "we are going to hear something about Monkey-face."

"Do you think so?"

"I would wager it. I am convinced the scamp is playing a double game, and cheats us all to his own profit."

"I have no great confidence in him, still I cannot believe that he could carry his effrontery so far."

"We shall soon see what we have to depend on; at any rate, though, promise me one thing."

"What is it?"

"That I be the first to speak. I know better than you how to deal with the Palefaces of the West."

"Be it so," Black-deer replied, "act as you think proper."

Five minutes after, they reached the colony. We related in the previous chapter how they were received, and what passed between them and Captain Watt.

This custom of the Indians of declaring war against their enemies may appear extraordinary to Europeans, who are accustomed to regard them as stupid savages, but we must make no mistake; the Redskins have an eminently chivalrous character, and never, except in the case of a horse robbery or such matter, will they attack an enemy before warning him that he may be on his guard.

In fact, it is by cleverly working on this chivalrous character, of which the North Americans, we regret to say, do not possess a particle, that the Whites have gained the majority of their victories over the Redskins.

When a few yards from the colony, the two men found again their horses which they had hobbled; they mounted, and went off at a rapid rate.

"Well," Tranquil asked the Chief, "what do you think of all this?"

"My brother was right, Monkey-face has constantly cheated us; it is evident that this deed emanates from him alone."

"What do you intend doing?"

"I do not know yet; perhaps it would be dangerous to unmask him at this moment."

"I am not of your opinion, Chief; the presence of this traitor among us can only injure our cause."

"Let us have a look at him first."

"Be it so! But permit me a remark."

"I am listening, my brother.'

"How is it that after recognizing the falseness of that deed of sale, you insisted on declaring war against this Long knife of the West, since he has proved to you that he was deceived by Monkey-face?"

The Chief smiled cunningly. "The Paleface was only deceived," he said, "because it suited him to be so."

"I do not understand you, Chief."

"I will explain myself. Does my brother know how a sale of land is effected?"

"No, I do not; and I confess to you, that, never having got to buy or sell, I have not troubled myself about it."

"Wah! In that case I will tell my brother."

"You will cause me pleasure, for I always like to gain information, and this may be useful to me at some time," the Canadian said with a grin.

"When a Paleface wishes to buy the hunting-ground of a tribe he goes to the principal Sachems of the nation, and after smoking the calumet of peace in council, he explains his meaning; the conditions are discussed; if the two contracting parties agree, a plan of the territory is drawn up by the principal sorcerer, the Paleface gives his goods, all the Chiefs place their sign manual at the foot of the plan, the trees are blazed with a tomahawk, the borders marked, and the purchaser takes immediate possession."

"Hum," Tranquil remarked, "that seems simple enough."

"In what council has the grey-head Chief smoked the calumet? Where are the sachems who have treated with him? Let him show me the trees that were marked."

"In truth, I fancy he would find that difficult."

"The Grey-head," the Chief continued, "knew that Monkey-face was cheating him; but the territory suited him, and he calculated on the strength of his arms to hold his own."

"That is probable."

"Conquered by evidence, and recognizing too late that he acted inconsiderately, he fancied he could recover all difficulties by offering us a few more bales of merchandize. Whenever did the Palefaces have a straight and honest tongue?"

"Thank you," the hunter said, laughingly.

"I do not speak of my brother's nation; I never had to complain of them, and I only refer to the Long knives of the West. Does my brother still think that I was wrong in throwing down the bloody arrows?"

"Perhaps, in that circumstance, Chief, you were a little too quick, and allowed your passion to carry you away, but you have so many reasons for hating the Americans that I dare not blame you."

"Then, I can still count on my brother's assistance?"

"Why should I refuse it to you, Chief? Your cause is still as it was, that is to say, just; it is my duty to help you, and I will do so, whatever may happen."

"Och! I thank my brother; his rifle will be useful to us."

"Here we are; it is time to form a determination with reference to Monkey-face."

"It is formed," the Chief answered, laconically.

At this moment, they entered a vast clearing, in the centre of which several fires were burning.

Five hundred Indian warriors, painted and armed for war, were lying about in the grass, while their horses, all harnessed, and ready for mounting, were hobbled, and eating their provender of climbing peas.

Round the principal fire several Chiefs were crouching and smoking silently.

The newcomers dismounted, and proceeded rapidly toward this fire, before which Monkey-face was walking up and down in considerable agitation.

The two men took their places by the side of the other Chiefs, and lit their calumets; although every one expected their arrival impatiently, no one addressed a word to them, Indian etiquette prohibiting a Chief from speaking, before the calumet was completely smoked out.

When Black-deer had finished his calumet, he shook out the ashes, passed it through his belt, and said:—

"The orders of the Sachems are accomplished; the bloody arrows have been delivered to the Palefaces."

The Chiefs bowed their heads in sign of satisfaction at these news.

Monkey-face walked up.

"Has my brother Black-deer seen Grey-head?" he asked.

"Yes," the Chief answered, drily.

"What does my brother think?" Monkey-face pressed him.

Black-deer gave him an equivocal glance.

"What matters the thought of a Chief at this moment," he answered, "since the Council of the Sachems has resolved on war?"

"The nights are long," Blue-fox then said, "will my brothers remain here smoking?"

Tranquil remarked in his turn—

"The Long knives are on their guard, they are watching at this moment, my brothers will remount their horses, and withdraw, for the hour is not propitious."

The Chiefs gave a sign of assent.

"I will go on the discovery," Monkey-face said.

"Good," Black-deer answered, with a stern smile; "my brother is skilful, he sees many things, he will inform us."

Monkey-face prepared to leap on a horse which a warrior led him up, but suddenly Black-deer rose, rushed toward him, and laying his hand roughly on his shoulder, compelled him to fall on his knees.

The warriors, surprised at this sudden aggression, the motive of which they did not divine, exchanged glances of surprise, though they did not make the slightest movement to interpose between the two Chiefs.

Monkey-face quickly raised his head.

"Does the Spirit of evil trouble my brother's brain?" he said, as he tried to free himself from the iron grip that nailed him to the ground.

Black-deer gave a sarcastic smile, and drew his scalping knife.

"Monkey-face is a traitor," he said in a sullen voice "he has sold his brothers to the Palefaces; he is about to die."

Black-deer was not only a renowned warrior, but his wisdom and honour were held in just repute by the tribe; hence no one protested against the accusation he had made, the more so, because, unfortunately for him, Monkey-face had been long known.

Black-deer raised his knife, whose bluish blade flashed in the fire-light, but by a supreme effort Monkey-face succeeded in freeing himself, bounded like a wild beast, and disappeared in the bushes with a hoarse laugh.

The knife had slipped, and only cut the flesh, without inflicting a serious wound on the clever Indian.

There was a moment of stupor, but then all rose simultaneously to rush in pursuit of the fugitive.

"Stay," Tranquil shouted in a loud voice, "it is now too late. Make haste to attack the Palefaces before that villain has warned them, for he is doubtless meditating fresh treachery."

The Chiefs recognized the justice of this, advice, and the Indians prepared for the combat.

CHAPTER X
THE BATTLE

In the meanwhile, as is stated a little while ago, Captain Watt had assembled all the members of the colony in front of the town.

The number of combatants amounted to sixty-two, including the females.

European ladies may think it singular that we count the females among the combatants: in truth, in the old world the days of Bradamante and Joan d'Arc have happily passed away for ever, and the fair sex, owing to the constant progress of civilization, is no longer reduced to the necessity of fighting side by side with men.

In North America, at the period of which we write, and even at the present day, on the prairies and the clearings, it is not so; when the war-yell of the Indians suddenly echoes on the ears of the pioneers, the women are constrained to give up the labour of their sex, to take a rifle in their delicate hands, and fight boldly in defence of the community.

We could, if necessary, cite several of these heroines with soft eyes and angelic countenances who, on occasion, have valiantly done their duty as soldiers and fought like perfect demons against the Indians.

Mrs. Watt was anything rather than a heroine, but she was the daughter and the wife of a soldier; she was born and brought up on the Indian borders; she had already smelt powder several times and seen blood flow, but, before all, she was a mother. As her children had to be defended, all her feminine timidity had disappeared and made way for a cold and energetic resolution.

Her example electrified all the other women of the colony, and all had armed, resolved to fight by the side of their husbands and fathers.

We repeat here that, what with men and women, the Captain had sixty-two combatants around him.

He tried to dissuade his wife from taking part in the fight, but the gentle creature whom he had seen hitherto so timid and obedient, plainly refused to give up her project, and the Captain was compelled to let her do as she pleased.

He therefore made his arrangements for defence. Twenty-four men were placed in the entrenchments under the orders of Bothrel. The Captain himself took the command of a second party of twenty-four hunters, intended to act anywhere and everywhere. The females, under the orders of Mrs. Watt, were left in charge of the tower, in which the children and the invalids were shut up, and the arrival of the Indians was then awaited.

It was about one in the morning when the Canadian hunter and the Pawnee Chief left the colony; by about half-past two all was ready for the defence.

The Captain made a last round of the entrenchment in order to ensure himself that all was in order, then, after ordering all the fires to be extinguished, he secretly left the colony by a concealed door in the palisades, of whose existence only himself and Sergeant Bothrel were cognizant.

A plank was placed across the ditch, and the Captain crossed, only followed by Bothrel and a Kentuckian of the name of Bob, a daring and broad-shouldered fellow, to whom we have already had occasion to refer.

The plank was carefully hidden so as to serve for their return, and the three men glided through the darkness like phantoms.

When they had gone about one hundred yards from the colony, the Captain halted.

"Gentlemen," he then said in a voice so faint that they were obliged to stoop down to hear him; "I have chosen you because the expedition we are about to attempt is dangerous, and I wanted resolute men with me."

"What is to be done?" Bothrel asked.

"The night is so dark that those accursed Pagans could if they liked reach the very edge of the ditch, and it would be impossible for us to notice them; I have, therefore, resolved to set fire to the piles of planks and roots. A man must know how to make sacrifices when needed; these fires which will burn a long while will spread a brilliant light, enabling us to see our enemies for a long distance and fire at them with certainty."

"The idea is excellent," Bothrel answered.

"Yes," the Captain continued, "still, we must not hide from ourselves that it is extremely perilous; it is plain that Indian scouts are already scattered over the prairies, perhaps very close to us, and when two or three fires have been lighted, if we see them, they will not fail to see us too. Each of us will take the necessary objects, and we will try by the rapidity of our movements to foil the tricks of these demons; remember that we shall act separately, and each of us will have four or five fires to light, so we cannot count on one another. To work!"

The combustibles and inflammable matters were shared between the three men and they separated.

Five minutes later a spark glistened, then a second, then a third; at the end of a quarter of an hour ten tires were lighted.

Weak at first, they seemed to hesitate for a while, but gradually the flame increased, gained consistency, and soon the whole plain was lit up by the blood-red glare of these immense torches.

The Captain and his comrades had been more fortunate than they anticipated in their expedition, for they had succeeded in lighting the piles of wood scattered over the valley, without attracting the attention of the Indians; and they hurried back to the entrenchments at full speed. It was high time, for suddenly a terrible war-yell burst forth behind them, and a large band of Indian warriors appeared on the skirt of the forest, galloping at full speed, and brandishing their weapons like a legend of demons.

But they came up too late to catch the Whites, who had crossed the ditch and were sheltered from their missiles.

A discharge of musketry greeted the arrival of the Indians, several fell from their horses, and the others turned and fled with great precipitation.

The fight had commenced, but the Captain cared little about that; thanks to his lucky expedient, a surprise was impossible, and they could see as well as in the daylight.

There was a moment's respite, by which the Americans profited to reload their rifles.

The colonists had felt anxious on seeing the immense fires lit up one after the other on the prairie; they believed in an Indian device, but were soon disabused, by the Captain's return, and congratulated themselves, on the contrary, upon this happy expedient, which enabled them to fire almost with certainty.

The Pawnees, however, had not given up their project of attack; in all probability they had only retired in order to deliberate.

The Captain, with his shoulder leant against the palisade, was attentively examining the deserted plain, when he fancied he perceived an unusual motion in a rather large field of Indian corn, about two rifle shots from the colony.

"Look out!" he said, "the enemy is approaching."

Every one put his finger on his trigger. All at once a great noise was heard, and the furthest pile of wood fell in, emitting myriads of sparks.

"By heaven!" the Captain shouted, "There is some Indian devilry behind that, for it is impossible for that enormous pile to be consumed."

At the same instant another fell in, followed immediately by a third, and then by a fourth.

There could no longer be a doubt as to the cause of these successive falls. The Indians, whose movements were neutralized by the light these monster beacons shed, had taken the very simple method of extinguishing them, which they were enabled to do in perfect safety, for they were out of rifle range.

No sooner was the wood down than it was scattered in every direction, and easily put out.

This expedient enabled the Indians to get very near to the palisades unnoticed.

Still, all the piles were not overthrown, and those that remained were near enough to the fort to be defended by its fire.

For all that, the Pawnees attempted to put them out. But the firing then recommenced, and the bullets fell in a hailstorm on the besiegers, who, after holding out for some minutes, were at last compelled to take to flight, for we cannot give the name of a retreat to the precipitation with which they withdrew.

The Americans began laughing and hooting at the fugitives.

"I think," Bothrel said facetiously, "that those fine fellows find our soup too hot, and regret having put their fingers in it."

"In truth," the Captain remarked, "they do not appear inclined to return this time."

He was mistaken; for, at the same instant, the Indians came back at a gallop.

Nothing could check them, and, in spite of the fusillade, to which they disdained to reply, they reached the very brink of the ditch.

It is true, that once there, they turned back, and retired as rapidly as they had come, though not without leaving on the way a great number of their comrades, whom the American bullets pitilessly laid low.

But the plan of the Pawnees had been successful, and the Whites soon perceived, to their great disappointment, that they had been too hasty in congratulating themselves on their facile victory.

Each Pawnee horseman carried on his croup a warrior, who, on reaching the ditch, dismounted, and profiting by the disorder and smoke, which prevented their being seen, sheltered themselves behind the trunks of trees and elevations of the soil so cleverly, that when the Americans leaned over the palisade to discover the results of the evening's charge, they were in their turn greeted by a discharge of bullets and long barbed arrows, which stretched fifteen on the ground.

There was a movement of blind terror among the Whites after this attack made by invisible enemies.

Fifteen men at one round was a fearful loss for the colonists; the combat was assuming serious proportions, which threatened to degenerate into a defeat; for the Indians had never before displayed so much energy and obstinacy in an attack.

No hesitation was possible; the daring force must be dislodged at any cost from the post where they had so rashly ambushed themselves.

The Captain formed his resolve.

Collecting some twenty resolute men, while the others guarded the palisades, he had the drawbridge lowered, and rushed out.

The enemies then met face to face.

The medley became terrible; the White men and Redskins intertwined like serpents, drunk with rage and blinded by hatred, only thought of killing each other.

All at once an immense glare illumined the scene of carnage, and cries of terror rose from the colony.

The Captain turned his head, and uttered a shriek of despair at the horrible sight that met his terror-stricken gaze.

The tower and principal buildings were on fire; in the light of the flames the Indians could be seen bounding like demons in pursuit of the defenders of the colony, who, grouped here and there, were attempting a resistance which had now become impossible.

This is what had occurred:—

While Black-deer, Blue-fox, and the other principal Pawnee Chiefs attempted an attack on the front of the colony, Tranquil, followed by Quoniam, and fifty warriors, on whom he could depend, had got into the buffalo-hide canoes, silently descended the river, and landed in the colony itself, before the alarm was given, for the very simple reason that the Americans did not at all apprehend an attack from the side of the Missouri.

Still, we must do the Captain the justice of saying that he had not left this side undefended; sentries had been posted there; but, unfortunately, in the disorder occasioned by the Indians' last charge, the sentries, thinking nothing was to be feared from the river, deserted their post to go whither they imagined the danger greatest, and help their comrades in repulsing the Indians.

This unpardonable fault ruined the defenders of the colony.

Tranquil disembarked his party without firing a shot.

The Pawnees, when they had once entered the fort, threw incendiary torches on the wooden buildings, and, uttering their war-yell, rushed on the Americans, whom they placed between two fires.

Tranquil, Quoniam, and some warriors who did not leave them, hurried up to the town.

Mrs. Watt, although taken by surprise, prepared, however, to defend the post confided to her.

The Canadian approached with hands upraised in sign of peace.

"Surrender, in Heaven's name!" he cried, "or you are lost; the colony is captured!"

"No!" she answered, boldly, "I will never surrender to a coward, who betrays his brothers to take the part of the Pagans!"

"You are unjust to me," the hunter answered, sadly— "I have come to save you."

"I will not be saved by you!"

"Unhappy woman! if not for your own sake, surrender on behalf of your children. See, the tower is on fire!"

The lady raised her eyes, uttered a thrilling shriek, and rushed wildly into the interior of the building.

The other females, trusting in the hunter's words, attempted no resistance, but laid down their arms.

Tranquil entrusted the guard of these poor women to Quoniam, with whom he left a few warriors, and then hurried off to put a stop to the carnage which was going on in all parts of the colony.

Quoniam entered the tower when he found Mrs. Watt half stifled and holding her children pressed to her heart with extraordinary strength. The worthy Negro threw the young lady across his shoulder, carried her out, and collecting all the females and children, led them to the banks of the

Missouri to get them out of range of the fire, and await the end of the fight, without exposing the prisoners to the fury of the victors.

It was now no longer a combat but a butchery, rendered more atrocious still by the barbarous refinements of the Indians, who attacked their unhappy enemies with indescribable fury.

The Captain, Bothrel, Bob, and some twenty Americans, the only colonists still alive, were collected in the centre of the esplanade defending themselves with the energy of despair against a cloud of Indians, and resolved to die sooner than fall into the hands of their ferocious enemies.

Tranquil, however, succeeded, by repeated entreaties and braving a thousand perils, in inducing them to lay down their arms and thus put an end to the carnage.

All at once cries, groans, and entreaties were heard from the riverside.

The hunter dashed off; agitated by a gloomy presentiment.

Black-deer and his warriors followed him. When they reached the spot where Quoniam had collected the women, a fearful sight presented itself to them.

Mrs. Watt and three other females lay motionless on the ground in a pool of blood, Quoniam lay extended in front of them with two wounds, one on his head, the other in his chest.

It was impossible to obtain any information from the other females as to what had occurred, for they were half mad with terror.

The Captain's children had disappeared.

End of Prologue.

CHAPTER XI
THE VENTA DEL POTRERO

Using now our privilege as romancer, we will transfer the scene of our narrative to Texas, and resume our story about sixteen years after the events recorded in the prologue.

Dawn was beginning to tinge the clouds with its opaline rays, the stars went out one after the other in the gloomy depths of the sky, and on the extreme blue line of the horizon a bright red reflection, precursor of sunrise, showed that day would ere long appear. Thousands of invisible birds, hidden beneath the foliage, suddenly woke up, and melodiously began their morning concert, while the yells of the wild beasts quitting the watering places, and returning slowly to their unexplored lairs, became gradually more dull and indistinct.

At this moment the breeze rose, burst into the dense cloud of steam which at sunrise exhales from the earth in these intertropical regions, whirled it round for an instant, then rent it asunder, and scattered it in space; thus displaying, without any apparent transition, the most delicious landscape the dreaming mind of poet or painter could imagine.

It is, before all, in America that Providence appears to have taken a pleasure in lavishing the most striking landscape effects, and in infinitely varying the contrasts and harmonies of that puissant nature which can only be found there.

Through the centre of an immense plain, circled on all sides by the tall foliage of a virgin forest, there ran in capricious windings a sandy road, whose golden colour contrasted harmoniously with the deep green of the grass and the silvery whiteness of a narrow stream which the first beams of the sun caused to sparkle like a casket of jewels. Not far from the stream, and at about the middle of the plain, rose a white house with a verandah running round it, and a roof of red tiles. This house, prettily covered with creepers that almost hid its walls, was a *Venta*, or hostelry, built on the top of a small mount. It was reached by an imperceptible ascent, and, owing to its position, commanded the immense and grand landscape.

Before the door of the venta several dragoons, picturesquely grouped, and about twenty in number, were saddling their horses while the arrieros were actively engaged in loading seven or eight mules.

Along the road and some paces from the venta, several horsemen, resembling black dots, could be seen just entering the forest to which we alluded, a forest which rose gradually, and was commanded by a girdle of lofty mountains, whose rugged and bare crests were almost confounded with the azure of the sky.

The door of the venta opened, and a young officer came out singing, accompanied by a stout and jolly-looking monk; after them, a charming maiden of eighteen or nineteen, fair-haired and fragile, with blue eyes and golden hair, appeared on the threshold.

"Come, come," the Captain said, for the young officer wore the marks of that grade, "we have lost too much time already, so to horse."

"Hum!" the monk growled, "we have had hardly time to breakfast; why the deuce are you in such a hurry, Captain?"

"Holy man," the officer went on with a laugh, "if you prefer remaining, you are at liberty to do so."

"No, no, I will go with you," the monk exclaimed, with a look of terror; "*caspita!* I want to take advantage of your escort."

"Then make haste, for I shall give orders to start within five minutes."

The officer, after looking round the plain, gave his *asistente* orders to bring up his horse, and mounted with that grace peculiar to Mexican riders. The monk stifled a sigh of regret, probably thinking of the savoury hospitality he was leaving, to run the risk of a long journey, and, aided by the arrieros, he contrived to lift himself on to a mule, whose loins gave way beneath the enormous load.

"Ouf!" he muttered, "Here I am."

"To horse!" the officer commanded.

The dragoons obeyed at once, and for a few seconds the clash of steel could be heard.

The maiden, to whom we have alluded, had hitherto stood silent and motionless in the doorway, apparently suffering from some secret agitation, and looking now and then anxiously at two or three Campesinos, who, leaning negligently against the wall of the venta, listlessly followed the movements of the party; but at the moment when the Captain was about to give the order to start, she resolutely went up to him and offered him a mechero.

"Your cigarette is not lighted, sir," she said, in a soft and melodious voice.

"On my honour, 'tis true," he replied, and bending gallantly down to her, he returned her the mechero, saying, "thanks, my pretty child."

The girl profited by this movement, which brought his face close to hers, to whisper hurriedly—

"Take care!"

"What?" he said, as he looked fixedly at her. Without replying, she laid her finger on her rosy lips, and turning quickly away, ran back into the venta.

The Captain drew himself up, frowned savagely, and bent a threatening glance on the two or three fellows leaning against the wall, but he soon shook his head.

"Bah!" he muttered, disdainfully, "they would not dare."

He then drew his sabre, whose blade glistened dazzlingly in the sunbeams, and placed himself at the head of the troop.

"Forward!" he shouted.

They started at once.

The mules followed the bell of the Néna, and the dragoons collected round the *recua* enclosed it in their midst.

For a few minutes the Campesinos, who had been watching the departure of the troop, looked after it along the winding road, then re-entered the venta one by one.

The girl was seated alone on an *equipal*, apparently busily engaged in sewing; still, through the almost imperceptible tremor that agitated her body, the flush on her brow, and the timid look she shot through her long eyelashes on the entrance of the Campesinos, it was easy to read that the calmness she affected was far from her heart, and that, on the contrary, a secret fear tormented her.

These Campesinos were three in number; they were men in the full vigour of life, with harshly marked features, firm glances, and brusque and brutal manners. They wore the Mexican border costume, and were well armed.

They sat down on a bench placed before a clumsily planed table, and one of them striking it sharply with his fist, turned to the girl and said roughly—

"Drink here."

She started, and raised her head quickly.

"What do you wish for, Caballeros?" she said.

"Mezcal."

She rose and hastened to serve them; the man who had spoken caught her by the dress at the moment she passed.

"An instant, Carmela," he said.

"Let go my dress, Ruperto," she replied, with a slight pout of ill-humour, "you will tear it for me."

"Nonsense!" he replied, with a coarse laugh, "you must fancy me very awkward."

"No, but your manner does not please me."

"Oh! oh! you are not always so wild, my charming bird."

"What do you mean?" she continued, with a blush.

"No matter, I understand it; but that is not the question just at present."

"What is it, then?" she asked with feigned surprise; "Have I not brought you the mezcal you ordered?"

"Yes, yes; but I have something to say to you."

"Well, say it quickly, and let me go."

"You are in a great hurry to escape from me; are you afraid lest your lover may surprise you in conversation with me?"

Ruperto's comrades began laughing, and the maiden stood quite abashed.

"I have no lover, Ruperto, and you know it very well," she answered with tears in her eyes; "it is cruel of you to insult a defenceless girl."

"Nonsense! I am not insulting you, Carmela; what harm is there in a pretty girl like you having a lover, if not two?"

"Let me go," she cried, as she made an angry movement to free herself.

"Not before you have answered my question."

"Ask it then, and let us have an end of this."

"Well, my wild little maid, be good enough to repeat to me what you whispered just now to that springald of a captain."

"I?" she replied in embarrassment; "what do you suppose I said to him?"

"That is the very point. Niña, I do not suppose what you said to him, I merely wish you to tell me what it was."

"Leave me alone, Ruperto, you only take a delight in tormenting me."

The Mexican looked at her searchingly.

"Do not turn the conversation, my beauty," he said drily, "for the question I ask you is serious."

"That is possible; but I have no answer to give you."

"Because you know you have done wrong."

"I do not understand you."

"Of course not! Well, I will explain myself; at the moment the officer was about to start, you said to him, 'Take care,' Would you venture to deny it?"

The girl turned pale.

"Since you heard me," she said, attempting to jest, "why do you ask me?"

The Campesinos had frowned on hearing Ruperto's accusation; the position was growing serious.

"Oh, oh!" one of them said, as he looked up; "Did she really say that?"

"Apparently, since I heard it," Ruperto retorted brutally.

The girl took a timid glance around, as if imploring an absent protector.

"He is not there," Ruperto remarked cruelly, "so it is of no use looking for him."

"Who?" she asked, hesitating between the shame of the supposition and the terror of her dangerous position.

"He," he answered with a grin. "Listen, Carmela; several times already you have learned more of our business than we liked; I repeat to you the remark you made a minute ago to the Captain, and try to profit by it; take care."

"Yes," the second speaker said brutally; "for we might forget that you are only a child, and make you pay dearly for your treachery."

"Nonsense," the third said, who had hitherto contented himself with drinking, and taking no part in the conversation; "the law must be equal for all; if Carmela has betrayed us, she must be punished."

"Well said, Bernardo," Ruperto exclaimed, as he smote the table; "there are just enough of us to pronounce the sentence."

"Good Heavens!" she screamed, as she freed herself by a sudden effort from the grasp of the arm which had hitherto held her; "Let me go, let me go!"

"Stay!" Ruperto shouted as he rose; "If you do not, some misfortune will happen."

The three men rushed on the maiden, and the latter, half wild with terror, sought in vain the door of the venta by which to escape.

But, at the moment when the three men laid their rough and horny hands on her white and delicate shoulders, the door, whose hasp she had been unable to lift in her terror, was thrown wide open, and a man appeared on the threshold.

"What is the matter here?" he asked in a harsh voice, as he crossed his hands on his chest; and he stood motionless, looking round at the company.

There was such menace in the voice of the new-comer, such a flash shot from his eyes, that the three terrified men fell back mechanically against the opposing wall, muttering—"The Jaguar! The Jaguar!"

"Save me! Save me!" the maiden shrieked, as she rushed wildly toward him.

"Yes," he said in a deep voice; "yes, I will save you, Carmela; woe to the man who causes a hair of your head to fall."

And softly raising her in his powerful arms, he laid her gently on a butacca, where she reclined in a half-fainting condition.

The man who appeared so suddenly was still very young; his beardless face would have seemed that of a child, if his regular features, with their almost feminine beauty, had not been relieved by two large black eyes, which possessed a brilliancy and magnetic power that few men felt themselves capable of enduring.

He was tall, but graceful and elegant, and his chest was wide; his long hair, black as the raven's wing, fell in clusters beneath his vicuna hat, which was ornamented with a deep gold toquilla.

He wore the brilliant and luxurious Mexican costume; his calzoneras of violet velvet, open above the knee, and decorated with a profusion of carved gold buttons, displayed his shapely leg, elegantly imprisoned in plaid silk stockings; his manga, thrown over, his shoulder, was bordered with a wide gold galoon, a girdle of white China crape confined his hips, and bore a pair of pistols and a sheathless machete, with a broad and glittering blade, passed through a ring of bronzed steel: an American rifle, studded with silver ornaments, was slung over his shoulder.

There was in the person of this man, still so young, an attraction so powerful, a dominating fire so strange, that it was impossible to see him without loving or hating him—so profound was the impression he unconsciously produced on all those, without exception, with whom chance brought him into relation.

No one knew who he was, or whence he came; his very name was unknown; and people had consequently been compelled to give him a sobriquet, with which, however, he did not appear at all offended.

As for his character, the following scenes will make it sufficiently well known for us to dispense for the present with entering into any lengthened details.

CHAPTER XII
LOVE AND JEALOUSY

The first feeling of terror which had caused the three men to recoil at the appearance of the Jaguar, had gradually worn off; their effrontery, if not their courage, had returned on seeing the inoffensive manner of the man they had long been accustomed to fear.

Ruperto, the biggest scoundrel of the three, was the first to regain his coolness, and, reflecting that the man who caused them such terror was alone, and therefore could not have the force on his side, he walked resolutely toward him.

"Rayo de Dios!" he said in a brutal voice, "Let that girl alone, for she deserves not only what has happened to her, but also the chastisement we are about to inflict on her at once."

The young man started as if a snake had stung him, and darted over his shoulder a glance full of menace at the man who had addressed him.

"Are you speaking to me in that way?" he asked.

"To whom else?" the other answered, resolutely, although in his heart he felt alarmed at the way in which his question had been taken up.

"Ah!" was all the Jaguar said; and without adding another word, he walked slowly toward Ruperto, whom he held motionless beneath his fascinating glance, and who watched him come up with a terror that momentarily increased.

On arriving about a yard from the Mexican the young man stopped.

This scene, apparently so simple, must, however, have possessed a terrible significance for the witnesses, for all bosoms were heaving, every brow was pallid.

The Jaguar, with livid face, crisped features, eyes inflamed with blood, and brows frowning, thrust forth his arm to seize Ruperto, who, overcome by terror, did not make a single movement to escape from this clutch, which he knew, however, would be mortal.

Suddenly Carmela bounded like a startled fawn, and cast herself between the two men.

"Oh!" she shrieked, as she clasped her hands; "have pity on him; do not kill him, in Heaven's name!"

The young man's face suddenly changed, and assumed an expression of ineffable gentleness.

"Be it so!" he said; "Since such is your wish, he shall not die; but he insulted you, Carmela, and must be punished. On your knees, villain!" he continued, as he turned to Ruperto and pressed his hand heavily on his shoulder; "On your knees, and ask pardon of this angel."

Ruperto sunk together beneath the weight of this iron hand, and fell at the maiden's feet, murmuring in a timid voice—

"Pardon, pardon!"

"Enough," the Jaguar then said, with a terrible accent; "rise, and thank your God for having escaped this time again from my vengeance. Open the door, Carmela."

The maiden obeyed.

"To horse!" the Jaguar continued; "Go and wait for me at the Rio Seco, and mind that not one stirs before my arrival, under penalty of death. Begone!"

The three men bowed their heads, and went out without reply; an instant later the gallop of their horses could be heard echoing on the sandy road.

The two young people remained alone in the venta.

The Jaguar sat down at the table where the men had been drinking a moment previously, buried his face in his hands, and seemed plunged in serious thought.

Carmela looked at him with a mixture of timidity and fear, not daring to address him.

At length, after a considerable period had elapsed, the young man raised his head, and looked around him, as if suddenly aroused from deep sleep.

"What, you remained here?" he said to her.

"Yes," she answered, softly.

"Thanks, Carmela—you are kind! You alone love me, when all else hates me."

"Have I not reason to do so?"

The Jaguar smiled mournfully, but answered this question by asking another, the usual tactics of persons who do not wish to let their thoughts be read.

"Now, tell me frankly what happened between you and those scoundrels."

The maiden seemed to hesitate for a moment, but made up her mind and confessed the warning she gave the Captain of Dragoons.

"You were wrong," the Jaguar said sternly to her; "your imprudence may produce serious complications. Yet I dare not blame you; you are a woman, and consequently ignorant of many things. Are you alone here?"

"Quite alone."

"What imprudence! How can Tranquil leave you thus?"

"His duties keep him at present at the Larch-tree hacienda, where there is going to be a grand hunt in a few days."

"Hum! At any rate, Quoniam ought to have remained with you."

"He could not, for Tranquil required his help."

"The devil is in the business, as it seems," he said, in an ill-humoured voice; "he must be mad thus to abandon a girl alone in a venta situated alone in the midst of such a desolate country, during whole weeks."

"I was not alone, for Lanzi was left with me."

"Ah! And what has become of him?"

"A little before sunrise I sent him to kill a little game."

"A capital reason; and you have been left exposed to the coarse language and ill-treatment of the first scoundrel who thought proper to insult you."

"I did not think there was any danger."

"Now, I trust you are undeceived."

"Oh!" she cried, with a start of terror, "That shall never happen again, I swear to you."

"Good! But I think I hear Lanzi's footsteps."

She looked out.

"Yes," she replied, "here he is."

The man shortly after entered. He was of about forty years of age, with an intelligent and bold face; he had on his shoulders a magnificent deer, fastened much in the way Swiss hunters carry a chamois, and in his right hand he held a gun.

He gave a look of annoyance on perceiving the young man; still, he bowed slightly to him as he placed the venison on the table.

"Oh, oh," the Jaguar said, in a good-humoured tone, "you have had a good hunt it seems, Lanzi; are the deer plentiful on the plain?"

"I have known the time when they were more numerous," he replied, gruffly; "but now," he added, shaking his head sorrowfully, "it is a hard matter for a poor man to kill one or two in a day."

The young man smiled.

"They will return," he said.

"No, no," Lanzi replied, "when the deer have been once startled, they do not return to the parts they have left, however much it might be to their benefit to do so."

"You must put up with it then, master, and take things as they are."

"Well, what else do I?" he growled, as he angrily turned his back on the speaker.

And, after this sally, he reloaded the game on his shoulders, and entered the other room.

"Lanzi is not amiable to-day," the Jaguar observed, when he found himself alone with Carmela.

"He is annoyed at meeting you here."

The young man frowned.

"Why so?" he asked.

Carmela blushed and looked down without answering.

The Jaguar looked at her searchingly for a moment.

"I understand," he said at last; "my presence in this hostelry displeases somebody—him, perhaps."

"Why should it displease him? He is not the master, I suppose."

"That is true; then it displeases your father—is that it?"

The maiden gave a nod of assent.

The Jaguar sprung up violently, and walked up and down the room, with his head down, and his arms behind his back; after a few minutes of this behaviour, which Carmela followed with an anxious eye, he stopped suddenly before her, raised his head, and looked at her fixedly.

"And does my presence here, Carmela, displease you also?"

The girl remained silent.

"Reply," he went on.

"I did not say so," she murmured, with hesitation.

"No," he said, with a bitter smile, "but you think so, Carmela, though you have not the courage to confess it to my face."

She drew herself up proudly.

"You are unjust to me," she replied, with peevish excitement, "unjust and unkind. Why should I—I, desire your absence? You never did me any harm; on the contrary, I have ever found you ready to defend me; this very day you did not hesitate to protect me from the ill-treatment of the wretches who insulted me."

"Ah! You allow it?"

"Why should I not allow it, since it is true? Do you consider me ungrateful, then?"

"No, Carmela, you are only a woman," he replied, bitterly.

"I do not understand your meaning, and do not wish to do so; I alone here defend you, when my father, or Quoniam, or anyone else accuses you. Is it my fault, if, owing to your character, and the mysterious life you lead, you are placed beyond the pale of ordinary existence? Am I responsible for the silence you insist on maintaining on all that concerns you personally? You know my father; you know how kind, frank, and worthy he is; many times he has tried, by circuitous ways, to lead you to an honourable explanation—but you have always repulsed his advances. You must, therefore, only blame yourself for the general isolation in which you are left, and the solitude formed around you; and do not address reproaches to the only person who, up to the present, has dared to support you against all."

"It is true," he answered, bitterly; "I am a madman. I acknowledge my wrongs towards you, Carmela, for you say truly; in all this world, you alone have been constantly kind and compassionate for the reprobate—for the man whom the general hatred pursues."

"Hatred as foolish as it is unjust."

"And which you do not share in—is it not?" he exclaimed, sharply.

"No, I do not share it; still, I suffer from your obstinacy; for, in spite of all that is said of you, I believe you to be honourable."

"Thank you, Carmela; I wish I had it in my power to prove immediately that you are right, and give a denial to those who insult me like cowards behind my back, and tremble when I stand before them. Unfortunately, that is impossible for the present; but the day will come, I hope, when it will be permitted me to make myself known as what I really am, and throw off the mask that stifles me; and then—"

"Then?" she repeated, seeing that he hesitated.

Again he hesitated.

"Then," he said, in a choking voice, "I shall have a question to ask you, and a request to make."

The maiden blushed, but recovered herself directly.

"You will find me ready to answer both," she murmured, in a low and inarticulate voice.

"Do you mean it?" he asked, joyfully.

"I swear it to you."

A flash of happiness lit up the young man's face like a sunbeam.

"My good Carmela," he said, in a deep voice, "when the moment arrives, I shall remind you of your promise."

She bowed her head in dumb assent.

There was a moment of silence. The maiden attended to her household duties with that bird-like lissomness and activity peculiar to women; the Jaguar walked up and down the room with a preoccupied air; after a few moments he went to the door and looked out.

"I must be gone," he said.

She gave him a scrutinizing glance.

"Ah," she said.

"Yes; then be kind enough to order Lanzi to prepare Santiago. Perhaps if I told him so myself he would feel disinclined to do it. I fancy I can see I am no longer in his good graces."

"I will go," she answered him with a smile.

The young man watched her depart with a stifled sigh.

"What is this I feel?" he muttered, as he pressed his hand powerfully against his heart, as if he suddenly felt a sudden pain: "Can it be what people call love? I am mad!" he went on, directly after; "How can I, the Jaguar, love? Can a reprobate be beloved?"

A bitter smile contracted his lips; he frowned and muttered, in a hollow voice—

"Every man has his task in this world, and I shall know how to accomplish mine."

Carmela came in again.

"Santiago will be ready in a moment. Here are your vaquera boots, which Lanzi begged me to give you."

"Thank you," he said.

And he began fastening on his legs those two pieces of stamped leather which in Mexico play the part of gaiters, and serve to protect the rider from the horse.

While the young man fastened on his botas, with one foot on the bench, and his body bent forward, Carmela examined him attentively, with an expression of timid hesitation.

The Jaguar noticed it.

"What do you want?" he asked her.

"Nothing," she said, stammering.

"You are deceiving me, Carmela. Come—time presses—tell me the truth."

"Well," she replied, with a hesitation more and more marked, "I have a prayer to make to you."

"Speak quickly, Niña, for you know that, whatever it may be, I grant it to you beforehand."

"You swear it?"

"I do."

"Well, whatever may happen, I desire that if you meet the Captain of Dragoons who was here this morning, you will grant him your protection."

The young man sprung up, as if stung by a viper.

"Ah, then," he shrieked, "what I was told was true, then?"

"I do not know what you are alluding to, but I repeat my request."

"I do not know the man, since I did not arrive until after his departure."

"Yes, you know him," she continued, boldly. "Why seek a subterfuge, if you wish to break the promise you made me? It would be better to be frank."

"It is well," he replied, in a gloomy voice and a tone of biting irony; "reassure yourself Carmela, I will defend your lover."

And he rushed madly from the venta.

"Oh!" the maiden exclaimed, as she fell on a bench, and melted into tears; "Oh! That demon is properly christened the Jaguar! He has a tiger's heart in his bosom."

She buried her face in her hands, and broke out into sobs.

At the same moment the rapid gallop of a retreating horse was heard.

CHAPTER XIII
CARMELA

Before we continue our story, it is indispensable for us to give our readers certain important and indispensable details about facts that have to come.

Among the provinces of the vast territory of New Spain, there is one, the most eastern of all, whose real value the Government of the Viceroys has constantly ignored. This ignorance was kept up by the Mexican Republic, which, at the period of the proclamation of Independence, did not think it worthy of being formed into a separate state, and, without dreaming of what might happen at a later date, negligently allowed it to be colonized by the North Americans, who even at that period seemed infected by that fever of encroachment and aggrandizement which has now become a species of endemic mania among these worthy citizens—we refer to Texas.

This magnificent country is one of the most fortunately situated in Mexico; territorially regarded, it is immense, no country is better watered, for considerable rivers pour into the sea, their waters swollen by countless streams which fertilize this country, as they traverse it in every direction; and these currents and rivers being deeply imbedded, never form those wide expanses of water by their overflow, which in other countries are transformed into fetid marshes.

The climate of Texas is healthy, and exempt from those frightful diseases which have given such a sinister celebrity to certain countries of the New World.

The natural borders of Texas are the Sabina on the East, Red River on the north, to the west a chain of lofty mountains, which enters vast prairies, and the Rio Bravo del Norte, and lastly, from the mouth of the latter river to that of the Sabina, the Gulf of Mexico.

We have said that the Spaniards were almost ignorant of the real value of Texas, although they had been acquainted with it for a very long time, for it is almost certain that in 1536, Cabeça de Vaca traversed it when he proceeded from Florida to the northern provinces of Mexico.

Still the honour of the first settlement attempted in this fine country belongs incontestably to France.

In fact, the unfortunate and celebrated Robert de la Salle, ordered by the Marquis de Siegnelay to discover the mouth of the Mississippi in 1684, made a mistake, and entered the Rio de Colorado, which he descended with countless difficulties, till he reached the San Bernardo lagoon, where he built a fort between Velasco and Matagorda, and took possession of the country. We will enter into no further details about this bold explorer, who twice attempted to reach the unknown lands to the east of Mexico, and was traitorously assassinated in 1687, by villains who belonged to his band.

A later reminiscence attaches France to Texas, for it was there that General Lallemand attempted in 1817 to found, under the name of *Champ d'Asyle*, a colony of French refugees, the unhappy relics of the invincible armies of the first empire. This colony, situated about ten leagues from Galveston, was utterly destroyed by the orders of the Viceroy Apodaca, by virtue of the despotic system, constantly followed by the Spaniards of the New World, of not allowing strangers, under any pretext, to establish themselves on any point of their territory.

We shall be forgiven these prosy details when our readers reflect that this country, scarce twenty years free, with a superficies of one hundred thousand acres and more, and inhabited by two hundred thousand persons at the most, has, however, entered on an era of prosperity and progress, which must inevitably arouse the attention of European Governments, and the sympathies of intelligent men of all nations.

At the period when the events occurred which we have undertaken to narrate, that is to say in the later half of 1829, Texas still belonged to Mexico, but its glorious revolution had begun, it was struggling valiantly to escape from the disgraceful yoke of the central government, and proclaim its independence.

Before, however, we continue our story, we must explain how it was that Tranquil, the Canadian hunter, and Quoniam, the Negro, who was indebted to him for liberty, whom we left on the Upper Missouri leading the free life of wood-rangers, found themselves established, as it were, in Texas, and how the hunter had a daughter, or, at any rate, called his daughter, the lovely fair-haired girl we have presented to the reader under the name of Carmela.

About twelve years before the day we visit the Venta del Potrero, Tranquil arrived at the same hostelry, accompanied by two comrades, and a child of five to six years of age, with blue eyes, ruddy lips, and golden hair, who was no other than Carmela; as for his comrades, one was Quoniam, the other an Indian half-breed, who answered to the name of Lanzi.

The sun was just about setting when the little party halted in front of the venta.

The host, but little accustomed in this desolate country, close to the Indian border, to see travellers, and especially at so late an hour, had already closed and barred his house, and was himself getting ready for bed, when the unexpected arrival of our friends forced him to alter his arrangements for the night.

It was, however, only with marked repugnance, and on the repeated assurances the travellers made him that he had nought to fear from them, that he at length decided to open his door, and admit them to his house.

Once that he had resolved to receive them, the host was as he should be to his guests, that is to say, polite and attentive, as far as that can enter into the character of a Mexican landlord, a race, be it noted in a parenthesis, the least hospitable in existence.

He was a short, stout man, with cat-like manners, and crafty looks, already of a certain age, but still quick and active.

When the travellers had placed their horses in the corral, before a good stock of alfalfa, and had themselves supped with the appetite of men who have made a long journey, the ice was broken between them and the host, thanks to a few tragos of Catalonian refino, liberally offered by the Canadian, and the conversation went on upon a footing of the truest cordiality, while the little girl, carefully wrapped up in the hunter's warm zarapé, was sleeping with that calm and simple carelessness peculiar to that happy age when the present is all in all, and the future does not exist.

"Well, gossip," Tranquil said gaily, as he poured out a glass of refino for the host; "I fancy you must lead a jolly life of it here."

"I?"

"Hang it, yes; you go to bed with the bees, and I feel certain you are in no hurry to get up in the morning."

"What else can I do in this accursed desert, where I have buried myself for my sins?"

"Are travellers so rare, then?"

"Yes and no; it depends on the meaning you give the word."

"Confound it! there are not two meanings, I should fancy."

"Yes, two very distinct meanings."

"Nonsense! I am curious to know them."

"That is easy enough: there is no lack of vagabonds of every colour in the country, and if I liked, they would fill my house the whole blessed day; but they would not shew me the colour of their money."

"Ah, very good; but these estimable Caballeros do not constitute the whole of your customers, I presume?"

"No; there are also the Indios Bravos, Comanches, Apaches, and Pawnees, and Heaven alone knows who else, who prowl about the neighbourhood from time to time."

"Hum! those are awkward neighbours, and if you have only such customers, I am beginning to be of your opinion; still, you must now and then receive pleasanter visits."

"Yes, from time to time, straggling travellers like yourself, of course; but the profits, in any case, are far from covering the expenses."

"That is true, here's your health."

"The same to you."

"In that case, though, allow me a remark which may appear to you indiscreet."

"Speak, speak, Caballeros, we are talking as friends, so have no chance of offence."

"You are right. If you are so uncomfortable here, why the deuce do you remain?"

"Why, where would you have me go?"

"Well, I do not know, but you would be better off anywhere than here."

"Ah! if it only depended on me," he said, with a sigh.

"Have you anybody with you here?"

"No, I am alone."

"Well, what prevents you going then?"

"Eh, Caramba, the money! All I possessed, and that was not much, was spent in building this house, and installing myself, and I could not have managed it had it not been for the peons."

"Is there a hacienda here?"

"Yes, the Larch tree hacienda, about four leagues off, so that, you understand, if I go, I must give up my all."

"Ah, ah," Tranquil said thoughtfully, "very good, go on. Why not sell it?"

"Where are the buyers? Do you fancy it so easy to find about here a man with four or five hundred piastres in his pocket; and, moreover, ready to commit an act of folly?"

"Well, I can't say, but I fancy by seeking he could be found."

"Nonsense, gossip, you are jesting!"

"On my word I am not," Tranquil said, suddenly changing his tone, "and I will prove it to you."

"Good."

"You say you will sell your house for four hundred piastres?"

"Did I say four hundred?"

"Don't finesse, you did."

"Very good, then; I admit it: what next?"

"Well, I will buy it, if you like."

"You?"

"Why not?"

"I will think about it."

"That is done; say yes or no, take it, or leave it; perhaps I may have altered my mind in five minutes, so decide."

The landlord gave the Canadian a searching glance. "I accept," he said.

"Good: but I will not give you four hundred piastres."

"How much?" the other said, crying off.

"I will give you six hundred."

The landlord looked at him in amazement.

"I am quite agreeable," he said.

"But on one condition."

"What is it?"

"That to-morrow, so soon as the sale is completed, you will mount your horse—you have one, I suppose?"

"Yes."

"Well, you will mount, start, and never show yourself here again."

"Oh! You may be quite certain on that point."

"It's settled then?"

"Perfectly."

"Then let your witnesses be ready at day-break."

"They shall be."

The conversation ended here. The travellers wrapped themselves in their fressadas and zarapés, lay down on the lumpy floor of the room, and fell asleep; the host followed their example.

As was arranged between them, the landlord, a little before daybreak, saddled his horse, and went to fetch the witnesses necessary for the validity of the transaction; for this purpose he galloped to the Larch-tree hacienda and returned by sunrise, accompanied by the major-domo and seven or eight peons.

The major-domo, the only one who could read and write, drew up the deed of sale, and after collecting all the persons, read it aloud.

Tranquil then took thirty-seven and a half gold onzas from his girdle, and spread them out on the table.

"Be witnesses, Caballeros," the major-domo said, addressing his audience, "that the Señor Tranquilo has paid the six hundred piastres agreed on for the purchase of the Venta del Potrero."

"We are witness," they replied.

Then all present, the major-domo at their head, passed into the corral behind the house.

On reaching it, Tranquil pulled up a tuft of grass which he cast over his shoulder; then picking up a stone, he hurled it over the opposite wall: according to the terms of Mexican law, he was now the owner.

"Be witness, Señores," the major-domo again spoke, "that Señor Tranquilo, here present, has legally taken possession of this estate. *Dios y libertad!*"

"*Dios y libertad!*" the others shouted; "Long life to the new huesped!"

All the formalities being performed, they now returned to the house, when Tranquil poured out bumpers for his witnesses, whom this unexpected liberality filled with delight.

The ex-landlord, faithful to his agreement, pressed the buyer's hand, mounted his horse, and went off, wishing him good luck. From that day they never heard of him again.

This was the manner in which the hunter arrived in Texas, and became a landed proprietor.

He left Lanzi and Quoniam at the venta with Carmela. As for himself, thanks to the patronage of the major-domo, who recommended him to his master, Don Hilario de Vaureal, he entered the Larch-tree hacienda in the capacity of tigrero or tiger-killer.

Although the country selected by the hunter to establish himself was on the confines of the Mexican border, and, for that reason, almost deserted, the vaqueros and peons cudgelled their brains for some time in trying to discover the reason which bad compelled so clever and brave a hunter as the Canadian to retire there. But all the efforts made to discover this reason, all the questions asked, remained without result; the hunter's comrades and himself remained dumb; as for the little girl, she knew nothing.

At length the disappointed people gave up trying to find the explanation of this enigma, trusting to time, that great clearer up of mysteries, to tell them at length the truth which was so carefully concealed.

But weeks, months, years elapsed, and nothing raised even a corner of the hunter's secret.

Carmela had grown an exquisite maiden, and the venta had increased the number of its customers. This border, hitherto so quiet, owing to its remoteness from the towns and pueblos, felt the movement which the revolutionary ideas imparted to the centre of the country; travellers became more frequent, and the hunter, who had up to this time appeared rather careless as to the future, trusting for his safety to the isolation of his abode, began to grow anxious, not for himself, but for Carmela, who was exposed almost definitively to the bold attempts not only of lovers, whom her beauty attracted, as honey does flies, but also to those of the ruffians whom the troublous times had drawn out of their lairs, and who wandered about all the roads like coyotes seeking prey to devour.

The hunter, wishful no longer to leave the maiden in the dangerous position into which circumstances had thrown her, was actively employed in warding off the misfortunes he foresaw; for, although it is impossible, for the present, to know what ties attached him to the girl who called him father, we will state here that he felt a really paternal affection and absolute devotion for her, in which, indeed, Quoniam and Lanzi imitated him. Carmela to these three men was neither girl nor woman; she was an idol they adored on their bended knees, and for whom they would have readily sacrificed their lives at the slightest sign it might please her to make them.

A smile from Carmela rendered them happy; the slightest frown from her made them sorrowful.

We must add, that although she was aware of the full extent of her power, Carmela did not abuse it, and it was her greatest joy to see herself surrounded by these three hearts which were so entirely devoted to her.

Now that we have given these details, doubtless very imperfect, but the only ones possible, we will resume our story at the point where we left it in the penultimate chapter.

CHAPTER XIV
THE CONDUCTA DE PLATA

We will now return to the caravan, which we saw leave the Potrero at sunrise, and in the Chief of which Carmela seemed so greatly interested.

This Chief was a young man of about five-and-twenty, with delicate, dashing, and distinguished features; he wore, with supreme elegance, the brilliant uniform of a Captain of Dragoons.

Although he belonged to one of the oldest and noblest families in Mexico, Don Juan Melendez de Gongora would only owe his promotion to himself; an extraordinary desire in a country where military honour is regarded almost as nothing, and where only the superior grades give those who hold them a degree of consideration which is rather the result of fear than of sympathy, on the part of the people.

Still Don Juan had persevered in his eccentric idea, and each step he won was not the result of a pronunciamento successfully carried out by any ambitious General, but that of a brilliant action. Don Juan belonged to that class of real Mexicans who honestly love their country, and who, jealous of its honour, dream for it a restoration, very difficult, if not impossible, to obtain.

The force of virtue is so great, even on the most depraved natures, that Captain Don Juan Melendez de Gongora was respected by all the men who approached him, even by those who loved him the least.

However, the Captain's virtue had nothing austere or exaggerated about it; he was a thorough soldier, gay, obliging, brave as his sword, and ever ready to help, either with his arm or purse, all those, friends or foes, who had recourse to him. Such, physically and morally, was the man who commanded the caravan, and granted his protection to the monk who rode by his side.

This worthy Frayle, about whom we have had already occasion to say a few words, deserves a detailed description.

Physically, he was a man of about fifty, almost as tall as he was wide, bearing a striking likeness to a barrel set on legs, and yet gifted with far from common strength and activity; his violet nose, his huge lips, and ruddy face, gave him a jovial appearance, which two little grey sunken eyes, full of fire and resolution, rendered ironical and mocking.

Morally, he was in no way distinguished from the majority of Mexican monks—that is to say, he was ignorant as a carp, prone to drinking, a passionate lover of the fair sex, and superstitious in the highest degree; but for all that, the best companion in the world, at home in all society, and always able to raise a laugh.

What singular accident could have brought him so far on the border? This no one knew or cared for, as everyone was aware of the vagabond humour of Mexican monks, whose life is constantly passed in roaming from one place to the other, without object, and generally without interest, but simply at the dictates of caprice.

At this period, Texas, joined to another province, formed a state called Texas and Cohahuila.

The party commanded by Don Juan de Melendez left Nacogdoches eight days previously, bound for Mexico; but the Captain, in accordance with the instructions he received, left the ordinary road, inundated at that moment with bands of brigands of every description, and made a long circuit to avoid certain ill-famed gorges of the Sierra de San Saba. He would still have to cross that range; but on the side of the great prairies, that is to say, at the spot where the plateaux, gradually descending, do not offer those variations of landscape which are so dangerous to travellers.

The ten mules the Captain escorted must be loaded with very precious merchandise, for the Federal Government—seeing the small number of troops it had in the State—to have resolved on having it convoyed by forty dragoons under an officer of Don Juan's reputation, whose presence, under existing circumstances, would have been highly necessary, not to say indispensable, in the interior of the State, in order to suppress revolutionary attempts, and keep the inhabitants in the path of duty.

In fact, the merchandise was very valuable; these ten mules transported three millions of piastres, which would assuredly be a grand windfall for the insurgents, if they fell into their hands.

The time was left far behind, when, under the rule of the Viceroys, the Spanish flag borne at the head of a train of fifty or sixty mules laden with gold, was sufficient to protect a conducta de plata effectually, and enable it to traverse, without the slightest risk, the whole width of Mexico, so great was the terror inspired by the mere name of Spain.

Now, it was not one hundred, or sixty mules; but ten, which forty resolute men seemed hardly sufficient to protect.

The government considered it advisable to employ the greatest prudence in sending off this conducta, which had long been expected at Mexico. The greatest silence was maintained as to the hour and day of departure, and the road it would follow.

The bales were made so as to conceal, as far as possible, the nature of the merchandise carried; the mules sent off one by one, in open day, only under the protection of the arriero, joined, fifteen leagues from the town, the escort which had been encamped for more than a month, under some plausible excuse, in an ancient presidio.

All had, therefore, been foreseen and calculated with the greatest care and intelligence to get this precious merchandise in safety to its destination; the arrieros, the only persons who knew the value of their load, would be careful not to speak about it, for the little they possessed was made responsible for the safety of their freight, and they ran the risk of being utterly ruined if their mules were robbed on the road.

The conducta advanced in the most excellent order, to the sound of the Néna's bells; the arrieros sang gaily their mules, urging them on by this eternal "arrea, Mula! Arrea, Linda!"

The pennons fastened to the long lances of the dragoons fluttered in the morning breeze, and the Captain listened idly to the monk's chatter, while at intervals taking a searching glance over the deserted plain.

"Come, come, Fray Antonio," he said to his stout companion, "you can no longer regret having set out at so early an hour, for the morning is magnificent, and everything forebodes a pleasant day."

"Yes, yes," the other replied with a laugh; "thanks to Nuestra Señora de la Soledad, honourable Captain, we are in the best possible state for travelling."

"Well, I am glad to find you in such good spirits, for I feared lest the rather sudden waking this morning might have stirred up your bile."

"I, good gracious, honourable Captain!" he replied, with feigned humility; "we unworthy members of the church must submit without murmuring to all the tribulations which it pleases the Lord to send us; and besides, life is so short, that it is better only to look at the bright side, not to lose in vain regret the few moments of joy to which we can lay claim."

"Bravo! That is the sort of philosophy I like; you are a good companion, Padre—I hope we shall travel together for a long while."

"That depends a little on you, Señor Captain."

"On me? how so?"

"Well, on the direction you propose following."

"Hum!" Don Juan said; "and pray where may you be going, Señor Padre?"

This old-fashioned tactic of answering one question by another, is excellent, and nearly always succeeds. This time the monk was caught; but, in accordance with the habit of his brethren, his answer was as it was meant to be, evasive.

"Oh, I," he said with affected carelessness; "all roads are pretty nearly the same to me; my gown assures me, wherever chance bends my steps, pleasant faces and hearty reception."

"That is true; hence I am surprised at the question you asked me an instant back."

"Oh, it is not worth troubling yourself about, honourable Captain. I should feel agonised at having annoyed you, hence I humbly beg you to pardon me."

"You have in no way annoyed me, Señor Padre. I have no reason for concealing the road I purpose following; this recua of mules I am escorting does not affect me in any way, and I propose leaving it to-morrow or the day after."

The monk could not restrain a start of surprise.

"Ah!" he said, as he looked searchingly at the speaker.

"Oh yes," the Captain continued, in an easy tone, "these worthy men begged me to accompany them for a few days, through fear of the gavillas that infest the roads; they have, it appears, valuable merchandize with them, and would not like to be plundered."

"I understand; it would not be at all pleasant for them."

"Would it? hence I did not like to refuse them the slight service which took me only a little way out of my road; but so soon as they consider themselves in safety, I shall leave them and enter the prairie, in accordance with the instructions I have received, for you know that the Indios Bravos are stirring."

"No, I was not aware of it."

"Well, in that case, I tell it you; there is a magnificent opportunity that presents itself to you, Padre Antonio, and you must not neglect it."

"A magnificent opportunity for me?" the monk repeated, in amazement; "What opportunity, honourable Captain?"

"For preaching to the Infidels, and teaching them the dogmas of our Holy Faith," he replied, with imperturbable coolness.

At this abrupt proposal the monk made a frightful face.

"Deuce take the opportunity!" he exclaimed, snapping his fingers; "I will leave that to other asses! I feel no inclination for martyrdom."

"As you please, Padre; still you are wrong."

"That is possible, honourable Captain, but hang me if I accompany you near those pagans; in two days I shall leave you."

"So soon as that?"

"Why, I suppose, that since you are going on to the prairie, you will leave the recua of mules you are escorting at the Rancho of San Jacinto, which is the extreme point of the Mexican possessions on the desert border."

"It is probable."

"Well, I will go on with the muleteers; as all the dangerous passes will then have been left behind, I shall have nothing to fear, and shall continue my journey in the most agreeable way possible."

"Ah," the Captain said to him, with a piercing glance; but he was unable to continue this conversation, which seemed highly interesting to him, for a horseman galloped up at full speed from the front, stopped before him, and stooping to his ear, whispered a few words.

The Captain looked scrutinizingly round him, drew himself up in the saddle, and addressed the soldier—

"Very good. How many are they?"

"Two, Captain."

"Watch them, but do not let them suspect they are prisoners; on arriving at the halting ground I will cross-question them. Rejoin your comrades."

The soldier bowed respectfully without reply, and went off at the same speed he had come up.

Captain Melendez had for a long time accustomed his subordinates not to discuss his orders, but obey them unhesitatingly.

We mention this fact because it is excessively rare in Mexico, where military discipline is almost a nullity, and subordination unknown.

Don Juan closed up the ranks of the escort, and ordered them to hurry on.

The monk had seen with secret alarm the conference between the officer and the soldier, of which he was unable to catch a word. When the Captain, after attentively watching the execution of his orders, returned to his place by his side, Father Antonio tried to jest about what had happened, and the cloud of gravity that had suddenly darkened the officer's face.

"Oh, oh," he said to him, with a loud laugh, "how gloomy you are, Captain! did you see three owls flying on your right? The pagans assert that such is an evil omen."

"Perhaps so," the Captain drily replied.

The tone in which the remark was uttered had nothing friendly or inviting about it. The monk understood that any conversation at this moment was impossible; he took the hint, bit his lips, and continued to ride silently by his companion's side.

An hour later they reached the bivouac; neither the monk nor the officer had said a word; but the nearer they came to the spot selected for the halt, the more anxious each seemed to grow.

CHAPTER XV
THE HALT

The sun had almost entirely disappeared on the horizon at the moment when the caravans reached the halting ground.

This spot, situated on the top of a rather scarped hill, had been selected with that sagacity which distinguishes Texan or Mexican arrieros; any surprise was impossible, and the aged trees that grew on the crest of the hill would, in the event of an attack, offer a secure protection against bullets.

The mules were unloaded, but, contrary to the usual custom, the bales, instead of being employed a breastwork for the camp, were piled up and placed out of reach of the marauders whom chance or cupidity might attract to this quarter when the darkness had set in.

Seven or eight large fires were lit in a circle, in order to keep off wild beasts; the mules received their ration of Indian corn on *mantas* or horsecloths laid on the ground; then, so soon as sentinels were posted round the camp, the troopers and arrieros were busily engaged in preparing the poor supper, which the day's fatigues rendered necessary.

Captain Don Juan and the monk, who had gone a little aside to a fire lit expressly for them, were beginning to smoke their husk cigarettes, while the officer's servant was hastily preparing his master's meal—a meal, we are bound to say, as simple as that of the other members of the caravan, but which hunger had the privilege of rendering not only appetising, but almost succulent, although it was only composed of a few *varas* of tocino, or meat dried in the sun, and four or five biscuits.

The Captain soon finished his supper. He then rose, and, as night had completely fallen, went to visit the sentries, and see that all was in order. When he resumed his place by the fire, Father Antonio, with his feet turned to the flame, and wrapped in a thick zarapé, was sleeping, or pretending to sleep, soundly.

Don Juan examined him for a moment with an expression of hatred and contempt, impossible to describe, shook his head twice or thrice thoughtfully, and then told his assistants, who were standing a few paces off in expectation of his orders, to have the two prisoners brought up.

These prisoners had hitherto been kept apart; though treated with respect, it was, however, easy for them to see that they were guarded with the greatest care; still, either through carelessness or some other reason, they did not appear to notice the fact, for their weapons had been left them, and, judging from their muscular force and energetic features, though both had reached middle life, there was fair ground for supposing when the moment arrived for them to insist on their liberty, they would be the men to try and regain it by force.

Without any remark they followed the Captain's servant, and soon found themselves before that officer.

Though the night was gloomy, the flames of the fire spread sufficient light around to illumine the faces of the new comers.

On seeing them Don Juan gave a start of surprise, but one of the prisoners laid his finger on his lip to recommend prudence to him, and at the same time glanced significantly at the monk lying near them.

The Captain understood this dumb warning, to which he replied by a light nod of the head, and then affected the utmost carelessness.

"Who are you?" he asked, as he idly rolled a cigarette between his fingers.

"Hunters," one of the prisoners answered, without hesitation.

"You were found a few hours back halting on the bank of a stream."

"Quite correct."

"What were you doing there?"

The prisoner bent a scrutinizing glance around, and then looked again boldly at the speaker.

"Before giving any further answer to your questions," he said, "I should like to ask you one in my turn."

"What is it?"

"Your right to cross-question me?"

"Look round you," the Captain lightly replied.

"Yes, I understand you, the right of force. Unluckily I do not recognize that right. I am a free hunter, acknowledging no other law but my will, no other master but myself."

"Oh, oh! your language is bold, comrade."

"It is that of a man not accustomed to yield to any arbitrary power; to take me you have abused—I do not say your strength, for your soldiers would have killed me, before compelling me to follow them, had not such been my intention—but the facility with which I confided in you: I therefore protest against it, and demand my immediate freedom."

"Your haughty language has no effect on me, and were it my good pleasure to force you to speak, I could compel you by certain irresistible arguments I possess."

"Yes," the prisoner said, bitterly, "the Mexicans remember the Spaniards their ancestors, and appeal to torture when necessary; well, try it, Captain—who prevents you? I trust that my gray hairs will not grow weak before your young moustache."

"Enough of this," the Captain said, angrily. "If I give you your liberty, should I deliver a friend or a foe?"

"Neither."

"Hum! what do you mean?"

"My answer is clear enough, surely."

"Still, I do not understand it."

"I will explain in two words."

"Speak."

"Both of us being placed in diametrically opposite positions, chance has thought proper to bring us together to-day: if we now part, we shall take with us no feeling of hatred through our meeting, because neither you nor I have had cause to complain of each other, and probably we shall never see each other again."

"Still, it is plain that when my soldiers found you, you were expecting somebody on this road."

"What makes you suppose that?"

"Hang it! you told me you were hunters; I do not see any game you could hunt along this road."

The prisoner began laughing.

"Who knows?" he replied, with a stress on his words, "Perhaps it was more precious game than you may fancy, and of which you would like to have your share."

The monk gave a slight start, and opened his eyes as awaking.

"What?" he said, addressing the Captain, and stifling a yawn. "You are not asleep, Don Juan?"

"Not yet," the latter answered. "I am questioning the two men my vanguard arrested some hours ago."

"Ah!" the monk remarked with a disdainful glance at the strangers, "these poor devils do not appear to me very alarming."

"You think so?"

"I do not know what you can have to fear from these men."

"Perhaps they are spies?"

Fray Antonio assumed a paternal air.

"Spies?" he said; "Do you fear an ambuscade?"

"Under the circumstances in which we now are, that supposition is not so improbable, I fancy."

"Nonsense! in a country like this, and with the escort you have at your service, that would be extraordinary; moreover, these two men let themselves be captured without resistance, as I heard, when they might easily have escaped."

"That is true."

"It is evident, then, that they had no bad intentions. If I were you, I would quietly let them go where they pleased."

"Is that your advice?"

"Indeed it is."

"You seem to take a great interest in these two strangers."

"I? Not the least in the world. I only tell you what is right, that's all: now you can act as you please. I wash my hands of it."

"You may be right, still I will not set these persons at liberty till they have told me the name of the person they were expecting."

"Were they expecting anybody?"

"They say so, at any rate."

"It is true, Captain," said the person who had hitherto spoken; "but though we knew you were coming, it was not you we were waiting for."

"Who was it, then?"

"Do you insist on knowing?"

"Certainly."

"Then answer, Fray Antonio," the prisoner said with a grin; "for you alone can reveal the name the Captain asks of us."

"I?" the monk said with a start of passion, and turning pale as a corpse.

"Ah, ah!" the Captain said, as he turned to him, "this is beginning to grow interesting."

It was a singular scene presented by the four men standing round the fire, whose flame fantastically lit up their faces.

The Captain carelessly smoked his cigarette, while looking sarcastically at the monk, on whose face impudence and fear were fighting a battle, every incident in which was easy to read; the two hunters, with their hands crossed over the muzzles of their long rifles, smiled cunningly, and seemed to be quietly enjoying the embarrassment of the man whom they had placed in this terrible dilemma.

"Don't pretend to look so surprised, Padre Antonio," the prisoner then at length said; "you know very well we were expecting you."

"Me?" the monk said in a choking voice; "the scoundrel is mad, on my soul."

"I am not mad, Padre, and I will trouble you not to employ such language toward me," the prisoner replied drily.

"Come, give in," the other, who had hitherto been silent, cried coarsely; "I do not care to dance at the end of a rope for your good pleasure."

"Which will inevitably happen," the Captain remarked quietly, "if you do not decide, Caballeros, on giving me a clear and explicit explanation of your conduct."

"There you see, Señor Frayle," the prisoner continued, "our position is growing delicate; come, behave like a man."

"Oh!" the monk exclaimed furiously, "I have fallen into a horrible trap."

"Enough," the Captain said in a thundering voice; "this farce has lasted only too long, Padre Antonio. It is not you who have fallen into a trap, but you tried to draw me into one. I have known you for a long time, and possess the most circumstantial details about the plans you were devising. It is a dangerous game you have been playing for a long time; a man cannot serve GOD and the devil simultaneously, without all being discovered at last; still, I wished to confront you with these worthy men, in order to confound you, and make the mask fall from your hypocritical face."

At this rude apostrophe the Monk was for a moment stunned, crushed as he was beneath the weight of the charges brought against him; at length he raised his head and turned to the Captain.

"Of what am I accused?" he asked haughtily.

Don Juan smiled contemptuously.

"You are accused," he replied, "of having wished to lead the conducta I command into an ambush formed by you, and where at this moment your worthy acolytes are waiting to massacre and rob us. What will you reply to that?"

"Nothing," he answered, drily.

"You are right, for your denials would not be accepted. Still, now that you are convicted by your own confession, you will not escape without an eternal recollection of our meeting."

"Take care of what you are about to do, Señor Captain: I belong to the church, and this gown renders me inviolable."

A mocking smile contracted the Captain's lips.

"No matter for that," he replied, "it shall be stripped off you."

Most of the troopers and arrieros, aroused by the loud voices of the monk and the officer, had gradually drawn nearer, and attentively followed the conversation.

The Captain pointed to the monk, and addressed the soldiers.

"Strip off the gown that covers that man," he said; "fasten him to a catalpa, and give him two hundred lashes with a *chicote*."

"Villains!" the monk exclaimed, nearly out of his mind; "Any man of you who dares to lay hands on me I curse; he will be eternally condemned for having insulted a minister of the altar."

The soldiers stopped in terror before this anathema, which their ignorance and stupid superstition robbed them of the courage to brave.

The monk folded his arms, and addressed the officer triumphantly —

"Wretched madman," he said, "I could punish you for your audacity, but I pardon you. Heaven will undertake to avenge me, and you will be punished when your last hour arrives. Farewell! Make room for me to pass, fellows!"

The dragoons, confused and timid, fell back slowly and hesitatingly before him; the Captain, forced to confess his impotence, clenched his fists, as he looked passionately around him.

The monk had all but passed through the ranks of the soldiers, when he suddenly felt his arm clutched; he turned with the evident intention of severely reprimanding the man who was so audacious as to touch him, but the expression of his face suddenly changed on seeing who it was that stopped him, and looked at him craftily, for it was no other than the strange prisoner, the first cause of the insult offered him.

"One moment, Señor Padre," the hunter said. "I can understand that these worthy fellows, who are Catholics, should fear your curse, and dare not lay a hand on you through their dread of eternal flames, but with me it is different. I am a heretic, as you know, hence I run no risk in taking off your gown, and, with your permission, I will do you that slight service."

"Oh!" the monk replied, as he ground his teeth; "I will kill you, John, I will kill you, villain!"

"Nonsense, threatened people live a long while," John replied, as he forced him to take off his monk's gown.

"There," he continued, "now, my fine fellows, you can carry out your Captain's orders in perfect safety; this man is no more to you than the first comer."

The hunter's bold action suddenly broke the spell that enchained the soldiers. So soon as the much-feared gown no longer covered the monk's shoulders, listening to neither prayers nor threats, they seized the culprit, fastened him, in spite of his cries, securely to a catalpa, and conscientiously administered the two hundred lashes decreed by the Captain, while the hunters played their part by counting the blows and laughing loudly at the contortions of the wretched man, whom pain caused to writhe like a serpent.

At the one hundred and twenty-eighth lash the monk became silent: his nervous system being completely overthrown, rendered him insensible; still, he did not faint, his teeth were clenched, a white foam escaped from his crisped lips, he looked fixedly before him without seeing anything, and giving no other signs of existence than the heavy sighs which at intervals upheld his muscular chest.

When the punishment was ended, and he was unfastened, he fell to the ground like a log, and lay there motionless.

His robe was handed back to him, and he was left to lie there, no one troubling himself further about him.

The two hunters then went off, after talking to the Captain for some minutes in a low voice.

The rest of the night passed away without incident.

A few minutes before sunrise, the soldiers and arrieros prepared to load the mules, and prepare everything for the start.

"Stay," the Captain suddenly exclaimed, "where is the monk? We cannot abandon him thus; lay him on a mule, and we will leave him at the first rancho we come to."

The soldiers hastened to obey, and look for Padre Antonio, but all their search was in vain; he had disappeared, and left no trace of his flight.

Don Juan frowned at the news, but, after a moment's reflection, he shook his head carelessly.

"All the better," he said, "he would have been in our way."

The conducta herewith started again.

CHAPTER XVI
A POLITICAL SKETCH

Before proceeding further, we will say in a few words what was the political situation of Texas at the moment when the story we have undertaken to tell took place.

During the Spanish domination, the Texans claimed their liberty, arms in hand; but after various successes, they were definitively crushed at the battle of Medina, on August 13th, 1815, a fatal date, by Colonel Arredondo, commanding the regiment of Estremadura, who was joined by the Militia of the State of Cohahuila. From that period up to the second Mexican Revolution, Texas remained bowed beneath the intolerable yoke of the military regime, and left defenceless to the incessant attacks of the Comanche Indians.

The United States had on many occasions raised claims to that country, declaring that the natural frontiers of Mexico and the Confederation were the Rio Bravo; but compelled in 1819 to allow ostensibly that their claims were not founded, they employed roundabout means to seize on this rich territory, and incorporate it in their borders.

It was at that time they displayed that astute and patiently Machiavellian policy, which finally led to their triumph.

In 1821, the first American emigrants made their appearance, timidly, and almost incognito, on the brazos, clearing the land, colonizing secretly, and becoming in a few years so powerful, that in 1824 they had made sufficient progress to form a compact mass of nearly 50,000 individuals. The Mexicans, incessantly occupied in struggling one against the other in their interminable civil wars, did not understand the purport of the American immigration, which they encouraged at the outset.

Hardly eight years had elapsed since the arrival of the first Americans in Texas, when they formed nearly the entire population.

The Washington Cabinet no longer concealed its intentions, and spoke openly of buying from the Mexicans the territory of Texas, in which the Spanish element had almost entirely disappeared, to make room for the daring and mercantile spirit of the Anglo-Saxons.

The Mexican Government, at last aroused from its long lethargy, understood the danger that threatened it from the double invasion of the inhabitants of Missouri and Texas into the State of Santa Fé. It tried to arrest the American emigration, but it was too late; the law passed by the Mexican Congress was powerless, and the colonization was not arrested, in spite of the Mexican military posts scattered along the border, with orders to turn the immigrants back.

General Bustamante, President of the Republic, seeing that he would soon have to fight with the Americans, silently prepared for the conflict, and sent under different pretexts to Red River and the Sabina various bodies of troops, which presently attained to the number of 1200 men.

Still, everything remained quiet apparently; and nothing evidenced the period when the struggle would commence, which a perfidy on the part of the Governor of the Eastern provinces caused to break out at the moment when least expected.

The facts were as follow: —

The Commandant of Anahuac arrested and put in prison several American colonists, without any plausible grounds.

The Texans had hitherto patiently endured the innumerable vexations which the Mexican officers made them undergo, but at this last abuse of force they rose as if by one accord, and went under arms to the Commandant, demanding with threats and angry shouts the immediate liberation of their fellow-citizens.

The Commandant, too weak to resist openly, feigned to grant what was asked of him, but represented that he required two days to fulfil certain formalities, and cover his own responsibility.

The insurgents granted this delay, by which the Commandant profited to send in all haste to the Nacogdoches garrison to help him.

This garrison arrived at the moment when the insurgents, confiding on the Governor's promise, were with-drawing.

Furious at having been so perfidiously deceived, the latter returned and made such an energetic demonstration that the Mexican officer considered himself fortunate in escaping a fight by surrendering his prisoners.

At this period, a *pronunciamento* in favour of Santa Anna hurled General Bustamante from power to the cry of "Long live the Federation!"

Texas was extremely afraid of the system of centralization, from which it would never have obtained the recognition of its independence as a separate State, and hence the people were unanimous for Federalism.

The colonists rose, and joining the insurgents of Anahuac who were still under arms, marched resolutely on Fort Velasco, to which they laid siege.

The rallying cry was still "Long live the Federation!" But this time it concealed the cry of Independence, which the Texans were as yet too weak to raise.

Fort Velasco was defended by a small Mexican garrison, commanded by a brave officer of the name of Ugartechea.

During this extraordinary siege, in which the assailants only replied to the cannon with rifle bullets, both Texans and Mexicans performed prodigies of valour and displayed extraordinary obstinacy.

The colonists, skilful marksmen, hidden behind enormous barricades, fired as at a mark, and killed the Mexican gunners whenever they showed themselves to load their guns. Matters reached such a point that the Commandant, seeing his bravest soldiers fall round him, devoted himself and set to work as artilleryman. Struck by this heroic courage, the Texans, who could have killed the brave Commandant twenty times, ceased their fire, and Ugartechea at length surrendered, giving up a defence which was henceforth impossible.

The success filled the colonists with joy, but Santa Anna was not deceived as to the object of the Texan insurrection; he understood that federalism concealed a well-devised revolutionary movement, and far from trusting to the apparent devotion of the colonists, so soon as his power was sufficiently strengthened to allow him to act energetically against them, he sent off Colonel Mexia with four hundred men, to reestablish in Texas the greatly shaken Mexican authority.

After many hesitations and diplomatic dodges, which had no possible result with parties, both of which employed perfidy as their chief weapon, the war at length broke out furiously; a committee of public safety was organized at San Felipe, and the people were called upon to take part in the struggle.

The civil war, however, had not yet officially broken out, when the man at length appeared who was destined to decide the fate of Texas, and for whom the glory of liberating it was reserved—we allude to Samuel Houston.

From this moment the timid and purposeless insurrection of Texas became a revolution. Still the Mexican government remained apparently the legitimate master of the colony, and the colonists were naturally denominated insurgents, and treated as such, when they fell into the hands of their enemies; that is to say, they were without trial hung, drowned, or shot, according as the spot where they were captured suited one of these three modes of death.

At the period when our story opens, the exasperation against the Mexicans and the enthusiasm for the noble cause of Independence had reached their acme.

About three weeks previously, a serious engagement had taken place between the garrison of Bejar and a detachment of Texan volunteers, commanded by Austin, one of the most renowned Chiefs of the insurgents; in spite of their inferiority in numbers and ignorance of military tactics, the colonists fought so bravely, and worked their solitary gun so skilfully, that the Mexican troops, after undergoing serious losses, were compelled to retreat precipitately on Bejar.

This action was the first on the west of Texas after the capture of Fort Velasco; it decided the revolutionary movement which ran through the country like a train of gunpowder.

On all sides the towns raised troops to join the army of liberation; resistance was organized on a grand scale and bold Guerilla Chiefs began traversing the country in every direction, making war on their own account, and serving after their fashion the cause they embraced and which they were supposed to be defending.

Captain Don Juan Melendez, surrounded by enemies the more dangerous because it was impossible for him to know their numbers or guess their movements; entrusted with an extreme delicate mission; having at each step a prescience of treachery incessantly menacing, though ignorant where, when, or how it would burst on him; was compelled to employ extreme precautions and a merciless severity, if he wished to get safe home the precious charge confided to him; hence he had not hesitated before the necessity of instituting an example by roughly punishing Padre Antonio.

For a long time past, grave suspicions had been gathering over the monk; his ambiguous conduct had aroused distrust, and caused presumptions in no way favourable to his honesty.

Don Juan had determined to clear up his doubts at the first opportunity that offered; we have stated in what way he had succeeded by springing a countermine, that is to say, by having the spy watched by others more skilful than himself, and catching him almost red-handed.

Still, we must do the worthy monk the justice of declaring that his conduct had not the slightest political motive; his thoughts were not so elevated as that; knowing that the Captain was entrusted with the charge of a conducta de plata, he had only tried to draw him into a trap, for the sake of having a share in the plunder, and making his fortune at a stroke, in order that he might enjoy those indulgences he had hitherto gone without; his ideas did not extend further, the worthy man was simply a highway robber, but there was nothing of the politician about him.

We will leave him for the present to follow the two hunters to whom he was indebted for the rude chastisement he received, and who quitted the camp immediately after the execution of the sentence.

These two men went off at a great speed, and, after descending the hill, buried themselves in a thick wood, where two magnificent prairie horses, half-tamed Mustangs, with flashing eye and delicate limbs, were quietly browsing, while waiting for their riders; they were saddled in readiness for mounting.

After unfastening the hobbles, the hunters put the bits in their mouths, mounted, and digging in their spurs, started at a sharp gallop.

They rode for a long distance, bent over their horses' necks, following no regular path, but going straight on, caring little for the obstacles they met on their passage, and which they cleared with infinite skill; about an hour before sunrise they at length stopped.

They had reached the entrance of a narrow gorge, flanked on both sides by lofty wooded hills, the spurs of the mountains, whose denuded crests seemed from their proximity to hang over the landscape. The hunters dismounted before entering the gorge, and after hobbling their horses, which they hid in a clump of floripondios, they began exploring the neighbourhood with the care and sagacity of Indian warriors seeking booty on the war-trail.

Their researches remained for a long time sterile, which could easily be perceived from the exclamations of disappointment they every now and then vented in a low voice: at length, after two hours, the first beams of the sun dissipated the darkness, and they perceived some almost imperceptible traces which made them start with joy.

Probably feeling now liberated from the anxiety that tormented them, they returned to their horses, lay down on the ground, and after fumbling in their alforjas, drew from them the materials for a modest breakfast, to which they did honour with the formidable appetite of men who have spent the whole night in the saddle, riding over mountains and valleys.

Since their departure from the Mexican camp the hunters had not exchanged a syllable, apparently acting under the influence of a dark preoccupation, which rendered any conversation unnecessary.

In fact, the silence of men accustomed to desert life is peculiar; they pass whole days without uttering a word, only speaking when necessity obliges them, and generally substituting for oral language that language of signs which, in the first place, has the incontestable advantage of not betraying the presence of those who employ it to the ears of invisible enemies constantly on the watch, and ready to leap, like birds of prey, on the imprudent persons who allow themselves to be surprised.

When the hunters' appetite was appeased, the one whom the Captain called John lit his short pipe, placed it in the corner of his month, and, handed the tobacco-pouch to his comrade.

"Well, Sam," he said in a low voice, as if afraid of being overheard, "I fancy we have succeeded, eh?"

"I think so too, John," Sam replied with a nod of affirmation; "you are deucedly clever, my boy."

"Nonsense," the other said disdainfully; "there is no merit in deceiving those brutes of Spaniards; they are stupid as bustards."

"No matter, the Captain fell into the hole in a glorious way."

"Hum! it was not he I was afraid of; for he and I have been good friends for a long time; but it was the confounded monk."

"Eh, eh, if he had not arrived just in time, he would probably have spoiled our fun; what is your opinion, John?"

"I think you are right, Sam. By Jabers, I laughed at seeing him writhe under the chicote."

"It was certainly a glorious sight; but are you not afraid that he may avenge himself? these monks are devilishly spiteful."

"Bah! what have we to fear from such vermin? He will never dare to look us in the face."

"No matter, we had better be on our guard. Our trade is a queer one, as you know, and it is very possible that some day or other this accursed animal may play us an ugly trick."

"Don't bother about him; what we did was all fair in war. Be assured that, under similar circumstances, the monk would not have spared us."

"That is true; so let him go to the deuce; the more so as the prey we covet could not be in a better situation for us. I should never pardon myself if I let it escape."

"Shall we remain here in ambush?"

"That is the safest way; we shall have time to rejoin our comrades when we see the recua enter the plain; and, besides, have we not to meet somebody here?"

"That is true, I forgot it."

"And stay, when you speak of the devil—here is our man."

The hunters rose quickly, seized their rifles, and hid themselves behind a rock, so as to be ready for any event.

The rapid gallop of a horse became audible, approaching nearer and nearer; ere long a rider emerged from the gorge, and pulled up calmly and haughtily at about two paces from the hunters.

The latter rushed from their ambuscade, and advanced toward him, with the right arm extended, and the palm of the hand open in sign of peace.

The horseman, who was an Indian warrior, responded to these pacific demonstrations by letting his buffalo robe float out; then he dismounted, and without further ceremony, shook the hands offered him.

"You are welcome, Chief," John said; "we were awaiting you impatiently."

"My Pale brothers can look at the sun," the Indian answered; "Blue-fox is punctual."

"That is true, Chief; there is nothing to be said, for you are remarkably punctual."

"Time waits for no man; warriors are not women; Blue-fox would like to hold a council with his Pale brothers."

"Be it so," John went on: "your observation is just. Chief, so let us deliberate; I am anxious to come to a definitive understanding with you."

The Indian bowed gravely to the speaker, sat down, lit his pipe, and, began smoking with evident pleasure; the hunters took seats by his side, and, like him, remained silent during the whole period their tobacco lasted.

At length, the Chief shook the ashes out of the bowl on his thumbnail, and prepared to speak.

At the same instant a detonation was heard, and a bullet cut away a branch just over the Chiefs head.

The three men leaped to their feet, and seizing their arms, prepared bravely to repulse the enemies who attacked them so suddenly.

CHAPTER XVII
THE PANTHER-KILLER

Between the Larch-tree hacienda and the Venta del Potrero, just half way between the two places, or at about forty miles from either, two men were sitting on the banks of a nameless stream, and conversing, as they supped on pemmican and a few boiled *camotes*.

These two men were Tranquil, the Canadian, and Quoniam, the Negro.

About fifty yards from them, in a copse of brambles and shrubs, a young colt about two months old was fastened to the trunk of a gigantic catalpa. The poor animal, after making vain efforts to break the cord that held it, had at length recognised the inutility of its attempts, and had sorrowfully lain down on the ground.

The two men, whom we left young at the end of our prologue, had now reached the second half of life. Although age had got but a slight grasp on their iron bodies, a few grey hairs were beginning to silver the hunter's scalp, and wrinkles furrowed his face, which was bronzed by the changes of the seasons.

Still, with the exception of these slight marks, which serve as a seal to ripened age, nothing denoted any weakening in the Canadian; on the contrary, his eye was still bright, his body equally straight, and his limbs just as muscular.

As for the Negro, no apparent change had taken place in him, and he seemed as young as ever; he had merely grown lustier, but had lost none of his unparalleled activity.

The spot where the two wood rangers had camped was certainly one of the most picturesque on the prairie.

The midnight breeze had swept the sky, whose dark blue vault seemed studded with innumerable spangles of diamonds, in the midst of which the southern cross shone; the moon poured forth its white rays, which imparted to objects a fantastic appearance; the night had that velvety transparence peculiar to twilight; at each gust of wind the trees shook their damp heads, and rained a shower, which pattered on the shrubs.

The river flowed on calmly between its wooded banks, looking in the distance like a silver riband, and reflecting in its peaceful mirror the trembling rays of the moon, which had proceeded about two-thirds of its course.

So great was the silence of the desert, that the fall of a withered leaf, or the rustling of a branch agitated by the passage of a reptile, could be heard.

The two men were conversing in a low voice; but, singularly enough with men so habituated to desert life, their night encampment, instead of being, according to the invariable rules of the prairie, situated on the top of a hillock, was placed on the slope that descended gently to the river, and in the mud of which numerous footprints of more than a suspicious nature were encrusted, the majority belonging to the family of the great Carnivora.

In spite of the sharp cold of night, and the icy dew which made them tremble, the hunters had lit no fire; still they would assuredly have derived great comfort from warming their limbs over the genial flames; the Negro especially, who was lightly attired in drawers that left his legs uncovered, and a fragment of a zarapé, full of holes, was trembling all over.

Tranquil, who was more warmly attired in the garb of Mexican Campesinos, did not appear to notice the cold at all; with his rifle between his legs, he gazed out into the darkness, or listened to any sound perceptible to him alone, while he talked to the Negro, disdaining to notice either his grimaces or the chattering of his teeth.

"So," he said, "you did not see the little one to-day Quoniam?"

"No, no, I have not seen her for two days," the Negro answered.

The Canadian sighed.

"I ought to have gone myself," he went on; "the girl is very solitary there, especially now that war has let loose on this side all the adventurers and border-ruffians."

"Nonsense! Carmela has beak and nails; she would not hesitate to defend herself if insulted."

"Confusion!" the Canadian exclaimed, as he clutched his rifle, "If one of those Malvados dared to say a word —"

"Do not trouble yourself thus, Tranquil; you know very well that if any one ventured to insult the Querida Niña, she would not want for defenders. Besides, Lanzi never leaves her for a moment, and you are aware how faithful he is."

"Yes," the hunter muttered, "but Lanzi is only a man after all."

"You drive me to desperation with the ideas which so unreasonably get into your head."

"I love the girl, Quoniam."

"Hang it, and I love her too, the little darling! Well, if you like, after we have killed the jaguar, we will go to the Potrero—does that suit you?"

"It is a long way from here."

"Nonsense! three hours' ride at the most. By the bye, Tranquil, do you know that it is cold? And I am getting literally frozen; cursed animal! I wonder what it is doing at this moment; I daresay it is amusing itself with wandering about instead of coming straight here."

"To be killed, eh?" Tranquil said, with a smile. "Hang it all! Perhaps it suspects what we have in store for it."

"That is possible, for those confounded animals are so cunning. Hilloah! the colt is quivering—it has certainly scented something."

The Canadian turned his head.

"No, not yet," he said.

"We shall have a night of it," the Negro muttered, with an ill-tempered look.

"You will ever be the same, Quoniam—impatient and headstrong. Whatever I may tell you, you obstinately refuse to understand me; how many times have I repeated to you that the jaguar is one of the most cunning animals in existence? Although we are to windward, I feel convinced it has scented us. It is prowling cunningly around us, and afraid to come too near us; as you say, it is wandering about without any apparent object."

"Hum! Do you think it will carry on that game much longer?"

"No, because it must be beginning to grow thirsty; three feelings are struggling in it at this moment—hunger, thirst, and fear; fear will prove the weakest, you may be assured; and it is only a question of time."

"I can see it; for nearly four hours we have been on the watch."

"Patience; the worst is over, and we shall soon have some news, I feel assured."

"May Heaven hear you, for I am dying of cold; is it a large animal?"

"Yes, its prints are wide, but, if I am not greatly mistaken, it has paired."

"Do you think so?"

"I could almost bet it, it is impossible for a single jaguar to do so much mischief in less than a week; from what Don Hilario told me, it seems that ten head of the Ganada have disappeared."

"In that case," Quoniam said, rubbing his hands gleefully, "we shall have a fine hunt."

"That is what I suppose; and it must have whelps to come so near the hacienda."

At this moment a hoarse bellowing, bearing some slight resemblance to the miauling of a cat, troubled the profound silence of the desert.

"There is its first cry," said Quoniam.

"It is still a long way off."

"Oh, it will soon come nearer."

"Not yet; it is not after us at this moment."

"Who else, then?"

"Listen."

A similar cry to the first, but coming from the opposite side, burst forth at this moment.

"Did I not tell you," the Canadian continued, quietly, "that it had paired?"

"I did not doubt it. If you do not know the habits of tigers, who should?"

The poor colt had risen; it was trembling all over, half dead with terror, and with its head buried between its front legs, it was standing up and uttering little plaintive cries.

"Hum!" Quoniam said, "poor innocent brute, it understands that it is lost."

"I hope not."

"The jaguar will strangle it."

"Yes, if we do not kill the brute first."

"By Jabus!" the Negro said, "I confess I should not be sorry if that wretched colt escaped."

"It will do so," the hunter answered; "I have chosen it for Carmela."

"Nonsense! Then why did you bring it here?"

"To make it used to the tiger."

"Well, that is an idea! Then I need not look any longer over there?"

"No, only think of the jaguar which will come on your right, while I take charge of the other."

"That's agreed."

Two other louder roars burst forth almost simultaneously.

"The beast is thirsty," Tranquil remarked; "its anger is aroused, and it is coming nearer."

"Good! shall we get ready?"

"Wait a while, our enemies are hesitating; they have not yet reached that paroxysm of rage which makes them forget all prudence."

The Negro, who had risen, sat down again philosophically.

A few minutes passed thus. At intervals the night breeze, laden with uncertain rumour, passed over the hunters' heads, and was lost in the distance like a sigh.

They were calm and motionless, with the eye fixed on space, the ear open to the mysterious noises of the desert, the finger on the rifle-trigger, ready at the first signal to face the still invisible foe, whose approach and imminent attack they, however, instinctively divined.

All at once the Canadian started, and stooped down to the ground.

"Oh!" he said, as he rose with marks of terrible anxiety, "What is taking place in the forest?"

The roar of the tiger burst forth like a clap of thunder.

A horrible shriek responded to it, and the wild gallop of a horse was heard, approaching at headlong speed.

"Quick! Quick!" Tranquil shouted, "Someone is in danger of death—the tiger is on his trail."

The two hunters rushed intrepidly in the direction of the roars.

The whole forest seemed quivering; nameless sounds issued from the hidden lairs, resembling at one moment mocking laughter, at another cries of agony.

The hoarse miauling of the jaguars went on uninterruptedly. The gallop of the horses which the hunters heard at first seemed multiplied and issuing from opposite points.

The panting hunters still ran on in a straight line, bounding over ravines and morasses with wonderful speed; the terror they felt for the strangers whom they wished to help gave them wings.

Suddenly a shriek of agony, louder and more despairing than the former, was heard a short distance off.

"Oh!" Tranquil shouted, in a paroxysm of madness, "It is she! It is Carmela!"

And, bounding like a wild beast, he rushed forward, followed by Quoniam, who, during the whole wild race, had never left him a hair's breadth.

Suddenly a deadly silence fell over the desert—every noise, every rumour, ceased as if by enchantment, and nothing could be heard save the panting of the hunters, who still ran on.

A furious roar uttered by the tigers burst forth; a crashing of branches agitated an adjoining thicket, and an enormous mass, bounding from the top of the tree, passed over the Canadian's head and disappeared; at the same instant a flash burst through the gloom and a shot was heard, answered almost immediately by a roar of agony and a shriek of horror.

"Courage, Niña, courage!" a masculine voice exclaimed, a short distance off, "You are saved!"

The hunters, by a supreme effort of their will, increased their speed, which was already incredible, and at length entered the scene of action.

A strange and terrible sight then offered itself to their horror-stricken gaze.

In a small clearing a fainting woman was stretched out on the ground, by the side of a ripped-up horse, which was struggling in the final convulsions.

This female was motionless, and appeared to be dead.

Two young tigers, crouching like cats, fixed their ardent eyes upon her, and were preparing to attack her; a few paces further on a wounded tiger was writhing on the ground with horrid roars, and trying to leap on a man, who, with one knee on the ground, with his left arm enveloped in the numerous folds of a zarapé, and the right armed with a long machete, was resolutely awaiting its attack.

Behind the man, a horse, with outstretched neck, smoking nostrils and laid-back ears, was quivering with terror, while a second tiger, posted on the largest branch of a larch tree, fixed its burning glances on the dismounted rider, while lashing the air with its tail, and uttering hoarse miauls.

What we have taken so long to describe, the hunters saw at a glance; quick as lightning the bold adventurers selected their parts, with a look of sublime simplicity.

While Quoniam leaped on the tiger cubs, and seizing them by the scurf, dashed their brains out against a rock, Tranquil shouldered his rifle, and killed the tigress at the moment when she was leaping on the horseman. Then turning with marvellous speed he killed the second tiger with the butt of his rifle, and laid it stiff at his feet.

"Ah!" the hunter said, with a feeling of pride, as he rested his rifle on the ground, and wiped his forehead, which was bathed in a cold perspiration.

"She lives!" Quoniam shouted, who understood what agony his friend's exclamation contained; "Fear alone made her faint, but she is otherwise unhurt."

The hunter slowly took off his cap, and raised his eyes to heaven.

"Thanks, O God!" he murmured, with an accent of gratitude impossible to render.

In the meanwhile, the horseman, so miraculously saved by Tranquil, had walked up to him.

"I will do the same for you, some day," he said, as he held out his hand.

"It is I who am your debtor," the hunter answered, frankly; "had it not been for your sublime devotion, I should have arrived too late."

"I have done no more than another in my place."

"Perhaps so. Your name, brother?"

"Loyal Heart. Yours?"

"Tranquil. We are friends for life and death."

"I accept, brother. And now let us attend to this poor girl."

The two men shook hands for a second time, and went up to Carmela, on whom Quoniam was lavishing every imaginable attention, though unable to recall her from the profound faint into which she had fallen.

While Tranquil and Loyal Heart took the Negro's place, the latter hastily collected a few dried branches and lit a fire.

After a few minutes, however, Carmela faintly opened her eyes, and was soon sufficiently recovered to explain the cause of her presence in the forest, instead of being quietly asleep in the Venta del Potrero.

This story, which, in consequence of the maiden's weakness, and the poignant emotions she had endured, it took her several hours to complete, we will tell the reader in a few words in the next chapter.

CHAPTER XVIII
LANZI

Carmela watched for a long time the Jaguar's irregular ride across country, and when he at length disappeared in the distance, in a clump of pine trees, she sadly bowed her head and re-entered the venta slowly and pensively.

"He hates him," she murmured, in a low, agitated voice; "he hates him. Will he be willing to save him?"

She fell into an equipal, and for some minutes remained plunged in a deep reverie.

At last she raised her head; a feverish flush covered her face, and her soft eyes seemed to emit flashes.

"I will save him!" she exclaimed, with supreme resolution.

After this exclamation she rose, and walking hurriedly across the room, opened the door leading into the corral.

"Lanzi?" she cried.

"Niña?" the half-breed replied, who was engaged at this moment in giving their alfalfa to two valuable horses belonging to the young lady, which were under his special charge.

"Come here."

"I will be with you in a moment."

Five minutes later at the most he appeared in the doorway.

"What do you want, señorita?" he said, with that calm obsequiousness habitual to servants who are spoiled by their masters; "I am very busy at this moment."

"That is possible, my good Lanzi," she answered softly; "but what I have to say to you admits of no delay."

"Oh, oh," he said, in a slightly suppressed tone, "what is the matter, then?"

"Nothing very extraordinary, my good man; everything in the venta is regular as usual. But I have a service to ask of you."

"Speak, señorita; you know that I am devoted to you."

"It is growing late, and it is probable that no traveller will arrive at the venta to-day."

The half-breed raised his head, and mentally calculated the position of the sun.

"I do not believe that any travellers will arrive to-day," he at length said, "for it is nearly four o'clock; still, they might come for all that."

"Nothing leads to the supposition."

"Nothing, indeed, señorita."

"Well, I wish you to shut up the venta."

"Shut up the venta! What for?"

"I will tell you."

"Is it really very important?"

"Very."

"Speak, then, Niña, I am all ears."

The maiden gave the half-breed, who was standing in front of her, a long and searching glance, leant her elbow gracefully on the table, and said, quietly—

"I am anxious, Lanzi."

"Anxious? What about?"

"At my father's long absence."

"Why, he was here hardly four days back."

"He never left me alone so long before."

"Still," the half-breed remarked, scratching his head with an embarrassed air—

"In a word," she interrupted him, resolutely, "I am anxious about my father, and wish to see him. You will close the venta, saddle the horses, and we will go to the Larch-tree hacienda; it is not far, and we shall be back in four or five hours."

"That will make it very late."

"The greater reason to start at once."

"Still—"

"No remarks; do as I order you—I insist on it."

The half-breed bowed without replying, for he knew that when his young mistress spoke thus he must obey.

The maiden walked forward a step, laid her white and delicate hand on the half-breed's shoulder, and putting her lovely face close to his, she added, with a gentle smile which made the poor fellow start with joy—

"Do not be vexed at my whim, my kind Lanzi, but I am suffering."

"Be vexed with you, Niña!" the half-breed answered with a significant shrug of his shoulders; "Why, do you not know that I would go into the fire for you? Much more, then, would I satisfy your slightest wish."

He then began carefully barricading the doors and windows of the venta, after which he proceeded to the corral to saddle the horses, while Carmela, suffering from nervous impatience, changed her attire for other clothes more convenient for the journey she designed, for she had deceived the old servant. It was not Tranquil she wished to find.

But Heaven had decreed that the plan she revolved in her pretty head should not succeed.

At the moment when she re-entered the sitting-room, fully dressed and ready to start, Lanzi appeared in the doorway of the corral with extreme agitation displayed in his face.

Carmela ran up to him eagerly, fancying that he had hurt himself.

"What is the matter with you?" she asked him, kindly.

"We are lost!" he replied, in a hollow voice, as he looked about him in terror.

"Lost!" she exclaimed, turning pallid as a corpse; "What do you mean?"

The half-breed laid a finger on his lip to command silence, made her a sign to follow him, and glided noiselessly into the corral.

Carmela followed him.

The corral was enclosed with a plank wall about six feet high; Lanzi went up to a spot where a wide cleft allowed a prospect of the plain.

"Look," he said to his mistress.

The girl obeyed, and laid her face against the plank.

Night was beginning to fall, and a denser shadow was each moment invading the plain. Still, the obscurity was not great enough to prevent Carmela distinguishing, about two hundred yards away, a numerous party of horsemen coming at full speed in the direction of the venta.

A glance sufficed the maiden to perceive that these horsemen were Indios Bravos.

The warriors, more than fifty in number, were in their full war paint; and as they bent over the necks of their horses, which were as untamable as themselves, they brandished their long lances over their heads with an air of defiance.

"These are Apaches," Carmela exclaimed, as she recoiled in terror. "How comes it that they have reached this place before we are warned of their arrival?"

The half-breed shook his head sadly.

"In a few minutes they will be here," he said; "what is to be done?"

"Defend ourselves!" the maiden replied, bravely; "They do not appear to have fire-arms. Behind the walls of our house we could easily hold out against them till daybreak."

"And then?" the half-breed asked, doubtfully.

"Then," she answered with exaltation, "Heaven will come to our aid."

"Amen!" the half-breed answered, less convinced than ever of the possibility of such a miracle.

"Make haste and bring down into the inn-room all the fire-arms we have; perhaps the heathens will fall back if they find themselves hotly received: and, after all, who knows whether they will attack us?"

"Hum! the demons are crafty, and know perfectly well how many persons dwell in this house. Do not expect that they will withdraw till they have carried it by storm."

"Well," she exclaimed, resolutely, "let us trust to Heaven; we shall die bravely fighting, instead of letting ourselves be captured like cowards, and becoming the slaves of those heartless and merciless villains."

"Be it so, then," the half-breed answered, electrified by his mistress's enthusiastic words, "we will fight. You know, señorita, that a combat does not terrify me. The pagans had better look out, for unless they take care, I may play them a trick they will remember for a long time."

This conversation broke off here for the present, owing to the necessity the speakers were under of preparing their means of defence, which they did with a speed and intelligence which proved that this was not the first time they found themselves in so critical a position.

The reader must not feel surprised at the virile heroism Carmela displayed under the present circumstances. On the border, where persons are incessantly exposed to the incursions of Indians and marauders of every description, the women fight by the side of the men, and forgetting the weakness of their sex, they can, on occasion, prove themselves as brave as their husbands and brothers.

Carmela was not mistaken, it was really a band of Indian Bravos coming up at a gallop, who soon reached the house, and completely surrounded it.

Usually the Indians in their expeditions proceed with extreme prudence, never showing themselves openly, and only advancing with great circumspection. This time it was easy to see that they believed themselves certain of success, and were perfectly well aware that the venta was stripped of its defenders.

On coming within twenty yards of the venta they stopped, dismounted, and seemed to be consulting for a moment.

Lanzi had profited by these few moments of respite to pile on the table all the weapons in the house, consisting of about a dozen rifles.

Although the doors and windows were barred, it was easy to follow the movements of the enemy through loopholes made at regular distances.

Carmela, armed with a rifle, had intrepidly stationed herself before the door, while the half-breed walked up and down anxiously, going out and coming in again, and apparently giving the last touch to an important and mysterious job.

"There," he said, a moment later, "that is all right; lay that rifle on the table again, señorita; we can only conquer those demons by stratagem, not by force, so leave me to act."

"What is your plan?"

"You will see. I have sawn two planks out of the enclosure of the corral; so soon as you hear me open the door, set off at full speed."

"But you?"

"Do not trouble yourself about me, but give your horse the spurs."

"I will not abandon you."

"Nonsense! No folly of that sort; I am old, my life only hangs by a thread, but yours is precious and must be saved; let me alone, I tell you."

"No, unless you tell me."

"I will tell you nothing. You will find Tranquil at the ford of the Venado; not a word more."

"Ah, that is it," she exclaimed; "well, I swear that I will not stir from your side, whatever may happen."

"You are mad; have I not told you I wished to play the Indians a famous trick?"

"Indeed!"

"Well, you will see. As, however, I fear some imprudence on your part, I wish to see you start before me, that is all."

"Are you speaking the truth?"

"Of course I am. In five minutes I shall have joined you again."

"Do you promise me, then?"

"Do you fancy I should find any fun in remaining here?"

"What do you intend doing?"

"Here are the Indians; begone, and do not forget to start at full gallop so soon as I open the door of the venta, and ride in the direction of the Venado ford."

"But I expect—"

"Begone, begone," he interrupted her quickly, as he pushed her toward the corral, "it is all settled."

The maiden unwillingly obeyed: but at this moment loud blows against the shutters were audible, and the half-breed profited by this demonstration of the Indians to close the door leading into the corral.

"I swore to Tranquil to protect her, whatever might happen," he muttered, "and I can only save her by desires for her. Well, I will die: but, Capa de Dios, I will have a fine funeral."

Fresh blows were dealt at the shutters, but with such violence that it was easy to see that they would be soon broken in.

"Who's there?" the half-breed asked quietly.

"Gente de paz," was the reply from without.

"Hum!" Lanzi said, "for peaceful people you have a singular way of announcing your presence."

"Open, open!" the voice outside repeated.

"I am very ready to do so, but what proves to me that you do not mean harm?"

"Open, or we will break down the door."

And the blows were renewed.

"Oh, oh," the half-breed said, "you are strong in the arms; do not trouble yourself further, I am going to open."

The blows ceased.

The half-breed unbarred the door, and opened it.

The Indians rushed into the interior with yells and howls of joy.

Lanzi slipped on one side to let them pass; he gave a start of joy on hearing a horse set out at full gallop.

The Indians paid no attention to this incident.

"Drink!" they shouted.

"What would you like to have?" the half-breed asked, seeking to gain time.

"Fire-water!" they yelled.

Lanzi hastened to serve them, and the orgy began.

Knowing they had nothing to fear from the inhabitants of the venta, the Redskins had rushed in so soon as the door was opened, without taking the precaution to post sentries; this negligence, on which Lanzi calculated, gave Carmela the opportunity of escaping unseen and undisturbed.

The Indians, and especially the Apaches, have a frenzied passion for strong liquors; the Comanches alone are teetotallers. Hitherto, they have succeeded in refraining from that mournful tendency to intoxication, which decimates and brutalizes their brothers.

Lanzi followed with a cunning look the evolutions of the Redskins, who crowded round the tables, drank deeply, and emptied the botas placed before them; their eyes were beginning to sparkle, their features were animated; they spoke loudly all at once, no longer knowing what they said, and only thinking about becoming intoxicated.

Suddenly the half-breed felt a hand laid on his shoulder.

He turned.

An Indian was standing with folded arms in front of him.

"What do you want?" he asked him.

"Blue-fox is a Chief," the Indian answered, "and has to speak with the Paleface."

"Is not Blue-fox satisfied with the way in which I have received him and his companions?"

"It is not that; the warriors are drinking, and the Chief wants something else."

"Ah," the half-breed said, "I am vexed, for I have given you all I had."

"No," the Indian replied drily.

"How so?"

"Where is the golden-haired girl?"

"I do not understand you, Chief," the half-breed said; on the contrary, understanding perfectly well.

The Indian smiled.

"The Paleface will look at Blue-fox," he said, "and will then see that he is a Chief, and not a child who can be put off with falsehoods. What has become of the girl with the golden hair, who lives here with my brother?"

"The person of whom you speak, if you mean the young lady to whom this house belongs—"

"Yes."

"Well! she is not here."

The Chief gave him a searching glance.

"The Paleface lies," he said.

"Look for her."

"She was here an hour ago."

"That is possible."

"Where is she?"

"Look."

"The Paleface is a dog whose scalp I will raise."

"Much good may it do you," the half-breed answered with a grin.

Unfortunately, while uttering these words, Lanzi gave a triumphant glance in the direction of the corral; the Chief caught it, rushed to the door, and uttered a yell of disappointment on seeing the hole in the palisade; the truth flashed upon him.

"Dog!" he yelled, and drawing his scalping knife, he hurled it furiously at his enemy.

But the latter, who was watching him, dodged the missile, which struck into the wall a few inches from his head.

Lanzi leaped over the bar, and rushed at Blue-fox.

The Indians rose tumultuously, and seizing their arms, bounded like wild beasts in pursuit of the half-breed.

The latter, on reaching the door of the corral, turned, fired his pistols among the crowd, leapt on his horse, and burying his spurs in its flanks, forced it to leap through the breach.

At the same moment a horrible noise was heard behind him, the earth trembled, and a confused mass of stones, beams, and fragments of every description fell around the rider and his horse, which was maddened with terror.

The Venta del Potrero was blown into the air, burying beneath its ruins the Apaches who had invaded it.

Such was the trick Lanzi had promised himself to play on the Indians.

We can now understand why he had insisted on Carmela setting off at full speed.

By a singular piece of good fortune, neither the half-breed nor his horse was wounded; the mustang, with foaming nostrils, flew over the prairie as if winged, incessantly urged on by its rider, who excited it with spur and force, for he fancied he could hear behind him the gallop of another horse in pursuit.

Unluckily the night was too dark for him to assure himself whether he were mistaken.

CHAPTER XIX
THE CHASE

The reader will probably consider that the means employed by Lanzi to get rid of the Indians were somewhat violent, and that he should not have had recourse to them save in the utmost extremity.

The justification of the half-breed is as simple as it is easy to give; the Indian braves, when they cross the Mexican border, indulge mercilessly in every possible riot, displaying the greatest cruelty toward the unhappy white men who fall into their hands, and for whom they testify a hatred which nothing can assuage.

Lanzi's position, alone, without help to expect from anyone, in an isolated spot, in the power of some fifty demons without faith or law, was most critical; the more so, as the Apaches, once they had been excited by strong liquors, the abuse of which causes them a species of raving madness, would no longer have recognized any restraint; their sanguinary character would have regained the upper hand, and they would have indulged in the most unjustifiable cruelty, for the mere pleasure of making an enemy of their race suffer.

The half-breed had, besides, peremptory reasons for behaving thus; he must, at all risks, ensure Carmela's safety, whom he had solemnly sworn to Tranquil to defend, even at the peril of his own life.

In the present case, he knew that his life or death depended solely on the caprice of the Indians, and hence he was quite reckless.

Lanzi was a cold, positive, and methodical man, who never acted till he had previously fully weighed the chances of success or failure. Under present circumstances, the half-breed ran no risk, for he knew that he was condemned by the Indians beforehand; if his plan succeeded, he might possibly escape; if not, he could die, but as a brave borderer should do, taking with him into the tomb a considerable number of his implacable foes.

His resolution once formed, it was carried out with the coolness we have described, and, thanks to his presence of mind, he had found time to leap on his horse and fly.

Still, all was not finished yet, and the galloping the half-breed heard behind him disturbed him greatly, by proving to him that his plan had not succeeded so well as he hoped, and that one of his enemies, at any rate, had escaped, and was on his track.

The half-breed redoubled his speed; he made his horse swerve from the straight line incessantly, in order to throw out his obstinate pursuer; but everything was of no avail, and still he heard him galloping behind him.

However brave a man may be, however great the energy is with which heaven has endowed him, nothing affects his courage so much as to feel himself menaced in the darkness by an invisible and unassailable foe; the obscurity of night, the silence that broods over the desert, the trees which in his mad race defile on his right and left like a legion of gloomy and threatening phantoms—all this combines to heighten the terrors of the hapless man who dashes along under the impression of a nightmare which is the more horrible, because he is conscious of danger, and knows not how to exorcise it.

Lanzi, with frowning brow, quivering lips, and forehead bathed with cold perspiration, rode thus for several hours across country, bowed over his horse's neck, following no settled course, but constantly pursued by the dry, sharp sound of the horse galloping after him.

Strangely enough, since he first heard this gallop, it had not appeared to draw any nearer; it might be thought that the strange horseman, satisfied with following the trail of the man he pursued, was not desirous of catching him up.

By degrees the half-breed's excitement calmed: the cold night air restored a little order to his ideas, his coolness returned, and with it the necessary clearness to judge of his position soundly.

Lanzi was ashamed of this puerile terror, so unworthy of a man like himself, which had for so long, through a selfish feeling, caused him to forget the sacred duty he had taken on himself, of protecting and defending at the peril of his life his friend's daughter.

At this thought, which struck him like a thunder-bolt, a burning blush flushed his face, a flash darted from his eyes, and he stopped his horse short, resolved on finishing once for all with his pursuer.

The horse, suddenly arrested in its stride, uttered a snort of pain, and remained motionless, at the same instant the galloping of the invisible steed ceased to be heard.

"Hilloah!" the half-breed muttered, "This is beginning to look ugly."

And drawing a pistol from his belt, he set the hammer. He immediately heard, like a funeral echo, the sharp sound of another hammer being set by his adversary.

Still, this sound, instead of increasing the half-breed's apprehensions, seemed, on the contrary, to calm them.

"What is the meaning of that?" he asked himself, mentally, as he shook his head, "Can I be mistaken? have I not to deal with an Apache?"

After this aside, during which Lanzi sought in vain to distinguish his unknown foe, he shouted in a loud voice:—

"Hilloah, who are you?"

"Who are you?" a masculine voice replied, emerging from the darkness, in a tone quite as resolute as that of the half-breed.

"That's a singular answer," Lanzi went on.

"Not more singular than the question."

These words were exchanged in excellent Spanish. The half-breed, now certain that he had to deal with a white man, banished all fear, and uncocking his pistol returned it to his girdle, as he said good-humouredly:—

"You must feel like myself, Caballero, inclined to draw breath after so long a ride; shall we rest together?"

"I wish for nothing better," the other answered.

"Why," a voice exclaimed, which the half-breed at once recognised, "it is Lanzi."

"Certainly," the latter shouted, joyfully, "*Voto à brios*, Doña Carmela, I did not hope to meet you here."

The three persons joined, and the explanations were short.

Fear does not calculate or reflect. Doña Carmela on one side, Lanzi on the other, filled with a vague terror, fled without attempting to account for the feeling that impelled them, exerted only by the instinct of self-preservation, that supreme weapon given by God to man with which to escape danger in extremities.

The only difference was, that the half-breed believed himself pursued by the Apaches, while Doña Carmela supposed them a-head of her.

When the young lady, on Lanzi's recommendation, left the venta, she rode blindly along the first path that presented itself.

Heaven willed it for her happiness that at the moment the house blew up with a terrible crash, Doña Carmela, half dead with fear and thrown from her horse, was found by a white hunter, who, moved with pity at the recital of the dangers that menaced her, generously offered to escort her to the Larch-tree hacienda, where she desired to proceed, in order to place herself under Tranquil's immediate protection.

Doña Carmela, after taking a scrutinizing glance at the hunter, whose honest look and open face were proofs of his loyalty, gratefully accepted his offer, fearing, as she did, that she might fall, in the darkness, among the Indian bands which were doubtless infesting the roads, and to which her ignorance of localities would have inevitably made her a prey.

The maiden and her guide set out therefore at once for the hacienda, but affected by numberless apprehensions, the gallop of the half-breed's horse made them believe a party of the enemy a-head of them, hence they had kept far enough behind to be able to turn and fly at the slightest suspicious movement on the part of their supposed enemies.

This explanation did away with all alarm, and Carmela and Lanzi were delighted at having met again thus providentially.

While the half-breed was telling his young mistress in what way he had disposed of the Apaches, the hunter, like a prudent man, had taken the horses by the bridle and led them into a thick coppice, where he carefully hid them. He then returned to his new friends, who had seated themselves on the ground, to enjoy a few moments of welcome rest.

At this moment, when the hunter returned, Lanzi was saying to his mistress—

"Why, señorita, should you fatigue yourself further this night? Our new friend and I will build you with a few axe strokes a jacal under which you will be famously sheltered; you will sleep till sunrise, and then we can start again for the hacienda. For the present you have no danger to fear, as you are protected by two men who will not hesitate to sacrifice their lives for you, if necessary."

"I thank you, my good Lanzi," the young lady answered; "your devotion is known to me, and I could not hesitate to trust to you if I were at this moment affected by fear of the Apaches. Believe me, that the thought of the perils I may have to incur from those pagans goes for nothing in my determination to start again immediately."

"What more important consideration can compel you, then, señorita?" the half-breed asked, in surprise.

"That, my friend, is an affair between my father and myself; it is sufficient for you to know that I must see and speak to him this very night."

"Be it so, as you wish it, señorita, I consent," the half-breed said, with a shake of his head; "still, you must allow that it is a very strange caprice on your part."

"No, my good Lanzi," she answered, sadly, "it is not a caprice; when you know the reasons that cause me, to act, I am convinced you will applaud me."

"That is possible; but if that is the case, why not tell me them, at once?"

"Because that is impossible."

"Silence!" the hunter interfered, quickly; "any discussion is unnecessary, for we must start as soon as we can."

"What do you mean?" they exclaimed, with a start of terror.

"The Apaches have found our trail; they are coming up quickly, and will be here within twenty minutes. This time there is no mistake, they are the men."

There was a lengthened silence.

Doña Carmela and Lanzi listened attentively.

"I hear nothing," the half-breed said, presently.

"Nor I," the maiden whispered.

The hunter smiled softly.

"You can hear nothing yet," he said, "for your ears are not accustomed, like mine, to catch the slightest sounds from the desert. Put faith in my words, trust to an experience which was never mistaken: your enemies are approaching."

"What is to be done?" Doña Carmela murmured.

"Fly," the half-breed exclaimed.

"Listen," the hunter said, quietly; "the Apaches are numerous, they are cunning, but we can only conquer them by cunning. If we try to resist we are lost; if we fly all three together, sooner or later we shall fall into their hands. While I remain here you will fly with señorita, but be careful to muffle your horses' hoofs so as to dull the sound."

"But you?" the maiden exclaimed quickly.

"Have I not told you? I shall remain here."

"Oh, in that case you will fall into the hands of the pagans, and be inevitably massacred."

"Perhaps so," he replied with an indescribable expression of sadness; "but at any rate my death will be of some service, as it will save you."

"Very well," said Lanzi; "I thank you for your offer, Caballero; unhappily, I cannot, and will not, accept it, for matters must not turn thus. I began the affair, and insist on ending it in my own way. Go away with the señorita, deliver her into her father's hands, and if you do not see me again, and he asks what has happened to me, tell him simply that I kept my promise, and laid down my life for her."

"I will never consent," Doña Carmela exclaimed energetically.

"Silence!" the half-breed hastily interrupted her, "Be off, you have not a moment to lose."

In spite of the young lady's resistance, he raised her in his muscular arms, and ran off with her into the thicket.

Carmela understood that nothing could change the half-breed's resolution, so she yielded to him.

The hunter accepted Lanzi's devotion as simply as he had offered his own, for the half-breed's conduct appeared to him perfectly natural; he therefore made not the slightest objection, but busied himself with getting the horses ready.

"Now begone," the half-breed said, so soon as the hunter and the maiden had mounted; "go, and may heaven be merciful to you!"

"And you, my friend?" Doña Carmela remarked sadly.

"I?" he answered with a careless toss of his head; "The red devils have not got me yet. Come, be off."

To cut short the conversation, the half-breed roughly lashed the horses with his chicote; the noble animals started at a gallop, and soon disappeared from his sight.

So soon as he was alone, the poor fellow gave vent to a sigh.

"Hum!" he muttered sadly; "This time I am very much afraid that it is all up with me; no matter, Canarios, I will fight to the last, and if the pagans catch me, it shall cost them dearly."

After forming this heroic resolution, which seemed to restore all his courage, the worthy man mounted his horse and prepared for action.

The Apaches dashed up with a noise resembling thunder.

The black outlines could already be distinguished through the darkness.

Lanzi took the bridle between his teeth, seized a pistol in either hand, and when he judged the moment propitious, he dug his spurs into his horse, dashed out in front of the Redskins, and crossed their front diagonally.

When within range, he fired his pistols into the group, gave a yell of defiance, and continued his flight with redoubled speed.

What the half-breed expected, really happened. His shots had told, and two Apaches fell with their chests pierced through and through. The Indians, furious at this audacious attack, which they were far from expecting from a single man, uttered a cry of fury, and dashed after him.

This was exactly what Lanzi wanted.

"There," he said on seeing the success of his scheme; "they are altogether now, and there is no fear of their scattering; the others are saved. As for me—bah, who knows?"

Doña Carmela and the hunter only escaped from the Apaches to fall in with the jaguars. We have seen how they were saved, thanks to Tranquil.

CHAPTER XX
THE CONFESSION

Tranquil attentively listened to the girl's story with drooping head and frowning brows; when she had finished, he looked at her for a moment enquiringly.

"Is that all?" he asked her.

"All," she answered timidly.

"And Lanzi, my poor Lanzi, have you no news of him?"

"None. We heard two shots, the furious galloping of several horses, the war-cry of the Apaches, and then all became silent again."

"What can have become of him?" the tigrero muttered sadly.

"He is resolute, and seems to me conversant with desert life," Loyal Heart said.

"Yes," Tranquil replied, "but he is alone."

"That is true," said the hunter; "alone against fifty, perhaps."

"Oh, I would give ten years of my life," the Canadian exclaimed, "to have some news of him."

"Caray, gossip," a merry voice replied; "I have brought you some all fresh, and shall charge you nothing for them."

The hearers started involuntarily at the sound of this voice, and turned quickly to the side where they heard it.

The branches parted, and a man appeared.

It was Lanzi.

The half-breed seemed as calm and composed as if nothing extraordinary had happened to him; but his face, usually so cold, now had an indescribable expression of cunning joy, his eyes sparkled, and a mocking smile played about his lips.

"By Jove! Our friend," Tranquil said as he offered him a hand; "you are a thousand times welcome, for our anxiety about you was great."

"Thank you, gossip; but, luckily for me, the danger was not so imminent as might be supposed, and I very easily succeeded in getting rid of those demons of Apaches."

"All the better; no matter how you contrived to escape, here you are safe and sound, so all is for the best; now that we have met again, they may come if their heart tells them to do so, and they will find somebody to talk to them."

"They will not do it; besides, they have something else on hand at this moment."

"Do you think so?"

"I am sure of it; they perceived the bivouac of Mexican soldiers escorting a conducta de plata, and are naturally trying to get hold of it; it was partly to that fortuitous circumstance I owe my safety."

"On my word! All the worse for the Mexicans," the Canadian said carelessly; "every man for himself: let them settle matters as they think proper, their affairs do not interest us."

"That is my opinion too."

"We have still three hours of night; let us profit by them to rest, in order to be ready to start for the hacienda at sunrise."

"The advice is good, and should be followed," said Lanzi, who immediately lay down with his feet to the fire, wrapped himself in his zarapé, and closed his eyes.

Loyal Heart, who doubtless shared his opinion, followed his example.

As for Quoniam, after conscientiously flaying the tigers and their cubs, he lay down in front of the fire, and for the last two hours had been sleeping with that careless indifference so characteristic of the Black race.

Tranquil then turned to Carmela. The maiden was seated a few paces from him; she was gazing into the fire pensively, and tears stood in her eyes.

"Well, daughter mine," the Canadian said to her softly, "what are you doing there? You must be exhausted with fatigue, so why not try to get a few minutes' rest?"

"For what good?" she asked sorrowfully.

"What do you mean?" the tigrero asked sharply, though the girl's accent made him start; "Why, to regain your strength of course."

"Let me remain awake, father; I could not sleep, however tired I might feel; sleep will fly my eyelids."

The Canadian examined her for a moment with the greatest attention.

"What is the meaning of this?" he asked, shaking his head meditatively.

"Nothing, father," she replied, as she tried to force a smile.

"Girl, girl," he muttered, "all this is not quite clear; I am only a poor hunter, very ignorant of matters of the world, and my mind is simple; but I love you, child, and my heart tells me you are suffering."

"I?" she exclaimed in denial; but all at once she burst into tears, and falling on the hunter's manly chest, she hid her face in his bosom, and murmured in a choking voice —

"Oh, father, father, I am so wretched."

Tranquil, at this exclamation, torn from her by the force of pain, started as if a serpent had stung him; his eye sparkled, he gave the girl a look full of paternal love, and compelled her with gentle constraint to look him in the face.

"Wretched? you, Carmela?" he exclaimed anxiously. "Great Heaven, what has happened then?"

By a supreme effort, the maiden succeeded in calming herself; her features reassumed their ordinary tranquillity, she wiped away her tears, and smiled at the hunter, who anxiously watched her.

"Pardon me, father," she said in an insinuating voice, "I am mad."

"No, no," he replied, shaking his head twice or thrice; "you are not mad, my child, but are concealing something from me."

"Father!" she said with a blush, and looked down in confusion.

"Be frank with me, child, for am I not your best friend?"

"That is true," she stammered.

"Have I ever refused to satisfy the slightest of your wishes?"

"Oh, never!"

"Have you ever found me severe to you?"

"Oh, no!"

"Well, then, why not confess to me frankly what is troubling you?"

"Because —" she murmured, in hesitation.

"What?" he answered, affectionately.

"I dare not."

"It must be very difficult to say, then?"

"Yes."

"Nonsense! Go on, girl, where will you find a confessor so indulgent as I am?"

"Nowhere, I know."

"Speak, then."

"I am afraid of vexing you."

"You will vex me a great deal more by obstinately remaining silent."

"But—"

"Listen, Carmela; while telling us a little while back what happened to-day at the venta, you confessed yourself that you wished to find me, no matter where I was, this very night; is that so?"

"Yes, father."

"Well, here I am, I am listening to you; besides, if what you have to say to me is so important as you led me to suppose, you will do well to make haste."

The maiden started; she gave a glance at the sky, where the gloom was beginning to be intersected by white stripes; all the hesitation disappeared from her face.

"You are right, father," she said, in a firm voice; "I hate to speak with you about an affair of the greatest importance, and perhaps I have deferred it too long, for it is a question of life and death."

"You startle me."

"Listen to me."

"Speak, child, speak, without fear, and reckon on my affection for you."

"I do so, my kind father, so you shall know all."

"It is well."

Doña Carmela seemed to collect herself for a moment, then, letting her dainty hand fall into her father's rough and large hand, while her long silken lashes drooped timidly, to serve as a veil to her eyes, she began in a weak voice at first, which, however, soon became more firm and distinct.

"Lanzi told you that meeting with a conducta de plata encamped a short distance from here, helped him to escape from the pursuit of the pagans. Father, this conducta spent last night at the venta, and the Captain who commands the escort is one of the most distinguished officers in the Mexican army; you have heard him spoken of before now in terms of praise, and I even think you are personally acquainted with him; his name is Don Juan Melendez de Gongora."

"Ah!" said Tranquil.

The maiden stopped, all palpitating.

"Go on," the Canadian said, gently.

Carmela gave him a side glance; as the tigrero was smiling, she resolved to continue.

"Already accident has brought the Captain several times to the venta; he is a true Caballero—gentle, polite, honourable, and we have never had the slightest ground of complaint against him, as Lanzi will tell you."

"I am convinced of it, my child, for Captain Melendez is exactly what you describe him."

"Is he not?" she quickly asked.

"Yes, he is a true Caballero; unfortunately, there are not many officers like him in the Mexican army."

"This morning, the conducta set out, escorted by the Captain; two or three ill-looking fellows, who remained at the venta, watched the soldiers depart with a cunning smile, then sat down, began drinking and saying to me things a girl ought not to hear, until at last they even threatened me."

"Ah!" Tranquil interrupted her, with a frown, "Do you know the scoundrels?"

"No, father, they are border ruffians, like those of whom there are too many about here; but, though I have seen them several times, I do not know their names."

"No matter, I will discover them, you may feel assured.

"Oh, father, you would do wrong to trouble yourself about that."

"Very well, that is my business."

"Fortunately for me, while this was occurring, a horseman arrived, whose presence was sufficient to impose silence on these men, and force them to become what they should always have been, that is to say, polite and respectful to me."

"Of course," the Canadian remarked, laughingly, "this caballero, who arrived so fortunately, was a friend of yours?"

"Only an acquaintance, father," she said, with a slight blush.

"Ah! very good."

"But he is a great friend of yours—at least, I suppose so."

"Hum! And pray do you know *his* name, my child?"

"Of course," she replied, quickly.

"And what is it, may I ask, if you have no objection to tell me?"

"None at all; he is called the Jaguar."

"Oh, oh!" the hunter continued, with a frown, "What could he have to do at the venta?"

"I do not know, father; but he said a few words in a low voice to the men of whom I have told you, who immediately left the talk, mounted their horses, and started at a gallop without making the slightest remark."

"That is strange," the Canadian muttered.

There was a rather lengthened silence; Tranquil was deep in thought, and was evidently seeking the solution of a problem, which appeared to him very difficult to solve.

At length he raised his head.

"Is that all you have to tell me?" he asked the girl; "up to the present I see nothing very extraordinary in all you have told me."

"Wait a while," she said.

"Then you have not finished yet?"

"Not yet."

"Very good—go on."

"Although the Jaguar spoke in a low voice with these men, through some words I overheard, without wishing to do so, I assure you, father—"

"I am fully persuaded of that. What did you guess from these few words?"

"I mean, I fancied I understood—"

"It is the same thing; go on."

"I fancied I understood, I say, that they were speaking of the conducta."

"And very naturally of Captain Melendez, eh?"

"I am certain that they mentioned his name."

"That is it. Then you supposed that the Jaguar intended to attack the conducta, and possibly kill the Captain, eh?"

"I do not say that," the maiden stammered, in extreme embarrassment.

"No, but you fear it."

"Good Heavens, father!" she went on, in a tone of vexation, "Is it not natural that I should take an interest in a brave officer who—"

"It is most natural, my child, and I do not blame you; even more, I fancy that your suppositions are very near the truth."

"Do you think so, father?" she exclaimed, as she clasped her hands in terror.

"It is probable," the Canadian quietly answered; "but reassure yourself, my child," he added, kindly; "although you have perhaps delayed too long in speaking to me, I may yet manage to avert the danger which is now suspended over the head of the man in whom you take such interest."

"Oh do so, father, I implore you."

"I will try, at any rate, my child, that is all I can promise you for the present; but what do you purpose doing?"

"I?"

"Yes, while my comrades and I are trying to save the Captain?"

"I will follow you, father, if you will let me."

"I think that is the most prudent course; but you must feel a great affection for the Captain, that you so ardently desire to save him?"

"I, father?" she replied with the most perfect frankness, "Not the least; it only seems to me terrible that so brave an officer should be killed, when there is a chance of saving him."

"Then you hate the Jaguar of course?"

"Not at all, father; in spite of his violent character, he seems to me a noble-hearted man—the more so, because he possesses your esteem, which is the most powerful reason with me; still it grieves me to see two men opposed who, I feel convinced, if they knew each other, would become fast friends, and I do not wish blood to be shed between them."

These words were uttered by the maiden with such simple frankness, that for some moments the Canadian remained completely stunned; the slight gleam of light he fancied he had found suddenly deserted him again, though it was impossible for him to say in what manner it had disappeared; he neither understood Doña Carmela's behaviour, nor the motives on which she acted—the more so, because he had no reason to doubt the good faith in all she had told him.

After looking attentively at the maiden for some minutes, he shook his head twice or thrice like a man completely at sea, and without adding a word, proceeded to arouse his comrades.

Tranquil was one of the most experienced wood-rangers in North America; all the secrets of the desert were known to him, but he was ignorant of the first word of that mystery which is called a woman's heart. A mystery the more difficult to fathom, because women themselves are nearly always ignorant of it; for they only act under the impression of the moment, under the influence of passion, and without premeditation.

In a few words the Canadian explained his plans to his comrades: the latter, as he anticipated, did not offer the slightest objection, but prepared to follow him.

Ten minutes later they mounted and left their bivouac under the guidance of Lanzi.

At the moment when they disappeared in the forest, the owl uttered its matutinal cry, the precursor of sunrise.

"Oh, Heavens!" the maiden murmured in agony; "Shall we arrive in time?"

CHAPTER XXI
THE JAGUAR

The Jaguar, when he left the Venta del Potrero, was suffering from extreme agitation, the maiden's words buzzed in his ears, with a mocking and ironical accent; the last look she had given him pursued him like a remorse. The young man was angry with himself for having so hastily broken off the interview with Doña Carmela, and dissatisfied with the way in which he had responded to her entreaties; in short, he was in the best possible temper to commit one of those acts of cruelty into which the violence of his character only too often led him, which had inflicted a disgraceful stigma on his reputation, and which he always bitterly regretted having committed, when it was too late.

He rode at full speed across the prairie, lacerating the sides of his horse, which reared in pain, uttering stifled maledictions, and casting around the ferocious glances of a wild beast in search of prey.

For a moment he entertained the idea of returning to the venta, throwing himself at the maiden's feet, and repairing the fault which his growing jealousy had forced him to commit, by abjuring all his hopes, and placing himself at Doña Carmela's service, to do whatever she might please to order.

But, like most good resolutions, this one lasted no longer than a lightning flash. The Jaguar reflected, and with reflection doubt and jealousy returned. The natural consequences of which was fresh fury, wilder and more insane than the first.

The young man galloped on thus for a long time, apparently following no settled direction; still at long intervals he stopped, rose in his stirrups, explored the plain with an eagle-glance, and then started again at full speed.

At about three in the afternoon he passed the conducta de Plata, but as he perceived it a long way off, it was easy for him to avoid it by swerving slightly to the right, and entering a thick wood of pine trees, which rendered him invisible long enough for him not to fear discovery from the scouts sent on ahead.

About an hour before sunset, the young man, who had perhaps stopped a hundred times to explore the neighbourhood, uttered a suppressed cry of joy; he had at length come up to the persons he was so anxious to join.

Not five hundred yards from the spot where the Jaguar had halted, a band of thirty to five and thirty horsemen was following the track complimented with the name of road, that led across the prairie.

This band, entirely composed of white men, as could be easily seen from their costume, appeared to assume something of a military air, and all were fully equipped with arms of every description.

At the beginning of this story we mentioned some horsemen just disappearing on the horizon; these were the men the Jaguar had just perceived.

The young man placed his open hands to his mouth in the shape of a speaking trumpet, and twice gave a sharp, shrill, and prolonged cry.

Although the troop was some distance off at the moment, still at this signal the riders stopped as if the feet of their horses had suddenly become embedded in the ground.

The Jaguar then bent over his saddle, leaped his horse over the bushes, and in a few minutes joined the men who had stopped for him.

The Jaguar was hailed with shouts of joy, and all pressed round him with marks of the deepest interest.

"Thanks, my friends," he said, "thanks for the proofs of sympathy you give me; but I must ask you to give me a moment's attention, for time presses."

Silence was re-established, as if by enchantment, but the flashing glances fixed on the young man said clearly that sympathy, though dumb, was not the less vivid.

"You were not mistaken, Master John," the Jaguar said, addressing one of the persons nearest to him; "the conducta is just behind us; we are not more than three or four hours' march ahead of it; as you warned me, it is escorted, and in proof that great importance is attached to its safety, the escort is commanded by Captain Melendez."

His audience gave a start of disappointment at these news.

"Patience," the Jaguar went on, with a sarcastic smile; "when force is not sufficient, stratagem remains; Captain Melendez is brave and experienced, I grant you, but are we not also brave men? Is not the cause we defend grand enough to excite us to carry out our enterprise at all hazards?"

"Yes, yes, hurrah, hurrah!" all the hearers shouted, as they brandished their weapons enthusiastically.

"Master John, you have already entered into relations with the Captain; he knows you, so you will remain here with another of our friends. Allow yourselves to be arrested. I entrust to you the duty of removing the suspicions that may exist in the Captain's mind."

"I will do it, you may be certain."

"Very good, but play close with him; for you have a strong opponent."

"Do you think so?"

"Yes. Do you know who accompanies him?"

"On my word, no."

"El Padre Antonio."

"What's that you say? by Jove, you did right to warn me."

"I thought so."

"Oh, oh! Does that accursed monk wish to poach on our manor?"

"I fear it. This man, as you know, is affiliated with all the scamps, no matter of what colour, who prowl about the desert: he is even reported to be one of their Chiefs; the idea of seizing the conducta may easily have occurred to him."

"By Heaven, I will watch him; trust to me, I know him too thoroughly and too long for him to care to oppose me; if he dared to attempt it, I could reduce him to impotence."

"That is all right. When you have obtained all the information we require to act, lose not a moment in informing us, for we shall count the minutes while waiting for you."

"That is settled. I suppose we meet at the Barranca del Gigante."

"Yes."

"One word more."

"Make haste."

"What about Blue-fox?"

"Hang it! I forgot all about him."

"Shall I wait for him?"

"Certainly."

"Shall I treat with him? You know but little reliance is to be placed in the word of an Apache."

"That is true," the young man answered, thoughtfully; "still, our position is at this moment most difficult. We are left to our own resources; our friends hesitate, and dare not yet decide in our favour; while, on the other hand, our enemies are raising their heads, regaining courage, and preparing to attack us vigorously. Although my heart heaves against such an alliance, it is still evident to me, that if the Apaches consent frankly to help us, their assistance will be very useful to us."

"You are right. In our present situation, outlawed by society, and tracked like wild beasts, it would, perhaps, be imprudent to reject the alliance of the Redskins."

"Well, my friend, I give you full liberty, and events must guide you. I trust entirely to your intelligence and devotion."

"I shall not deceive your expectations."

"Let us part now; and luck be with you."

"Goodbye, till we meet again."

"Goodbye, till to-morrow."

The Jaguar gave a parting nod to his friend or accomplice, whichever the reader pleases to call him, placed himself at the head of the band, and started at a gallop.

This John was no other than John Davis, the slave-dealer, whom the reader probably remembers to have come across in the earlier chapters of this story. How it is we find him again in Texas, forming part of a band of outlaws, and become the pursued instead of the pursuer, would be too long to explain at this moment. Let us purpose eventually to give the reader full satisfaction on the point.

John and his comrades let themselves be apprehended by Captain Melendez's scouts, without offering the slightest opposition. We have already described how they behaved in the Mexican camp; so we will follow the Jaguar at present.

The young man seemed to be, and really was, the chief of the horsemen at whose head he rode.

These individuals all belonged to the Anglo-Saxon race, and to a man were North Americans.

What trade were they carrying on? Surely a very simple one.

For the moment they were insurgents; most of them came to Texas at the period when the Mexican government authorized American immigration. They had settled in the country, colonized it, and cleared it; in a word, they ended by regarding it as a new country.

When the Mexican government inaugurated that system of vexations, which it never gave up again, these worthy fellows laid down the pick and the spade to take up the Kentucky rifle, mounted their horses, and broke out in overt insurrection against an oppressor who wished to ruin and dispossess them.

Several bands of insurgents were thus hastily formed on various points of the Texan territory, fighting bravely against the Mexicans wherever they met with them. Unfortunately for them, however, these bands were isolated; no tie existed among them to form a compact and dangerous whole; they obeyed chiefs, independent one of the other, who all wished to command, without bowing their own will to a supreme and single will, which would have been the only way of obtaining tangible results, and conquering that independence, which, owing to this hapless dissension, was still regarded as a Utopia by the most enlightened men in the country.

The horsemen we have brought on the stage were placed under the orders of the Jaguar, whose reputation for courage, skill, and prudence was too firmly established in the country for his name not to inspire terror in the enemies whom chance might bring him across.

The sequel will prove that, in choosing their chiefs, the colonists had made no mistake about him.

The Jaguar was just the chief these men required. He was young, handsome, and gifted with that fascination which improvises kingdoms; he spoke little, but each of his words left a reminiscence.

He understood what his comrades expected of him, and had achieved prodigies; for, as ever happens with a man born for great things, who rises proportionately and ever remains on a level with events, his position, by extending, had, as it were, enlarged his intellect; his glance had become infallible, his will of iron; he identified himself so thoroughly with his new position, that he no longer allowed himself to be mastered by any human feeling. His face seemed of marble, both in joy and sorrow. The enthusiasm of his comrades could produce neither flame nor smile on his countenance.

The Jaguar was not an ordinary ambitious man; he was grieved by the disagreement among the insurgents; he most heartily desired a fusion, which had become indispensable, and laboured with all his might to effect it; in a word, the young man had faith; he believed; for, in spite of the innumerable faults committed since the beginning of the insurrection by the Texans, he found such vitality in the work of liberty hitherto so badly managed, that he learned at length that in every human question there is something more powerful than force, than courage, even than genius, and that this something is the idea whose time has come, whose hour has struck by the clock of Deity. Hence he forgot all his annoyances in hoping for a certain future.

In order to neutralize, as far as possible, the isolation in which his band was left, the Jaguar had inaugurated certain tactics which had hitherto proved successful. What he wanted was to gain time, and perpetuate the war, even though waging an unequal contest. For this purpose he was obliged to envelop his weakness in mystery, show himself everywhere, stop nowhere, enclose the foe in a network of invisible adversaries, force him to stand constantly on guard, with his eyes vainly fixed on all points of the horizon, and incessantly harassed, though never really and seriously attacked by respectable forces. Such was the plan the Jaguar inaugurated against the Mexicans, whom he enervated thus by this fever of expectation and the unknown, the most terrible of all maladies for the strong.

Hence the Jaguar and the fifty or sixty horsemen he commanded were more feared by the Mexican government than all the other insurgents put together.

An extraordinary prestige attached to the terrible chief of these unsiegeable men; a superstitious fear preceded them, and their mere approach produced disorder among the troops sent to fight them.

The Jaguar cleverly profited by his advantages to attempt the most hazardous enterprises and the most daring strokes. The one he meditated at this moment was one of the boldest he had hitherto conceived, for it was nothing less than to carry off the conducta de plata and make a prisoner of Captain Melendez, an officer whom he justly considered one of his most dangerous adversaries, and with whom he, for that very reason, longed to measure himself, for he foresaw the light such a victory would shed over the insurrection, and the partisans it would immediately attract to him.

After leaving John Davis behind him, the Jaguar rapidly advanced toward a thick forest, whose dark outline stood out on the horizon, and in which he prepared to bivouac for the night, as he could not reach the Barranca del Gigante till late the following day. Moreover, he wished to remain near the two men he had detached as scouts, in order the sooner to learn the result of their operations.

A little after sunset, the insurgents reached the forest, and instantaneously disappeared under covert.

On reaching the top of a small hill which commanded the landscape, the Jaguar halted, and ordered his men to dismount and prepare to camp.

A bivouac is soon organized in the desert.

A sufficient space is cleared with axes, fires are lighted at regular distances to keep off wild beasts; the horses are picketed, and sentries placed to watch over the common safety, and then everybody lies down before the fire, rolls himself in his blanket, and that is all. These rough men, accustomed to brave the fury of the seasons, sleep as profoundly under the canopy of the sky, as the denizens of towns in their sumptuous mansions.

The young man, when everybody had lain down to rest, went the rounds to assure himself that all was in order, and then returned to the fire, when he fell into earnest thought.

The whole night passed and he did not make the slightest movement; but he did not sleep, his eyes were open and fixed on the slowly expiring embers.

What were the thoughts that contracted his forehead and made his eyebrows meet?

It would be impossible to say.

Perhaps he was travelling in the country of fancy, dreaming wide awake one of those glorious dreams we have at the age of twenty, which are so intoxicating and so deceitful!

Suddenly he started and sprung up as if worked by a spring.

At this moment the sun appeared in the horizon, and began slowly dispersing the gloom.

The young man bent forward and listened.

The sharp snap of a gun being cocked was heard a short distance off, and a sentry concealed in the shrubs shouted in a harsh, sharp voice:—

"Who goes there?"

"A friend," was the reply from the bushes. The Jaguar started.

"Tranquil here!" he muttered to himself; "For what reason can he seek me?"

And he rushed in the direction where he expected to find the Panther-killer.

CHAPTER XXII
BLUE-FOX

We will now return to Blue-fox and his two comrades, whom, in a previous chapter, we left at the moment when, after hearing bullets "ping" past their ears, they instinctively entrenched themselves behind rocks and trunks of trees.

So soon as they had taken this indispensable precaution against the invisible assailants, the three men carefully inspected their weapons to be ready to reply; and then waited with finger on trigger, and looking searchingly in all directions.

They remained thus for a rather lengthened period, though nothing again disturbed the silence of the prairie, or the slightest sign revealed to them that the attack made upon them would be renewed.

Suffering from the deepest anxiety, not knowing to what they should attribute this attack, or what enemies they had to fear, the three men knew not what to do, or how to escape with honour from the embarrassing position into which chance had thrown them. At length Blue-fox resolved to go reconnoitring.

Still, as the Chief was justly afraid of falling into an ambuscade, carefully prepared to capture him and his comrades, without striking a blow, he thought it prudent, ere he started, to take the most minute precautions.

The Indians are justly renowned for their cleverness; forced, through the life they lead from their birth, to employ continually the physical qualities with which Providence has given them, in them hearing, smell, and, above all, sight have attained such a development, that they can fairly contend with wild beasts, of whom, after all, they are only plagiarists; but, as they have at their disposal one advantage over animals in the intelligence which permits them to combine their actions and see their probable consequences, they have acquired a cat-like success, if we may be allowed to employ the expression, which enables them to accomplish surprising things, of which only those who have seen them at work can form a correct idea, so greatly does their skill go beyond the range of possibility.

It is before all when they have to follow a trail, that the cleverness of the Indians, and the knowledge they possess of the laws of nature, acquire extraordinary proportions. Whatever care their enemy may have taken, whatever precautions he may have employed to hide his trail and render it invisible, they always succeed in discovering it in the end; from them the desert has retained no secrets, for them this virgin and majestic nature is a book, every page of which is known to them, and in which they read fluently, without the slightest—we will not say mistake, but merely—hesitation.

Blue-fox, though still very young, had already gained a well-deserved reputation for cleverness and astuteness; hence under the present circumstances, surrounded in all probability by invisible enemies, whose eyes, constantly fixed on the spot that served as his refuge, watched his every movement, he prepared with redoubled prudence to foil their machinations and countermine their plans.

After arranging with his comrades a signal in the probable event of their help being required, he took off his buffalo robe, whose wide folds might have impeded his movements, removed all the ornaments with which his head, neck, and chest were loaded, and only retained his *mitasses*, a species of drawers made in two pieces, fastened from distance to distance with hair, bound round the loins with a strip of untanned deer-hide, and descending to his ankles.

Thus clothed, he rolled himself several times in the sand, for his body to assume an earthy colour. Then he passed through his belt his tomahawk and scalping knife, weapons an Indian never lays aside, seized his rifle in his right hand, and, after giving a parting nod to his comrades who attentively watched his different preparations, he lay down on the ground, and began crawling like a serpent through the tall grass and detritus of every description.

Although the sun had risen for some time, and was pouring its dazzling beams over the prairie, Blue-fox's departure was managed with such circumspection that he was far out on the plain, while his comrades fancied him close to them; not a blade of grass had been agitated in his passage, or a pebble slipped under his feet.

From time to time Blue-fox stopped, took a peering glance around, and then, when he felt assured that all was quiet, and nothing had revealed his position, he began crawling again on his hands and knees in the direction of the forest covert, from which he was now but a short distance.

He then reached a spot entirely devoid of trees, where the grass, lightly trodden down at various spots, led him to suppose he was reaching the place where the men who fired must have been ambushed.

The Indian stopped, in order to investigate more closely the trail he had discovered.

It apparently belonged to only one man; it was clumsy, wide, and made without caution, and rather the footsteps of a white man ignorant of the customs of the prairie, than of a hunter or Indian.

The bushes were broken as if the person who passed through them had done so by force, running along without taking the trouble to part the brambles; while at several spots the trampled earth was soaked with blood.

Blue-fox could not at all understand this strange trail, which in no way resembled those he was accustomed to follow.

Was it a feint employed by his enemies to deceive him more easily by letting him see a clumsy trail intended to conceal the real one? Or was it, on the other hand, the trail of a white man wandering about the desert, of whose habits he was ignorant?

The Indian knew not what opinion to adhere to, and his perplexity was great. To him it was evident that from this spot the shot was fired which saluted him at the moment when he was about to begin his speech; but for what object had the man, whoever he was, that had chosen this ambush, left such manifest traces of his passage? He must surely have supposed that his aggression would not remain unpunished, and that the persons he selected as a target would immediately start in pursuit of him.

At length, after trying for a long time to solve this problem, and racking his brains in vain to arrive at a probable conclusion, Blue-fox adhered to his first one, that this trail was fictitious, and merely intended to conceal the true one.

The great fault of cunning persons is to suppose that all men are like themselves, and only employ cunning; hence they frequently deceive themselves, and the frankness of the means employed by their opponent completely defeats them, and makes them lose a game which they had every chance of winning.

Blue-fox soon perceived that his supposition was false, that he had given his enemy credit for much greater skill and sagacity than he really possessed, and that what he had regarded as an extremely complicated scheme intended to deceive him, was, in fact, what he had at first thought it, namely, the passing of a man.

After hesitating and turning back several times, the Indian at length resolved on pushing forward, and following what he believed to be a false trail, under the conviction that he would speedily find the real one; but, as he was persuaded that he had to do with extremely crafty fellows, he redoubled his prudence and precautions, only advancing step by step, carefully exploring the bushes and the chaparral, and not going on till he was certain he had no cause to apprehend a surprise.

His manoeuvres occupied a long time; he had left his comrades for more than two hours, when he found himself all at once at the entrance of a rather large clearing, from which he was only separated by a curtain of foliage.

The Indian stopped, drew himself up gently, parted the branches, and looked into the clearing.

The forests of America are full of these clearings, produced either by the fall of trees crumbling with old age, or of those which have been struck by lightning, and laid low by the terrible hurricanes which frequently utterly uproot the forests of the New World. The clearing to which we allude here was rather large; a wide stream ran through it, and in the mud of its banks might be seen the deeply-imprinted footprints of the wild beasts that came here to drink.

A magnificent mahogany tree, whose luxuriant branches overshadowed the whole clearing, stood nearly in the centre. At the foot of this gigantic denizen of the forest, two men were visible.

The first, dressed in a monk's gown, was lying on the ground with closed eyes, and face covered with a deadly pallor; the second, kneeling by his side, seemed to be paying him the most anxious attention.

Owing to the position occupied by the Redskin, he was enabled to distinguish the features of this second person, whose face was turned toward him.

He was a man of lofty stature, but excessively thin; his face, owing to the changes of weather to which it must have been long exposed, was of a brick colour, and furrowed by deep wrinkles; a snow-white beard fell on his chest, mingled with the long curls of his equally white hair, which fell in disorder on his shoulders. He wore the garb of the American rangers combined with the Mexican costume; thus a vicuña-skin hat, ornamented with a gold *golilla*, covered his head; a zarapé served as his cloak, and his cotton velvet violet trousers were thrust into long deer-skin gaiters, that came up to his knees.

It was impossible to guess this man's age; although his harsh and marked features, and his wild eyes, which burned with a concentrated fire and had a wandering expression, revealed that he had attained old age, still no trace of decrepitude was visible in any part of his person; his stature seemed not to have lost an inch of its height, so straight was he still; his knotted limbs, full of muscles hard as ropes, seemed endowed with extraordinary strength and suppleness; in a word, he had all the appearance of a dangerous wood-ranger, whose eye must be as sure, and arm as ready, as if he were only forty years of age.

In his girdle he carried a pair of long pistols, and a sword with a straight and wide blade, called a machete, passed through an iron ring instead of a sheath, hung on his left side. Two rifles, one of which doubtless belonged to him, were leant against the trunk of the tree, and a magnificent mustang, picketed a few yards off, was nibbling the young tree shoots.

What it has taken us so long to describe, the Indian saw at a glance; but it appeared as if this scene, which he was so far from anticipating, was not very cheering to him, for he frowned portentously, and could hardly restrain an exclamation of surprise and disappointment on seeing the two persons.

By an instinctive movement of prudence he cocked his rifle, and after he had done this, he went on watching what was doing in the clearing.

At length the man dressed in the monk's gown made a slight movement as if to rise, and partly opened his eyes; but too weak yet, probably, to endure the brilliancy of the sunbeams, though they were filtered through the dense foliage, he closed them again; still, the individual who was nursing him, saw that he had regained his senses, by the movement of his lips, which quivered as if he were murmuring a prayer in a low voice.

Considering, therefore, that, for the present at least, his attentions were no longer needed by his patient, the stranger rose, took his rifle, leant his crossed hands on the muzzle, and awaited stoically, after giving a look round the clearing, whose gloomy and hateful expression caused the Indian Chief to give a start of terror in his leafy hiding place.

Several minutes elapsed, during which no sound was audible, save the rustling of the stream over its bed, and the mysterious murmur of the insects of all descriptions hidden beneath the grass.

At length the man lying on the ground made a second movement, stronger than the first, and opened his eyes.

After looking wildly around him, his eyes were fastened with a species of strange fascination on the tall old man, still standing motionless by his side, and who gazed on him in return with a mingled feeling of ironical compassion and sombre melancholy.

"Thanks," he at last murmured, in a weak voice.

"Thanks for what?" the stranger asked, harshly.

"Thanks for having saved my life, brother," the sufferer answered.

"I am not your brother, monk," the stranger said, mockingly; "I am a heretic, a gringo, as you are pleased to call us; look at me, you have not examined me yet with sufficient attention; have I not horns and goat's feet?"

These words were uttered with such a sarcastic accent, that the monk was momentarily confounded.

"Who are you, then?" he at length asked, with secret apprehension.

"What does that concern you?" the other said, with an ill-omened laugh; "The demon, mayhap."

The monk made a sudden effort to rise, and crossed himself repeatedly.

"May Heaven save me from falling into the hands of the Evil Spirit!" he added.

"Well, you ass," the other said, as he shrugged his shoulders contemptuously, "reassure yourself, I am not the demon, but a man like yourself, perhaps not quite so hypocritical, though, that's the only difference."

"Do you speak truly? Are you really one of my fellow men, disposed to serve me?"

"Who can answer for the future?" the stranger replied, with an enigmatical smile; "Up to the present, at any rate, you have had no cause of complaint against me.

"No, oh no, I do not think so, although since my fainting fit my ideas have been quite confused, and I can remember nothing."

"What do I care? That does not concern me, for I ask nothing of you; I have enough business of my own not to trouble myself with that of others. Come, do you feel better? Have you recovered sufficiently to continue your journey?"

"What! continue my journey?" the monk asked timidly; "Do you intend to abandon me then?"

"Why not? I have already wasted too much time with you, and must attend to my own affairs."

"What?" the monk objected, "After the interest you have so benevolently taken in me, you would have the courage to abandon me thus when almost dead, and not caring what may happen to me after your departure?"

"Why not? I do not know you, and have no occasion to help you. Accidentally crossing this clearing, I noticed you lying breathless and pale as a corpse. I gave you that ease which is refused to no one in the desert; now that you have returned to life, I can no longer be of service to you, so I am off; what can be more simple or logical? Goodbye, and may the demon, for whom you took me just now, grant you his protection!"

After uttering these words in a tone of sarcasm and bitter irony, the stranger threw his rifle over his shoulder, and walked a few paces toward his horse.

"Stay, in Heaven's name!" the monk exclaimed, as he rose with greater haste than with his weakness seemed possible, but fear produced the strength; "What will become of me alone in this desert?"

"That does not concern me," the stranger answered, as he coolly loosed the arm of his zarapé, which the monk had seized; "is not the maxim of the desert, each for himself?"

"Listen," the monk said eagerly; "my name is Fray Antonio, and I am wealthy: if you protect me, I will reward you handsomely."

The stranger smiled contemptuously.

"What have you to fear? you are young, stout, and well armed; are you not capable of protecting yourself?"

"No, because I am pursued by implacable enemies. Last night they inflicted on me horrible and degrading torture, and I only managed with great difficulty to escape from their clutches. This morning accident brought me across two of these men. On seeing them a species of raging madness possessed me; the idea of avenging myself occurred to me; I aimed at them, and fired, and then fled, not knowing whither I was going, mad with rage and terror; on reaching this spot I fell, crushed and exhausted, as much through the sufferings I endured this night, as through the fatigues caused by a long and headlong race along abominable roads. These men are doubtless pursuing me; if they find me—and they will do so, for they are wood-rangers, perfectly acquainted with the desert—they will kill me without pity; my only hope is in you, so in the name of what you hold dearest on earth, save me! Save me, and my gratitude will be unbounded."

The stranger had listened to this long and pathetic pleading without moving a muscle of his face. When the monk ceased, with breath and argument equally exhausted, he rested the butt of his rifle on the ground.

"All that you say may be true," he answered drily, "but I care as little for it as I do for a flash in the pan; get out of the affair as you think proper, for your entreaties are useless; if you knew who I am, you would very soon give up tormenting my ears with your jabbering."

The monk fixed a terrified look on the strange man, not knowing what to say to him, or the means he should employ to reach his heart.

"Who are you then?" he asked him, rather for the sake of saying something than in the hope of an answer.

"Who I am?" he said, with an ironical smile, "You would like to know. Very good, listen in your turn; I have only a few words to say, but they will ice the blood in your veins with terror; I am the man called the White Scalper, the Pitiless one!"

The monk tottered back a few paces, and clasped his hands with an effort.

"Oh, my God!" he exclaimed, frenziedly; "I am lost!"

At this moment the hoot of an owl was heard a short distance off. The hunter started.

"Some one was listening to us!" he exclaimed, and rushed rapidly to the side whence the signal came, while the monk, half dead with terror, fell on his knees, and addressed a fervent prayer to Heaven.

CHAPTER XXIII
THE WHITE SCALPER

We must now stop our story for a little while, in order to give the reader certain details about the strange man whom we introduced in our previous chapter, details doubtless very incomplete, but still indispensable to the proper comprehension of facts that have to follow.

If, instead of telling a true story, we were inventing a romance, we should certainly guard ourselves against introducing into our narrative persons like the one we have to deal with now; unhappily, we are constrained to follow the line ready traced before us, and depict our characters as they are, as they existed, and as the majority still exist.

A few years before the period at which the first part of our story begins, a rumour, at first dull, but which soon attained a certain degree of consistency and a great notoriety in the vast deserts of Texas, arose almost suddenly, icing with fear the Indios Bravos, and the adventurers of every description who continually wander about these vast solitudes.

It was stated that a man, apparently white, had been for some time on the desert, pursuing the Redskins, against whom he seemed to have declared an obstinate war. Acts of horrible cruelty and extraordinary boldness were narrated about this man, who was said to be always alone; wherever he met Indians, no matter their number, he attacked them; those who fell into his power were scalped, and their hearts torn out, and in order that it might be known that they had fallen under his blows, he made on their stomach a wide incision, in the shape of a cross. At times this implacable enemy of the red race glided into their villages, fired them during the night, when all were asleep, and then he made a frightful butchery, killing all who came in his way; women, children, and old men, he made no exception.

This gloomy redresser of wrongs, however, did not merely pursue Indians with his implacable hatred—half-breeds, smugglers, pirates, in a word, all the bold border ruffians accustomed to live at the expense of society had a rude account to settle with him; but the latter he did not scalp, but merely contented himself with fastening them securely to trees, where he condemned them to die of hunger, and become the prey of wild beasts.

During the first years, the adventurers and Redskins, drawn together by the feeling of a common danger, had several times banded to put an end to this ferocious enemy, bind him, and inflict the law of retaliation on him; but this man seemed to be protected by a charm, which enabled him to escape all the snares laid for him, and circumvent all the ambuscades formed on his road, It was impossible to catch him; his movements were so rapid and unexpected, that he often appeared at considerable distances from the spot where he was awaited, and where he had been seen shortly before. According to the Indians and adventurers, he was invulnerable; bullets and arrows rebounded from his chest; and soon, through the continual good fortune that accompanied all his enterprises, this man became a subject of universal terror on the prairie; his enemies, convinced that all they might attempt against him would prove useless, gave up a struggle which they regarded as waged against a superior power. The strangest legends were current about him; every one feared him as a maleficent spirit; the Indians named him *Kiein-Stomann,* or the White Scalper, and the Adventurers designated him among themselves by the epithet of Pitiless.

These two names, as we see, were justly given to this man, with whom murder and carnage seemed the supreme enjoyment, such pleasure did he find in feeling his victims quivering beneath his blood-red hand, and tearing the heart out of their bosom; hence his mere name, uttered in a whisper, filled the bravest with horror.

But who was this man? Whence did he come? What fearful catastrophe had cast him into the fearful mode of life he led?

No one could answer these questions. This individual was a horrifying enigma, which no person could solve.

Was he one of those monstrous organizations, which, beneath the envelope of man, contain a tiger's heart?

Or, else, a soul ulcerated by a frightful misfortune, all whose faculties are directed to one object, vengeance?

Both these hypotheses were equally possible; perhaps both were true.

Still, as every medal has its reverse, and man is not perfect in either good or evil, this individual had at times gleams, not of pity, but perhaps of fatigue, when blood mounted to his gorge, choked him, and rendered him a little less cruel, a little less implacable, almost human, in a word. But these moments were brief, these attacks, as he called them himself, very rare; nature regained the upper hand almost at once, and he became only the more terrible, because he had been so near growing compassionate.

This was all known about this individual at the moment when we brought him on the stage in so singular a fashion. The assistance he had given the monk was so contrary to all his habits, that he must have been suffering at the moment from one of his best attacks, to have consented not only to give such eager attention to one of his fellows, but also to waste so much time in listening to his lamentations and entreaties.

To finish the information we have to give about this person, we will add that no one knew whether he had a permanent abode; he was not known to have any woman to love, or any follower; he had ever been seen alone; and during the ten years he had roamed the desert in every direction, his countenance had undergone no change; he had ever the same appearance of old age and strength, the same long and white beard, and the same wrinkled face.

As we have said, the scalper rushed into the chaparral to discover who had given the signal that startled him; his researches were minute, but they produced no other result than that of enabling him to discover that he was not mistaken, and that a spy hidden in the bushes had really seen all that took place in the clearing, and heard all that was said.

Blue-fox, after summoning his comrades, cautiously retired, convinced that if he fell into the hands of the Scalper, he would be lost in spite of all his courage.

The latter returned thoughtfully to the side of the monk, whose praying still went on, and had assumed such proportions that it threatened to become interminable.

The Scalper looked for a moment at the Fray, an ironical smile playing round his pale lips the while, and then gave him a hearty blow with the butt of his rifle between the shoulders.

"Get up!" he said, roughly.

The monk fell on his hands, and remained motionless. Believing that the other intended to kill him, he resigned himself to his fate, and awaited the death-blow which, in his opinion, he must speedily receive.

"Come, get up, you devil of a monk!" the Scalper went on; "Have you not mumbled paternosters enough?"

Fray Ambrosio gently raised his head; a gleam of hope returned to him.

"Forgive me, Excellency," he replied; "I have finished; I am now at your orders; what do you desire of me?"

And he quickly sprung up, for there was something in the other's eye which told him that disobedience would lead to unpleasant results.

"That is well, scoundrel! You seem to me as fit to pull a trigger as to say a prayer. Load your rifle, for the moment has arrived for you to fight like a man, unless you wish to be killed like a dog."

The monk took a frightened glance around.

"Excellency," he stammered, with great hesitation, "is it necessary that I should fight?"

"Yes, if you wish to keep a whole skin; if you do not, why, you can remain quiet."

"But perhaps there is another mode?"

"What is it?"

"Flight, for instance," he said, insinuatingly.

"Try it," the other replied, with a grin.

The monk, encouraged by this semi-concession, continued, with slightly increased boldness—

"You have a very fine horse."

"Is it not?"

"Magnificent," Fray Antonio went on, enthusiastically.

"Yes, and you would not be vexed if I let you mount it, to fly more rapidly, eh?"

"Oh! do not think that," he said, with a gesture of denial.

"Enough!" the Scalper roughly interrupted; "Think of yourself, for your enemies are coming."

With one bound he was in the saddle, made his horse curvet, and hid himself behind the enormous stem of the mahogany tree.

Fray Antonio, aroused by the approach of danger, quickly seized his rifle, and also got behind the tree.

At the same moment a rather loud rustling was heard in the bushes, which then parted, and several men appeared.

They were about fifteen in number, and Apache warriors; in the midst of them were Blue-fox, John Davis, and his companions.

Blue-fox, though he had never found himself face to face with the White Scalper, had often heard him spoken of, both by Indians and hunters; hence, when he heard him pronounce his name, an indescribable agony contracted his heart, as he thought of all the cruelty to which his brothers had been victims from this man; and the thought of seizing him occurred to him. He hastened to give the signal agreed on with the hunters, and rushing through the chaparral with the velocity characteristic of Indians, went to the spot where his warriors were waiting, and bade them follow him. On his return, he met the two hunters who had heard the signal, and were hurrying to his help.

In a few words Blue-fox explained to them what was occurring. To tell the truth, we must confess that this confidence, far from exciting the warriors and hunters, singularly lowered their ardour, by revealing to them that they were about to expose themselves to a terrible danger, by contending with a man who was the more dangerous because no weapon could strike him; and those who had hitherto dared to assail him, had ever fallen victims to their temerity.

Still, it was too late to recoil, and flight was impossible; the warriors, therefore, determined to push on, though much against the grain.

As for the two hunters, if they did not completely share in the blind credulity of their comrades, and their superstitious fears, this fight was far from pleasing them. Still, restrained by the shame of abandoning men to whom they fancied themselves superior in intelligence, and even in courage, they resolved to follow them.

"Excellency!" the monk exclaimed in a lamentable voice, when he saw the Indians appear, "Do not abandon me."

"No, if you do not abandon yourself, scoundrel!" the Scalper answered.

On reaching the skirt of the clearing, the Apaches, following their usual tactics, sheltered themselves behind trees, so that this confined clearing, in which so many men were on the point of beginning an obstinate struggle, seemed absolutely deserted.

There was a moment of silence and hesitation. The Scalper at length decided on being the first to speak.

"Halloh!" he cried, "What do you want here?"

Blue-fox was going to answer, but John Davis prevented him.

"Leave him to me," he said.

Quitting the trunk of the tree behind which he was sheltered, he then boldly walked a few paces forward, and stopped almost in the centre of the clearing.

"Where are you, you who are speaking?" he asked in a loud and firm voice; "Are you afraid of letting yourself be seen?"

"I fear nothing," the squatter replied.

"Show yourself, then, that I may know you again," John said impudently.

Thus challenged, the Scalper came up within two paces of the hunter.

"Here I am," he said, "What do you want of me?"

Davis let the horse come up without making any movement to avoid it.

"Ah," he said, "I am not sorry to have had a look at you."

"Is that all you have to say to me?" the other asked gruffly.

"Hang it, you are in a tremendous hurry! Give me time to breathe, at any rate."

"A truce to jests, which may cost you dearly; tell me at once what your proposals are—I have no time to lose in idle talk."

"How the deuce do you know that I have proposals to make to you?"

"Would you have come here without?"

"And I presume that you are acquainted with these proposals?"

"It is possible."

"In that case, what answer do you give me?"

"None."

"What, none!"

"I prefer attacking you."

"Oh, oh, you have a tough job before you; there are eighteen of us, do you know that?"

"I do not care for your numbers. If there were a hundred of you, I would attack you all the same."

"By Heaven! For the rarity of the fact, I should be curious to see the combat of one man against twenty."

"You will do so ere long."

And, while saying this, the Scalper pulled his horse back several paces.

"One moment, hang it," the hunter exclaimed sharply; "let me say a word to you."

"Say it."

"Will you surrender?"

"What?"

"I ask you if you will surrender."

"Nonsense," the Scalper exclaimed with a grin; "you are mad. I surrender! It is you who will have to ask mercy ere long."

"I would not believe it, even if you killed me."

"Come, return to your shelter," the Scalper said with a shrug of his shoulders; "I do not wish to kill you defencelessly."

"All the worse for you, then," the hunter said; "I have warned you honourably, now I wash my hands of it; get out of it as you can."

"Thanks," the Scalper answered energetically; "but I am not yet in so bad a state as you fancy."

John Davis contented himself with shrugging his shoulders, and returned slowly to his shelter in the forest, whistling Yankee Doodle.

The Scalper had not imitated him; although he was perfectly well aware that a great number of enemies surrounded him and watched over his movements, he remained firm and motionless in the centre of the clearing.

"Hola!" he shouted in a mocking voice, "You valiant Apaches, who hide yourselves like rabbits in the shrubs, must I come and smoke you out of your holes in order to make you show yourselves? Come on, if you do not wish me to believe you old cowardly and frightened squaws."

These insulting words raised to the highest pitch the exasperation of the Apache warriors, who replied by a prolonged yell of fury.

"Will my brothers allow themselves any longer to be mocked by a single man?" Blue-fox exclaimed; "Our cowardice causes his strength. Let us rush with the speed of the hurricane on this genius of evil; he cannot resist the shock of so many renowned warriors. Forward, brothers, forward! To us be the honour of having crushed the implacable foe of our race."

And uttering his war-cry, which his comrades repeated, the valiant Chief rushed upon the Scalper, resolutely brandishing his rifle over his head; all the warriors followed him.

The Scalper awaited them without stirring; but so soon as he saw them within reach, drawing in the reins, and pressing his knees, he made his noble stud leap into the thick of the Indians. Seizing his rifle by the barrel, and employing it like a club, he began smiting to the right and left with a vigour and rapidity that had something supernatural about them.

Then a frightful medley commenced; the Indians rushed on this man, who, being a skilful horseman, made his steed go through the most unexpected curvets, and by the rapidity of his movements prevented the enemy leaping on his bridle and stopping him.

The two hunters at first remained quiet, convinced that it was impossible for a single man even to resist for a few moments such numerous and brave foes; but they soon perceived, to their great amazement, that they were mistaken; several Indians were already stretched on the ground, their skulls split by the Scalper's terrible club, all whose blows went home.

The hunters then began changing their opinion as to the result of the fight, and wished to help their comrades, but their rifles were useless to them in the continued changes of the scene of action, and their bullets might as easily have struck friend as foe; hence they threw away their rifles, drew their knives, and hurried to the assistance of the Apaches, who were already beginning to give way.

Blue-fox, dangerously wounded, was lying in a state of insensibility. The warriors, still on their legs, were beginning to think of a retreat, and casting anxious glances behind them.

The Scalper still fought with the same fury, mocking and insulting his enemies; his arm rose and fell with the regularity of a pendulum.

"Ah, ah!" he exclaimed, on noticing the hunters; "So you want your share. Come on, come on."

The latter did not allow it to be repeated, but rushed wildly upon him.

But they fared badly; John Davis, struck by the horse's chest, was hurled twenty feet, and fell to the ground; at the same instant his comrade's skull was broken, and he expired without a groan.

This last incident gave the finishing stroke to the Indians, who, unable to overcome the terror with which this extraordinary man inspired them, began flying in all directions with yells of terror.

The Scalper gave a glance of triumph and satisfied hatred at the sanguinary arena, where a dozen bodies lay stretched out, and urging his horse on, he caught up a fugitive, lifted him by the hair, and threw him over his saddle-bow, and disappeared in the forest with a horrible grin.

Once again the Scalper had opened a bloody passage for himself.

As for Fray Antonio, so soon as he saw that the fight had begun, he thought it needless to await its issue; he, therefore, took advantage of the opportunity, and gliding gently from tree to tree, he effected a skilful retreat and got clear off.

CHAPTER XXIV
AFTER THE FIGHT

For more than half an hour the silence of death hovered over the clearing, which offered a most sad and lugubrious aspect through the fight we described in the preceding chapter.

At length John Davis, who in reality had received no serious wound, for his fall was merely occasioned by the shock of the Scalper's powerful horse, opened his eyes and looked around him in amazement; the fall had been sufficiently violent to cause him serious bruises, and throw him into a deep fainting fit; hence, on regaining consciousness, the American, still stunned, did not remember a single thing that had happened, and asked himself very seriously what he had been doing to find himself in this singular situation.

Still, his ideas grew gradually clearer, his memory returned, and he remembered the strange and disproportioned fight of one man against twenty, in which the former remained the victor, after killing and dispersing his assailants.

"Hum!" he muttered to himself, "Whether he be man or demon, that individual is a sturdy fellow."

He got up with some difficulty, carefully feeling his paining limbs; and when he was quite assured he had nothing broken, he continued with evident satisfaction—

"Thank Heaven! I got off more cheaply than I had a right to suppose, after the way in which I was upset." Then he added, as he gave a glance of pity to his comrade, who lay dead near him; "That poor Jim was not so lucky as I, and his fun is over. What a tremendous machete stroke he received! Nonsense!" he then said with the egotistic philosophy of the desert; "We are all mortal, each has his turn; to-day it's he, to-morrow I, so goes the world."

Leaning on his rifle, for he still experienced some difficulty in walking, he took a few steps on the clearing in order to convince himself by a conclusive experiment that his limbs were in a sound state.

After a few moments of an exercise that restored circulation to his blood and elasticity to his joints, completely reassured about himself, the thought occurred to him of trying whether among the bodies lying around him any still breathed.

"They are only Indians," he muttered, "but, after all, they are men; although they are nearly deprived of reason, humanity orders me to help them; the more so, as my present situation has nothing very agreeable about it, and if I succeed in saving any of them, their knowledge of the desert will be of great service to me."

This last consideration determined him on helping men whom probably without it he would have abandoned to their fate, that is to say, to the teeth of the wild beasts which, attracted by the scent of blood, would have certainly made them their prey after dark.

Still it is our duty to render the egotistic citizen of the United States the justice of saying that, so soon as he had formed this determination, he acquitted himself conscientiously and sagaciously of his self-imposed task, which was easy to him after all; for the numerous professions he had carried on during the course of his adventurous life had given him a medical knowledge and experience which placed him in a position to give sick persons that care their condition demanded.

Unfortunately, most of the persons he inspected had received such serious wounds that life had long fled their bodies, and help was quite unavailing.

"Hang it, hang it!" the American muttered at every corpse he turned over, "These poor savages were killed by a master-hand. At any rate they did not suffer long, for with such fearful wounds they must have surrendered their souls to the Creator almost instantaneously."

He thus reached the spot where lay the body of Blue-fox, with a wide gaping wound in his chest.

"Ah, ah! Here is the worthy Chief," he went on. "What a gash! Let us see if he is dead too."

He bent over the motionless body, and put the blade of his knife to the Indian's lips.

"He does not stir," he continued, with an air of discouragement; "I am afraid I shall have some difficulty in bringing him round."

In a few minutes, however, he looked at the blade of his knife and saw that it was slightly tarnished.

"Come, he is not dead yet; so long as the soul holds to the body, there is hope, so I will have a try."

After this aside, John Davis fetched some water in his hat, mixed a small quantity of spirits with it, and began carefully laving the wound; this duty performed, he sounded it and found it of no great depth, and the abundant loss of blood had in all probability brought on the state of unconsciousness. Reassured by this perfectly correct reflection, he pounded some *oregano* leaves between two stones, made a species of cataplasm of them, laid it on the wound, and secured it with a strip of bark; then unclenching the wounded man's teeth with the blade of his knife, he thrust in the mouth of his flask, and made him drink a quantity of spirits.

Success almost immediately crowned the American's tentatives, for the Chief gave vent to a deep sigh, and opened his eyes almost instantaneously.

"Bravo!" John exclaimed, delighted at the unhoped for result he had achieved. "Courage, Chief, you are saved. By Jove! You may boast of having come back a precious long distance."

For some minutes the Indian remained stunned, looking around him absently, without any consciousness of the situation in which he was, or of the objects that surrounded him.

John attentively watched him, ready to give him help again, were it necessary; but it was not so. By degrees the Redskin appeared to grow livelier; his eyes lost their vacant expression, he sat up and passed his hand over his dank brow.

"Is the fight over?" he asked.

"Yes," John answered, "in our complete defeat; that was a splendid idea we had of capturing such a demon."

"Has he escaped, then?"

"Most perfectly so, and without a single wound, after killing at least a dozen of your warriors, and cleaving my poor Jim's skull down to the shoulders."

"Oh!" the Indian muttered hoarsely, "He is not a man, but the spirit of evil."

"Let him be what he likes," John exclaimed, energetically; "I intend to fight it out some day, for I hope to come across this demon again."

"May the Wacondah preserve my brother from such a meeting, for this demon would kill him."

"Perhaps so; as it is, if he did not do so to-day, it was no fault of his, but let him take care; we may some day stand face to face with equal weapons, and then—"

"What does he care for weapons? Did you not see that they have no power over him, and that his body is invulnerable?"

"Hum! That is possible; but for the present let us leave the subject and attend to matters that affect us much more closely. How do you find yourself?"

"Better, much better; the remedy you have applied to my wound does me great good; I am beginning to feel quite comfortable."

"All the better; now try to rest for two or three hours, while I watch over your sleep; after that, we will consult as to the best way of getting out of this scrape."

The Redskin smiled on hearing this remark.

"Blue-fox is no cowardly old woman whom a tooth-ache or ear-ache renders incapable of moving."

"I know that you are a brave warrior, Chief; but nature has limits, which cannot be passed, and, however great your courage and will may be, the abundant haemorrhage which your wound has caused you must have reduced you to a state of extreme weakness."

"I thank you, my brother; those words come from a friend; but Blue-fox is a Sachem in his nation, death alone can render him unable to move. My brother will judge of the Chief's weakness."

While uttering these words, the Indian made a supreme effort; fighting against pain, with the energy and contempt of suffering that characterize the Red race, he succeeded in rising, and not only stood firmly on his feet, but even walked several yards without assistance, or the slightest trace of emotion appearing on his face.

The American regarded him with profound admiration; he could not imagine, though he himself justly enjoyed a reputation for braver, that it was possible to carry so far the triumph of moral over physical force.

The Indian smiled proudly on reading in the American's eyes the astonishment his performance caused him.

"Does my brother still believe that Blue-fox is so weak?" he asked him.

"On my word, Chief, I know not what to think; what you have just done confounds me; I am prepared to suppose you capable of accomplishing impossibilities."

"The Chiefs of my nation are renowned warriors, who laugh at pain, and for them suffering does not exist," the Redskin said, proudly.

"I should be inclined to believe it, after your way of acting."

"My brother is a man; he has understood me. We will inspect together the warriors lying on the ground, and then think of ourselves."

"As for your poor comrades, Chief, I am compelled to tell you that we have no occasion to trouble ourselves about them, for they are all dead."

"Good! they fell nobly while fighting; the Wacondah will receive them into his bosom, and permit them to hunt with him on the happy prairies."

"So be it!"

"Now, before all else, let us settle the affair we began this morning, and which was so unexpectedly broken off."

John Davis, in spite, of his acquaintance with desert life, was confounded by the coolness of this man, who, having escaped death by a miracle, still suffering from a terrible wound, and who had regained possession of his intellectual faculties only a few moments before, seemed no longer to think of what had occurred, considered the events to which he had all but fallen a victim as the very natural accidents of the life he led, and began again, with the greatest freedom of mind, a conversation interrupted by a terrible fight, at the very point where he left it. The fact was, that, despite the lengthened intercourse the American had hitherto had with the Redskins, he had never taken the trouble to study their character seriously, for he was persuaded, like most of the whites indeed, that these men are beings almost devoid of intelligence, and that the life they lead places them almost on a level with the brute, while, on the contrary, this life of liberty and incessant perils renders danger so familiar to them that they have grown to despise it, and only attach a secondary importance to it.

"Be it so," he said presently; "since you wish it, Chief, I will deliver the message intrusted to me for you."

"My brother will take a place by my side."

The American sat down on the ground by the Chief, not without a certain feeling of apprehension through his isolation on this battle-field strewn with corpses; but the Indian appeared so calm and tranquil that John Davis felt ashamed to let his anxiety be seen, and affecting carelessness he was very far from feeling, he began to speak.

"I am sent to my brother by a great warrior of the Palefaces."

"I know him; he is called the Jaguar. His arm is strong, and his eye flashes like that of the animal whose name, he bears."

"Good! The Jaguar wishes to bury the hatchet between his warriors and those of my brother, in order that peace may unite them, and that, instead of fighting with each other, they may pursue the buffalo on the same hunting grounds, and avenge themselves on their common enemies. What answer shall I give the Jaguar?"

The Indian remained silent for a long time; at length he raised his head.

"My brother will open his ears," he said, "a Sachem is about to speak."

"I am listening," the American answered.

The Chief went on—

"The words my bosom breathes are sincere—the Wacondah inspires me with them; the Palefaces, since they were brought by the genius of evil in their large medicine-canoes to the territories of my fathers, have ever been the virulent enemies of the Red men; invading their richest and most fertile hunting grounds, pursuing them like wild beasts whenever they met with them, burning their callis, and dispersing the bones of their ancestors to the four winds of Heaven. Has not such constantly been the conduct of the Palefaces? I await my brother's answer."

"Well," the American said, with a certain amount of embarrassment, "I cannot deny, Chief, that there is some truth in what you say; but still, all the men of my colour have not been unkind to the Redskins, and several have tried to do them good."

"Wah! two or three have done so, but that only goes to prove what I assert. Let us come to the question we wish to discuss at present."

"Yes, I believe that will be the best," the American replied, delighted in his heart at not having to sustain a discussion which he knew would not result in victory to him.

"My nation hates the Palefaces," the Chief continued; "the condor does not make its nest with the maukawis, or the grizzly bear pair with the antelope. I, myself, have an instinctive hatred for the Palefaces. This morning, then, I should have peremptorily declined the Jaguar's proposals, for how do the wars the Palefaces wage together concern us? When the coyotes devour each other, the deer rejoice: we are happy to see our cruel oppressors tearing one another; but now, though my hatred is equally vivid, I am bound to bury it in my heart. My brother has saved my life; he helped when I was stretched out on the ground, and the Genius of Death was hovering over my head; ingratitude is a white vice, gratitude a red virtue. From this day the hatchet is buried between the Jaguar and Blue-fox for five succeeding moons; for five moons the enemies of the Jaguar will be those of Blue-fox; the two Chiefs will fight side by side, like loving brothers: in three suns from this one, the Sachem will join the Paleface Chief at the head of five hundred renowned warriors, whose heels are adorned with numerous coyote tails, and who form the pick of the nation. What will the Jaguar do for Blue-fox and his warriors?"

"The Jaguar is a generous Chief; if he is terrible for his enemies, his hand is always open for his friends; each Apache warrior will receive a rifle, one hundred charges of powder, and a scalping knife, The Sachem will also receive in addition to these presents two vicuna skins filled with fire-water."

"Wah!" the Chief exclaimed, with evident satisfaction, "My brother has said truly that the Jaguar is a generous Chief. Here is my totem as signal of alliance, as well as my feather of command."

While thus speaking the Chief drew from his game bag or medicine bag, which he wore slung, a square piece of parchment, on which was clumsily drawn the totem or animal emblematic of the tribe, handed it to the American, who placed it in his bosom; then removing the eagle feather fixed in his war-lock, he also gave him that.

"I thank my brother the Sachem," John Davis then said, "for having acceded to my proposal; he will have no cause to repent it."

"A Chief has given his word; but see, the sun is lengthening the shadows of the trees, the maukawis will soon strike up the evening song; the hour has come to pay the last duties to the Chiefs who are dead, and then separate to rejoin our common friends."

"On foot as we are, that appears to me rather difficult," John remarked.

The Indian smiled.

"The warriors of Blue-fox are watching over him," he said.

In fact, the Chief had hardly twice given a private signal, ere fifty Apache warriors burst into the clearing, and assembled silently around him.

The fugitives who escaped from the Scalper's terrible arm, soon collected again; they returned to their camp and announced the news of their defeat to their comrades, and then a detachment was sent off under the orders of a subaltern Chief, to look for their Sachem, But these horsemen, seeing Blue-fox in conference with a Paleface, remained under covert, patiently waiting till it pleased him to summon them.

The Sachem gave orders to bury the dead. The funeral ceremony then began, which circumstances compelled them to abbreviate.

The bodies were carefully washed, wrapped in new buffalo robes, and then placed in a sitting posture in trenches dug for each of them, with their weapons, bit, and provisions by their side, in order that they might want for nothing on their journey to the happy hunting grounds, and be able to mount and hunt so soon as they joined the Wacondah.

When these several rites had been performed, the hunters were filled up, and covered with heavy stones, lest the wild beasts should grub up and devour the bodies.

The sun was just disappearing on the horizon, when the Apaches finished the last duties to their brothers. Blue-fox then walked up to the hunter, who had hitherto been a silent, if not indifferent, spectator of the ceremony.

"My brother wishes to return to the warriors of his nation?" he said to him.

"Yes," the American laconically answered.

"The Paleface has lost his horse, so he will mount the mustang Blue-fox offers him; within two hours he can have returned to his friends."

John Davis gratefully accepted the present so generously made him, mounted at once, and, after taking leave of the Apaches, set off at full speed.

On their side, the Indians, at a signal from their Chief, buried themselves in the forest and clearing where such terrible events had occurred, and fell back into silence and solitude.

CHAPTER XXV
AN EXPLANATION

Like all men the greater portion of whose life is spent in the desert, the Jaguar was gifted with excessive prudence joined to extreme circumspection.

Though still very young, his life had been composed of such strange incidents, he had been an actor in such extraordinary scenes, that from an early age he had grown accustomed to shut up his emotions in his heart, and preserve on his countenance, whatever he might see or experience, that marble-like stoicism which characterizes the Indians, and which the latter have converted into such a tremendous weapon against their enemies.

On hearing Tranquil's voice all at once so close to him, the young man gave a start, frowned, and asked himself mentally how it was that the hunter came to find him thus in his camp, and what reason was powerful enough to impel him to do so; the more so, because his intimacy with the Canadian, ever subject to intermittences, was at this moment on terms far from amicable, if not completely hostile.

Still the young man, in whom the feeling of honour spoke loudly, and whom the steps taken by Tranquil flattered more than he cared to let anyone see, concealed the apprehensions that agitated him, and walked quickly, and with a smile on his lips, to meet the hunter.

The latter was not alone; Loyal Heart accompanied him.

The Canadian's manner was reserved, and his face was covered by a cloud of sorrow.

"You are welcome to my camp, hunter," the Jaguar said kindly, as he offered his hand.

"Thank you," the Canadian answered laconically, not touching the proffered hand.

"I am glad to see you," the young man went on, without any display of annoyance; "what accident has brought you in this direction?"

"My comrade and I have been hunting for a long time; fatigue is crushing us, and the smoke of your camp attracted us."

The Jaguar pretended to accept as gospel this clumsy evasion of a man who justly prided himself as being the healthiest and strongest wood-ranger of the desert.

"Come, then, and take a seat at my camp fire, and be good enough to regard everything here as belonging to you, and act in accordance with it."

The Canadian bowed, but made no answer, and with Loyal Heart followed the hunter who preceded them, and guided them through the mazes of the camp.

On reaching the fire, upon which the young man threw a few handfuls of dry wood, the hunters sat down on buffalo skulls placed there as seats, and then, without breaking the silence, filled their pipes and began smoking.

The Jaguar imitated them.

Those white men who traverse the prairie, and whose life is spent in hunting or trapping on these vast solitudes, have unconsciously assumed most of the habits and customs of the Redskins, with whom the exigencies of their position bring them constantly into contact.

A thing worthy of remark, is the tendency of civilized men to return to savage life, and the facility with which hunters, born for the most part in the great centres of population, forget their habits of comfort, surrender the customs of towns, and renounce the usages by which they were governed during the earlier part of their life, in order to adopt the manners, and even the habits, of the Redskins.

Many of these hunters carry this so far, that the greatest compliment which can be paid them is to pretend to take them for Indian warriors.

We must confess that, per contra, the Redskins are not at all jealous of our civilization, in which they take but slight interest, and that those whom accident or commercial reasons carry to cities, and by such we mean cities like New York, or New Orleans;—these Indians, we say, far from being astounded at what they see, look around them with glances of pity, not understanding how men can voluntarily consent to shut themselves up in the smoky cages called houses, and expend their life in ungrateful toil, instead of living in the open air among the vast solitudes, hunting the buffalo, bear, and jaguar, under the immediate eye of Heaven.

Are the savages completely wrong in thinking so? Is their reasoning false? We do not believe it.

Desert life possesses, for the man whose heart is still open enough to comprehend its moving incidents, intoxicating delights which can only be experienced there, and which the mathematically ruled customs of towns cannot at all cause to be forgotten, if they have once been tasted.

According to the principles of Indian etiquette on matters of politeness, no question must be addressed to strangers who sit down at the camp-fire, until they are pleased to begin the conversation.

In an Indian's wigwam a guest is regarded as sent by the Great Spirit; he is sacred to the man he visits as long as he thinks proper to remain with him, even if he be his mortal enemy.

The Jaguar, thoroughly conversant with Redskin customs, remained silently by the side of his guests, smoking and thinking, and waiting patiently till they decided on speaking.

At length, after a considerable lapse of time, Tranquil shook the ashes from his pipe on his thumbnail, and turned to the young man.

"You did not expect me, I fancy?" he said.

"I did not," the other answered; "still be assured that the visit, though unexpected, is not less agreeable to me."

The hunter curled his lip in a singular fashion.

"Who knows?" he muttered, answering his own thoughts rather than the Jaguar's remark; "perhaps yes, perhaps no; man's heart is a mysterious and undecipherable book, in which only madmen fancy they can read."

"It is not so with me, hunter, as you know from experience."

The Canadian shook his head.

"You are still young; the heart to which you refer is still unknown to yourself; in the short period your existence has passed through, the wind of passion has not yet blown over you and bowed you down before its powerful impetus: wait, in order to reply with certainty, until you have loved and suffered; when you have bravely sustained the shock, and resisted the hurricane of youth, it will be time for you to speak."

These words were uttered with a stern accent, but there was no bitterness about them.

"You are harsh to me, to-day, Tranquil," the young: man answered sorrowfully; "how have I sunk in your esteem? What reprehensible act have I done?"

"None—at any rate, it pleases me to believe so; but I fear that soon—"

He stopped and shook his head mournfully.

"Finish the sentence," the young man quickly exclaimed.

"For what end?" he answered; "Who am I that I should impose on you a line of conduct which you would probably despise, and advice which would prove unwelcome? It is better to be silent."

"Tranquil!" the young man said, with an emotion he could not master, "For a long time we have known each other, you are aware of the esteem and respect I hold you in, so speak; whatever you have to say, however rude your reproaches may be, I will listen to you, I swear it."

"Nonsense; forget what I said to you; I was wrong to think of meddling in your affairs; on the prairie, a man should only think about himself, so let us say no more."

The Jaguar gave him a long and profound glance. "Be it so," he answered; "we will say no more about it."

He rose and walked a few yards in agitation, then he brusquely returned to the hunter.

"Pardon me," he said, "for not having thought of offering you refreshment, but breakfast time has now arrived. I trust that your comrade and yourself will do me the honour of sharing my frugal meal."

While speaking thus, the Jaguar bent on the Canadian a most meaning glance.

Tranquil hesitated for a second.

"This morning at sunrise," he then said, "my friend and myself ate, just before entering your camp."

"I was sure of it," the young man burst out. "Oh, oh! Now my doubts are cleared up; you refuse water and salt at my fire, hunter."

"I? But you forget that—"

"Oh!" he interrupted, passionately, "No denial, Tranquil; do not seek for pretexts unworthy of yourself and me; you are too honest and sincere a man not to be frank, cuerpo de Cristo! Likewise, you know the law of the prairies; a man will not break his fast with an enemy. Now, if you still have in your heart a single spark of that kindly feeling you entertained toward me at another period, explain yourself clearly, and without any beating round the bush—I insist on it."

The Canadian seemed to reflect for a few moments, and then suddenly exclaimed, with great resolution—

"Indeed, you are right, Jaguar; it is better to have an explanation like honest hunters, than try to deceive each other like Redskins; and besides, no man is infallible. I may be mistaken as well as another, and Heaven is my witness that I should like it to be so."

"I am listening to you, and on my honour, if the reproaches you make are well founded, I will recognize it."

"Good!" the hunter said, in a more friendly tone than he had hitherto employed; "you speak like a man; but, perhaps," he added, pointing to Loyal Heart, who discreetly made a move to withdraw, "you would prefer our interview being private?"

"On the contrary," the Jaguar answered, eagerly, "this hunter is your friend; I hope he will soon be mine, and I do not wish to have any secrets from him."

"I desire ardently for my part," Loyal Heart said, with a bow, "that the slight cloud which has arisen between you and Tranquil may be dispersed like the vapour driven away by the morning breeze, in order that I may become better acquainted with you; as you wish it, I will listen to your conversation."

"Thanks, Caballero. Now speak, Tranquil, I am ready to listen to the charges you fancy you have to bring against me."

"Unluckily," said Tranquil, "the strange life yon have led since your arrival in these parts gives occasion for the most unfavourable surmises; you have formed a band of adventurers and border-ruffians, outlawed by society, and living completely beyond the ordinary path of civilized peoples."

"Are we prairie-hunters and wood-rangers obliged to obey all the paltry exigencies of cities?"

"Yes, up to a certain point; that is to say, we are not allowed to place ourselves in open revolt against the institutions of men who, though we have separated from them, are no less our brothers, and to whom we continue to belong by our colour, religion, origin, and the family ties which attach us to them, and which we have been unable to break.

"Be it so, I admit to a certain extent the justice of your reasoning; but even supposing that the men I command are really bandits, border-ruffians as you call them, do you know from what motives they act? Can you bring any accusation against them?"

"Patience, I have not finished yet."

"Go on, then."

"Next, in addition to this band of which you are the ostensible Chief, you have contracted alliances with the Redskins, the Apaches among others, the most impudent plunderers on the prairie; is that so?"

"Yes, and no, my friend; in the sense that the alliance which you charge me with never existed until the present hour; but this morning it was probably concluded by two of my friends with Blue-fox, one of the most renowned Apache Chiefs."

"Hum! that is an unlucky coincidence."

"Why so?"

"Are you aware what your new allies did last night?"

"How should I? Since I do not know where they are, and have not even received the official report of the treaty being made."

"Well, I will tell you; they attacked the Venta del Potrero, and burned it to the ground."

The Jaguar's savage eye emitted a flash of fury; he bounded to his feet, and convulsively seized his rifle.

"By Heaven!" he shouted, loudly, "Have they done that?"

"They did; and it is supposed at your instigation."

The Jaguar shrugged his shoulders disdainfully.

"For what object?" he said. "But Doña Carmela, what has become of her?"

"She is saved, thank Heaven!"

The young man heaved a sigh of relief.

"And you believed in such infamy on my part?" he asked, reproachfully.

"I do not believe it now," the hunter replied.

"Thanks, thanks! but by Heaven! The demons shall pay dearly, I swear, for the crime they have committed; now go on."

"Unluckily, if you have exculpated yourself from my first accusation, I doubt whether you will be able to do so with the second."

"You can tell me it, at any rate."

"A conducta de plata, commanded by Captain Melendez, is on the road for Mexico."

The young man gave a slight start.

"I know it," he said, shortly.

The hunter gave him an inquiring glance.

"They say—" he went on, with considerable hesitation.

"They say," the Jaguar interrupted him, "that I am following the conducta, and when the propitious moment arrives, I mean to attack it at the head of my bandits, and carry off the money; that is the story?"

"Yes."

"They are right," the young man answered, coldly; "that is really my intention; what next?"

Tranquil started in surprise and indignation at this cynical answer.

"Oh!" he exclaimed, in great grief, "What is said of you is true, then? You are really a bandit?"

The young man smiled bitterly.

"Perhaps I am," he said, in a hollow voice; "Tranquil, your age is double mine; your experience is great; why do you judge rashly on appearances?"

"What! Appearances! Have you not confessed it yourself?"

"Yes, I have."

"Then you meditate a robbery?"

"A robbery!" he exclaimed, blushing with indignation, but at once recovering himself, he added, "It is true, you are bound to suppose that."

"What other name can be given to so infamous a deed?" the hunter exclaimed, violently.

The Jaguar raised his head quickly, as if he intended to answer, but his lips remained dumb.

Tranquil looked at him for a moment with mingled pity and tenderness, and then turned to Loyal Heart.

"Come, my friend," he said, "we have remained here only too long."

"Stay!" the young man exclaimed, "Do not condemn me thus; I repeat to you that you are ignorant of the motives through which I act."

"Whatever these motives may be, they cannot be honourable; I see no other than pillage and murder."

"Oh!" the young man exclaimed, as he buried his face sorrowfully in his hands. "Let us go," Tranquil repeated.

Loyal Heart had watched this strange scene attentively and coldly.

"A moment," he said; then, slipping forward, he laid his hand on the Jaguar's shoulder.

The latter raised his head.

"What do you want of me?" he asked.

"Listen to me, Caballero," Loyal Heart answered in a deep voice; "I know not why, but a secret foreboding tells me that your conduct is not so infamous as everything leads us to suppose, and that some day you will be permitted to explain it, and exculpate yourself in the sight of all."

"Oh! were it but possible for me to speak!"

"How long do you believe that you will be compelled to remain silent?"

"How do I know? That depends on circumstances independent of my will."

"Then, you cannot fix a period?"

"It is impossible; I have taken an oath, and am bound to keep it."

"Good: then promise me only one thing."

"What is it?"

"To make no attempt on the life of Captain Melendez."

The Jaguar hesitated.

"Well?" Loyal Heart went on.

"I will do everything to save it."

"Thanks!" then, turning to Tranquil, who stood motionless by his side, he said—

"Take your place again, brother, and breakfast with this caballero, I answer for him body for body; if in two months from this day he does not give you a satisfactory explanation of his conduct, I, who am bound by no oath, will reveal to you this mystery, which appears, and really is, inexplicable for you."

The Jaguar started, and gave Loyal Heart a searching glance, which produced no effect, however, on the hunter's indifferently placid face.

The Canadian hesitated for a few moments, but at length took his place again by the fire, muttering—.

"In two months, be it so;" and he added in an aside, "but till then I will watch him."

CHAPTER XXVI
THE EXPRESS

Captain Melendez was anxious to pass through the dangerous defile near which the conducta had bivouacked; he knew how great was the responsibility he had taken on himself in accepting the command of the escort, and did not wish, in the event of any misfortune happening, that a charge of carelessness or negligence could be brought against him.

The sum conveyed by the recua of mules was important. The Mexican government, ever forced to expedients to procure money, was impatiently expecting it; the Captain did not conceal from himself that the whole responsibility of an attack would be mercilessly thrown on him, and that he would have to endure all the consequences, whatever might be the results of an encounter with the border rifles.

Hence his anxiety and alarm increased with every moment; the evident treachery of Fray Antonio only heightened his apprehensions, by making him suspect a probable trap. Though it was impossible for him to guess from what quarter the danger would come, he felt it, as it were, approaching him inch by inch, and besetting him on all sides, and he expected a terrible explosion at any moment.

This secret intuition, this providential foreboding, which told him to be on his guard, placed him in a state of excitement impossible to describe, and threw him into an intolerable situation, from which he resolved to escape at all hazards, preferring to run the danger and confront it, to remaining longer with bayonets pointed at unseen foes.

Hence he doubled his vigilance, himself inspecting the vicinity of the camp, and watching the loading of the mules, which, fastened to each other, would, in the event of an attack, be placed in the centre of the most devoted and resolute men of the escort.

Long before sunrise, the Captain, whose sleep had been an uninterrupted series of continued starts, quitted the hard bed of skins and horsecloths on which he had vainly sought a few hours of rest, which his nervous condition rendered impossible, and began walking sharply up and down the narrow space that composed the interior of the camp, involuntarily envying the careless and calm slumbers of the troopers, who were lying here and there on the ground, wrapped up in their zarapés.

In the meanwhile day gradually broke. The owl, whose matin hoot announces the appearance of the sun, had already given its melancholy note. The Captain kicked the arriero Chief, who was lying by the fire, and aroused him.

The worthy man rubbed his eyes several times, and when the last clouds of sleep were dissipated, and order was beginning to be re-established in his ideas, he exclaimed, while stifling a last sigh—

"Caray, Captain, what fly has stung you that you awake me at so early an hour? Why, the sky has scarce turned white yet; let me sleep an hour longer. I was enjoying a most delicious dream, and will try to catch it up again, for sleep is a glorious thing."

The Captain could not refrain from smiling at this singular outburst; still, he did not consider himself justified in listening to the arriero's complaints, for circumstances were too serious to lose time in futile promises.

"Up, up! Cuerpo de Cristo!" he shouted; "Remember that we have not yet reached the Rio Seco, and that if we wish to cross this dangerous passage before sunset, we must make haste."

"That is true," the arriero said, who was on his legs in a moment, as fresh and lively as if he had been awake for an hour; "forgive me, Captain, for I have quite as much interest as yourself in making no unpleasant encounter; according to the law, my fortune answers for the load I am conveying, and if an accident happened, I and my family would be reduced to beggary."

"That is true, I did not think of that clause in your contract."

"That does not surprise me, for it cannot at all interest you; but I cannot get it out of my head, and I declare to you, Captain, that since I undertook this unlucky journey, I have very often repented having accepted the conditions imposed on me; something tells me that we shall not arrive safe and sound on the other side of these confounded mountains."

"Nonsense, that is folly, no Bautista. You are in a capital condition, and well escorted; what cause can you have for fear?"

"None, I know, and yet I am convinced that I am not mistaken, and this journey will be fatal to me."

The same presentiments agitated the officer; still, he must not allow the arriero to perceive any of his internal disquietude; on the contrary, he must comfort him, and restore that courage which seemed on the point of abandoning him.

"You are mad, on my soul," he exclaimed; "to the deuce with the absurd notions you have got in your wool-gathering noddle."

The arriero shook his head gravely.

"You are at liberty, Don Juan Melendez," he answered, "to laugh at these ideas; you are an educated man, and naturally believe in nothing. But I, Caballero, am a poor ignorant Indian, and set faith in what my fathers believed before me; look you, Captain, we Indians, whether civilized or savage, have hard heads, and your new ideas cannot get through our thick skulls."

"Come, explain yourself," the Captain continued, desirous to break off the conversation without thwarting the arriero's prejudices; "what reason leads you to suppose that your journey will be unlucky? You are not the man to be frightened at your own shadow; I have been acquainted with you for a long while, and know that you possess incontestable bravery."

"I thank you, Captain, for the good opinion you are pleased to have of me; yes, I am courageous, and believe I have several times proved it, but it was when facing dangers which my intellect understood, and not before perils contrary to the natural laws that govern us."

The Captain twisted his moustache impatiently at the arriero's fatiguing prolixity: but, as he reminded him, he knew the worthy man, and was aware by experience that attempting to cut short what he had to say was a loss of time, and he must be allowed to do as he liked.

There are certain men with whom, like the spur with restiff horses, any attempt to urge them on is a sure means of making them go back.

The young man, therefore, mastered his impatience, and coldly said:—

"I presume, then, you saw some evil omen at the moment of your departure?"

"Indeed I did, Captain; and certainly, after what I saw, I would not have started, had I been a man easily frightened."

"What was the omen, then?"

"Do not laugh at me, Captain; several passages of Scripture itself prove that GOD is often pleased to grant men salutary warnings, to which unhappily," he added with a sigh, "they are not wise enough to give credence."

"That is true," the Captain muttered in the style of an interjection.

"Well," the arriero continued, flattered by this approval from a man like the one he was talking with; "my mules were saddled, the recua was waiting for me in the corral, guarded by the peons, and I was on the point of starting. Still, as I did not like separating from my wife, for a long time probably, without saying a last good bye, I proceeded toward the house to give her a parting kiss, when, on reaching the threshold, I mechanically raised my eyes, and saw two owls sitting on the azotea, who fixed their eyes on me with infernal steadiness. At this unexpected apparition, I shuddered involuntarily and turned my eyes away. At this very moment, a dying man, carried by two soldiers on a litter, came down the street, escorted by a monk who was reciting the Penitential Psalms, and preparing him to die like an honest and worthy Christian; but the wounded man made no other answer than laughing ironically at the monk. All at once this man half rose on the litter, his eyes grew brilliant, he turned to me, gave me a glance full of sarcasm, and fell back, muttering these two words evidently addressed to me:—

"*Hasta luego* (we shall meet soon)."

"Hum!" the Captain said.

"The species of rendezvous this individual gave me, had nothing very flattering about it, I fancy!" the arriero continued. "I was deeply affected by the words, and I rushed toward him with the intention of reproaching him, as I thought was proper—but he was dead."

"Who was the man—did you learn?"

"Yes, he was a Salteador, who had been mortally wounded in a row with the citizens, and was being carried to the steps of the Cathedral, to die there."

"Is that all?" the Captain asked.

"Yes.'

"Well, my friend, I did well in insisting upon knowing the motives of your present uneasiness."

"Ah!"

"Yes, for you have interpreted the omen with which you were favoured, in a very different way from what you should have done."

"How so?"

"Let me explain: this foreboding signifies, on the contrary, that with prudence and indefatigable vigilance you will foil all treachery, and lay beneath your feet any bandits who dare to attack you."

"Oh!" the arriero exclaimed, joyfully; "Are you sure of what you assert?"

"As I am of salvation in the other world," the Captain replied, crossing himself fervently.

The arriero had a profound faith in the Captain's words, for he held him in great esteem, owing to his evident superiority; he did not dream, consequently, of doubting the assurance the latter gave him of the mistake he had made in the interpretation of the omen which had caused him such alarm; he instantly regained his good spirits, and snapped his fingers mockingly.

"Caray, if that is the case, I run no risk; hence it is useless for me to give Nuestra Señora de la Soledad the wax taper I promised her."

"Perfectly useless," the Captain assured him.

Now, feeling perfectly at his ease again, the arriero hastened to perform his ordinary duties.

In this way, the Captain, by pretending to admit the ideas of this ignorant Indian, had led him quietly to abandon them.

By this time all were astir in the camp, the arrieros were rubbing down and loading the mules, while the troopers were saddling their horses and making all preparations for a start.

The Captain watched all the movements with feverish energy, spurring some on, scolding others, and assuring himself that his orders were punctually carried out.

When all the preparations were completed, the young officer ordered that the morning meal should be eaten all standing, and with the bridle passed over the arm, in order to lose no time, and then gave the signal for departure.

The soldiers mounted, but at the moment when the column started to leave the camp finally, a loud noise was heard in the chaparral, the branches were violently pulled back, and a horseman dressed in a dragoon uniform appeared a short distance from the party, toward which he advanced at a gallop.

On coming in front of the Captain, he stopped short, and raised his hand respectfully to the peak of his forage cap.

"*Dios guarde a Vm!*" he said, "have I the honour of speaking with Captain Don Juan Melendez?"

"I am he," the Captain answered in great surprise; "what do you want?"

"Nothing personally," the trooper said, "but I have to place a despatch in your Excellency's hands."

"A despatch—from whom?"

"From his most Excellent General Don José-Maria Rubio, and the contents of the despatch must be important, for the General ordered me to make the utmost diligence, and I have ridden forty-seven leagues in nineteen hours, in order to arrive more quickly."

"Good!" the Captain answered; "Give it here."

The dragoon drew from his bosom a large letter with a red seal, and respectfully offered it to the officer.

The latter took it and opened it, but, before reading it, he gave the motionless and impassive soldier before him a suspicious glance, which he endured, however, with imperturbable assurance.

The man seemed to be about thirty years of age, tall and well built; he wore his uniform with a certain amount of ease; his intelligent features had an expression of craft and cunning, rendered more marked still by his incessantly moving black eyes, which only rested with considerable hesitation on the Captain.

Sum total, this individual resembled all Mexican soldiers, and there was nothing about him that could attract attention or excite suspicion.

Still it was only with extreme repugnance that the Captain saw himself compelled to enter into relations with him; the reason for this it would certainly have been very difficult, if not impossible for him to say; but there are in nature certain laws which cannot be gainsaid, and which cause us at the mere sight of a person, and before he has even spoken, to feel a sympathy or antipathy for him, and be attracted or repulsed by him. Whence comes this species of secret presentiment which is never wrong in its appreciation? That we cannot explain: we merely confine ourselves to mentioning a fact, whose influence we have often undergone and efficacy recognized, during the course of our chequered life.

We are bound to assert that the Captain did not feel at all attracted toward the man to whom we refer, but, on the contrary, was disposed to place no confidence in him.

"At what place did you leave the General?" he asked, as he mechanically turned in his fingers the open despatch, at which he had not yet looked.

"At Pozo Redondo, a little in advance of the Noria de Guadalupe, Captain."

"Who are you—what is your name?"

"I am the assistente of his most excellent General; my name is Gregorio Lopez."

"Do you know the contents of this despatch?"

"No; but I suppose it is important."

The soldier replied to the Captain's questions with perfect freedom and frankness. It was evident that he was telling the truth.

After a final hesitation, Don Juan made up his mind to read; but he soon began frowning, and an angry expression spread over his features.

This is what the despatch contained:—

"Pozo Redondo."

"General Don José-Maria Rubio, Supreme Military Commandant of the State of Texas, has the honour to inform Captain Don Juan Melendez de Gongora, that fresh troubles have broken out in the state; several parties of bandits and border-ruffians, under the orders of different Chiefs, are going about the country pillaging and burning haciendas, stopping convoys, and interrupting the communications. In the presence of such grave facts, which compromise the public welfare and the safety of the inhabitants, the government, as their duty imperiously orders, have thought fit, in the interest of all, to take general measures to repress these disorders, before they break out on a larger scale. In consequence, Texas is declared under martial law—(here followed the measures adopted by the General to suppress the rebellion, and then the despatch went on as follows)—General Don José-Maria Rubio having been informed by spies, on whose devotion he can trust, that one of the principal insurgent Chiefs, to whom his comrades have given the name of the Jaguar, is preparing to carry off the conducta de plata confided to the escort of Captain Don Juan Melendez de Gongora, and that, for this purpose, the said cabecilla purposes to form an ambuscade on the Rio Seco, a spot favourable for a surprise; General Rubio orders Captain Melendez to let himself be guided by the bearer of the present despatch, a sure and devoted man, who will lead the conducta to the Laguna del Venado, where this conducta will form a junction with a detachment of cavalry sent for the purpose, whose numerical strength will protect it from any aggression. Captain Melendez will take the command of the troops, and join the General at head quarters with the least possible delay."

"Dios y libertad."

"The supreme Military General commanding in the State of Texas,

"DON JOSE-MARIA RUBIO."

After reading this despatch carefully, the Captain raised his head and examined the soldier for an instant with the deepest and most earnest attention.

The latter, leaning on the hilt of his sword, was carelessly playing with his knot, and apparently paying no attention to what was going on around him.

"The order is positive," the Captain repeated several times, "and I must obey it, although everything tells me that this man is a traitor."

Then he added aloud—

"Are you well acquainted with this part of the country?"

"I was born here, Captain," the dragoon replied; "there is not a hidden track I did not traverse in my youth."

"You know that you are to serve as my guide?"

"His Excellency the General did me the honour of telling me so, Captain."

"And you feel certain of guiding us safe and sound to the spot where we are expected?"

"At least I will do all that is necessary."

"Good. Are you tired?"

"My horse is more so than I. If you would grant me another, I would be at your orders immediately, for I see that you are desirous of setting out."

"I am. Choose a horse."

The soldier did not let the order be repeated. Several remounts followed the escort, and he selected one of them, to which he transferred the saddle. In a few minutes he was mounted again.

"I am at your Excellency's orders," he said.

"March," the Captain shouted, and added mentally, "I will not let this scoundrel out of sight during the march."

CHAPTER XXVII
THE GUIDE

Military law is inflexible—it has its rules, from which it never departs, and discipline allows of neither hesitation nor tergiversation; the oriental axiom, so much in favour at despotic courts, "to hear is to obey," is rigorously true from a military point of view. Still, however hard this may appear at the first blush, it must be so, for if the right of discussion were granted inferiors with reference to the orders their superiors gave them, all discipline would be destroyed; the soldiers henceforth only obeying their caprices, would grow ungovernable, and the army, instead of rendering the country the services which it has a right to expect from it, would speedily become a scourge.

These reflections, and many others, crossed the Captain's mind, while he thoughtfully followed the guide whom his General's despatch had so singularly forced on him; but the order was clear and peremptory, he was obliged to obey, and he did obey, although he felt convinced that the man to whom he was compelled to trust was unworthy of the confidence placed in him, if he were not an utter traitor.

As for the trooper, he galloped carelessly at the head of the caravan, smoking, laughing, singing, and not seeming to suspect the doubts entertained about him.

It is true that the Captain carefully kept secret the ill opinion he had formed of the guide, and ostensibly placed the utmost confidence in him: for prudence demanded that in the critical situation in which the conducta was placed, those who composed it should not suspect their Chief's anxiety, lest they might be demoralized by the fear of an impending, treachery.

The Captain, before starting, had given the most severe orders that the arms should be in a good state; he sent off scouts ahead, and on the flanks of the troops, to explore the neighbourhood, and be assured that the road was free, and no danger to be apprehended; in a word, he had taken most scrupulously all the measures prudence dictated, in order to guarantee the safety of the journey.

The guide, who was an impassive witness of all these precautions, on whose behalf they were taken with so much ostentation, appeared to approve of them, and even drew attention to the skill the border-ruffians have in gliding through bushes and grass without leaving traces, and the care the scouts must devote to the accomplishment of the mission entrusted to them.

The further the conducta advanced in the direction of the mountains, the more difficult and dangerous the march became; the trees, at first scattered over a large space, became imperceptibly closer, and at last formed a dense forest, through which, at certain spots, they were compelled to cut their way with the axe, owing to the masses of creepers intertwined in each other, and forming an inextricable tangle; then again, there were rather wide streams difficult of approach, which the horses and mules were obliged to ford in the midst of iguanas and alligators, having frequently the water up to their girths.

The immense dome of verdure under which the caravan painfully advanced, utterly hid the sky, and only allowed a few sunbeams to filter through the foliage, which was not sufficient entirely to dissipate the gloom which prevails almost constantly in the virgin forests, even at mid-day.

Europeans, who are only acquainted with the forests of the old world, cannot form even a remote idea of those immense oceans of verdure which in America are called virgin forests.

There the trees form a compact mass, for they are so entwined in each other, and fastened together by a network of lianas which wind round their stems and branches, plunging in the ground to rise again like the pipes of an immense organ, or forming capricious curves, as they rise and descend incessantly amid tufts of the parasite called Spanish beard, which falls from the ends of the branches of all the trees; the soil, covered with detritus of every sort, and humus formed of trees that have died of old age, is hidden beneath a thick grass several feet in height. The trees, nearly all of the same species, offer so little variety, that each of them seems only a repetition of the others.

These forests are crossed in all directions by paths formed centuries agone by the feet of wild beasts, and leading to their mysterious watering-places; here and there beneath the foliage are stagnant marshes, over which myriads of mosquitoes buzz, and from which dense vapours rise that fill the forest with gloom; reptiles and insects of all sorts crawl on the ground, while the cries of birds and the hoarse calls of the wild beasts form a formidable concert which the echoes of the lagoons repeat.

The most hardened wood-rangers enter in tremor the virgin forests, for it is almost impossible to find one's way with certainty, and it is far from safe to trust to the tracks which cross and are confounded; the hunters know by experience that once lost in one of these forests, unless a miracle supervene, they must perish within the walls formed by the tall grass and the curtain of lianas, without hope of being helped or saved by any living being of their own species.

It was a virgin forest the caravan entered at this moment.

The guide pushed on, without the least hesitation, appearing perfectly sure of the road he followed, contenting himself by giving at lengthened intervals a glance to the right or left, but not once checking the pace of his horse.

It was nearly mid-day; the heat was growing stifling, the horses and men, who had been on the march since four in the morning along almost impracticable roads, were exhausted with fatigue, and imperiously claimed a few hours' rest, which was indispensable before proceeding further.

The Captain resolved to let the troop camp in one of those vast clearings, so many of which are found in these parts, and are formed by the fall of trees overthrown by a hurricane, or dead of old age.

The command to halt was given. The soldiers and arrieros gave a sigh of relief, and stopped at once.

The Captain, whose eyes were accidentally fixed at this moment on the guide, saw a cloud of dissatisfaction on his brow; still, feeling he was watched, the man at once recovered himself, pretended to share the general joy, and dismounted.

The horses and mules were unsaddled, that they might browse freely on the young tree shoots and the grass that grew abundantly on the ground.

The soldiers enjoyed their frugal meal, and lay down on their zarapés to sleep.

Ere long, the individuals composing the caravan were slumbering, with the exception of two, the Captain and the guide.

Probably each of them was troubled by thoughts sufficiently serious to drive away sleep, and keep them awake, when all wanted to repose.

A few paces from the clearing, some monstrous iguanas were lying in the sun, wallowing in the grayish mud of a stream whose water ran with a slight murmur through the obstacles of every description that impeded its course. Myriads of insects filled the air with the continued buzzing of their wings; squirrels leaped gaily from branch to branch; the birds, hidden beneath the foliage, were singing cheerily, and here and there above the tall grass might be seen the elegant head and startled eyes of a deer or an ashata, which suddenly rushed beneath the covert with a low of terror.

But the two men were too much occupied with their thoughts to notice what was going on around them.

The Captain raised his head at the very moment when the guide had fixed on him a glance of strange meaning: confused at being thus taken unawares, he tried to deceive the officer by speaking to him—old-fashioned tactics, however, by which the latter was not duped.

"It is a hot day, Excellency," he said, with a nonchalant air.

"Yes," the Captain answered, laconically.

"Do you not feel any inclination for sleep?"

"No."

"For my part, I feel my eyelids extraordinarily heavy, and my eyes close against my will; with your permission I will follow the example of our comrades, and take a few moments of that refreshing sleep they seem to enjoy so greatly."

"One moment—I have something to say to you."

"Very good," he said, with an air of the utmost indifference.

He rose, stifling a sigh of regret, and seated himself by the Captain's side, who withdrew to make room for him under the protecting shadow of the large tree which stretched out above his head its giant arms, loaded with vines and Spanish beard.

"We are about to talk seriously," the Captain went on.

"As you please."

"Can you be frank?"

"What?" the soldier said, thrown off his guard by the suddenness of the question.

"Or, if you prefer it, can you be honest?"

"That depends."

The Captain looked at him.

"Will you answer my questions?"

"I do not know."

"What do you say?"

"Listen, Excellency," the guide said, with a simple look, "my mother, worthy woman that she was, always recommended me to distrust two sorts of people, borrowers and questioners, for she said, with considerable sense, the first attack your purse, the others your secrets."

"Then you have a secret?"

"Not the least in the world."

"Then what do you fear?"

"Not much, it is true. Well, question me, Excellency, and I will try to answer you."

The Mexican peasant, the Manzo or civilized Indian, has a good deal of the Norman peasant about him, in so far as it is impossible to obtain from him a positive answer to any question asked him. The Captain was compelled to be satisfied with the guide's half promise, so he went on:—

"Who are you?"

"I?"

"Yes, you."

The guide began laughing.

"You can see plainly enough," he said.

The Captain shook his head.

"I do not ask you what you appear to be, but what you really are."

"Why, señor, what man can answer for himself, and know positively who he is?"

"Listen, scoundrel," the Captain continued, in a menacing tone, "I do not mean to lose my time in following you through all the stories you may think proper to invent. Answer my questions plainly, or, if not—"

"If not?" the guide impudently interrupted him.

"I blow out your brains like a dog's!" he replied, as he drew a pistol from his belt, and hastily cocked it.

The soldier's eye flashed fire, but his features remained impassive, and not a muscle of his face stirred.

"Oh, oh, señor Captain," he said, in a sombre voice, "you have a singular way of questioning your friends."

"Who assures me that you are a friend? I do not know you."

"That is true, but you know the person who sent me to you; that person is your Chief as he is mine. I obeyed him by coming to find you, as you ought to obey him by following the orders he has given you."

"Yes, but those orders were sent me through you."

"What matter?"

"Who guarantees that the despatch you have brought me was really handed to you?"

"Caramba, Captain, what you say is anything but flattering to me," the guide replied with an offended look.

"I know it; unhappily we live at a time when it is so difficult to distinguish friends from foes, that I cannot take too many precautions to avoid falling into a snare; I am entrusted by Government with a very delicate mission, and must therefore behave with great reserve toward persons who are strangers to me."

"You are right, Captain; hence, in spite of the offensive nature of your suspicions, I will not feel affronted by what you say, for exceptional positions require exceptional measures. Still, I will strive by my conduct to prove to you how mistaken you are."

"I shall be glad if I am mistaken; but take care. If I perceive anything doubtful, either in your actions or your words, I shall not hesitate to blow out your brains. Now that you are warned, it is your place to act in accordance."

"Very good, Captain, I will run the risk. Whatever happens. I feel certain that my conscience will absolve me, for I shall have acted for the best."

This was said with an air of frankness which, in spite of his suspicions, had its effect on the Captain.

"We shall see," he said; "shall we soon get out of this infernal forest in which we now are?"

"We have only two hours' march left; at sunset we shall join the persons who are awaiting us."

"May Heaven grant it!" the Captain muttered.

"Amen!" the soldier said boldly.

"Still, as you have not thought proper to answer any of the questions I asked you, you must not feel offended if I do not let you out of sight from this moment, and keep you by my side when we start again."

"You can do as you please, Captain; you have the power, if not the right, on your side, and I am compelled to yield to your will."

"Very good, now you can sleep if you think proper."

"Then you have nothing more to say to me?"

"Nothing."

"In that case I will avail myself of the permission you are kind enough to grant me, and try to make up for lost time."

The soldier then rose, stiffing a long yawn, walked a few paces off, lay down on the ground, and seemed within a few minutes plunged in a deep sleep.

The Captain remained awake. The conversation he had held with his guide only increased his anxiety, by proving to him that this man concealed great cunning beneath an abrupt and trivial manner. In fact, he had not answered one of the questions asked him, and after a few minutes had succeeded in making the Captain turn from the offensive to the defensive, by giving him speciously logical arguments to which the officer was unable to raise any objection.

Don Juan was, therefore at this moment in the worst temper a man of honour can be in, who is dissatisfied with himself and others, fully convinced that he was in the right, but compelled, to a certain extent, to allow himself in the wrong.

The soldiers, as generally happens in such cases, suffered from their chief's ill temper; for the officer, afraid of adding the darkness to the evil chances he fancied he had against him, and not at all desirous to be surprised by night in the inextricable windings of the forest, cut the halt short much sooner than he would have done under different circumstances.

At about two o'clock P.M. he ordered the boot and saddle to be sounded, and gave the word to start.

The greatest heat of the day had passed over, the sunbeams being more oblique, had lost a great deal of their power, and the march was continued under conditions comparatively better than those which preceded it.

As he had warned him, the Captain intimated to the guide that he was to ride by his side, and, so far as was possible, did not let him out of sight for a second.

The latter did not appear at all troubled by this annoying inquisition; he rode along quite as gaily as heretofore, smoking his husk cigarette, and whistling fragments of jarabés between his teeth.

The forest began gradually to grow clearer, the openings became more numerous, and the eye embraced a wider horizon; all led to the presumption that they would soon reach the limits of the covert.

Still, the ground began rising slightly on both sides, and the path the conducta followed grew more and more hollow, in proportion as it advanced.

"Are we already reaching the spurs of the mountains?" the Captain asked.

"Oh, no, not yet," the guide answered.

"Still we shall soon be between two hills?"

"Yes, but of no height."

"That is true; still, if I am not mistaken, we shall have to pass through a defile."

"Yes, but of no great length."

"You should have warned me of it."

"Why so?"

"That I might have sent some scouts ahead."

"That is true, but there is still time to do so if you like; the persons who are waiting for us are at the end of that gorge."

"Then we have arrived?"

"Very nearly so."

"Let us push on in that case."

"I am quite ready."

They went on; all at once the guide stopped.

"Hilloh!" he said, "Look over there, Captain; is not that a musket barrel glistening in the sunbeams?"

The Captain sharply turned his eyes in the direction indicated by the soldier.

At the same moment a frightful discharge burst forth from either side of the way, and a shower of bullets poured on the conducta.

Before the Captain, ferocious at this shameful treachery, could draw a pistol from his belt, he rolled on the ground, dragged down by his horse, which had a ball right through its heart.

The guide had disappeared, and it was impossible to discover how he had escaped.

CHAPTER XXVIII
JOHN DAVIS

John Davis, the ex-slave dealer, had too powerful nerves for the scenes he had witnessed this day, and in which he had even played a very active and dangerous part, to leave any durable impressions on his mind.

After quitting Blue-fox, he galloped on for some time in the direction where he expected to find the Jaguar; but gradually he yielded to his thoughts, and his horse, understanding with that admirable instinct which distinguishes these noble animals, that its rider was paying no attention to it, gradually reduced its pace, passing from the gallop to a trot, and then to a foot-pace, walking with its head down, and snapping at a few blades of grass as it passed.

John Davis was considerably perplexed by the conduct of one of the persons with whom accident had brought him in contact on this morning so fertile in events of every description. The person who had the privilege of arousing the American's attention to no eminent degree was the White Scalper.

The heroic struggle sustained by this man alone against a swarm of obstinate enemies, his herculean strength, the skill with which he managed his horse—all in this strange man seemed to him to border on the marvellous.

During bivouac watches on the prairie he had frequently heard the most extraordinary and exaggerated stories told about this hunter by the Indians with, a terror, the reason of which he comprehended, now that he had seen the man; for this individual who laughed at weapons directed against his chest, and ever emerged safe and sound from the combats he engaged in, seemed rather a demon than a being appertaining to humanity. John Davis felt himself shudder involuntarily at this thought, and congratulated himself in having so miraculously escaped the danger he had incurred in his encounter with the Scalper.

We will mention, in passing, that no people in the world are more superstitious than the North Americans. This is easy to understand: this nation—a perfect harlequin's garb—is an heterogeneous composite of all the races that people the old world; each of the representatives of these races arrived in America, bearing in his emigrants' baggage not only his vices and passions, but also his creed and his superstitions, which are the wildest, most absurd, and puerile possible. This was the more easily effected, because the mass of emigrants, who have at various periods sought a refuge in America, was composed of people for the most part devoid of all learning, or even of a semblance of education; from this point of view, the North Americans, we must do them the justice of saying, have not at all degenerated; they are at the present day at least as ignorant and brutal as were their ancestors.

It is easy to imagine the strange number of legends about sorcerers and phantoms which are current in North America. These legends, preserved by tradition, passing from mouth to mouth, and with time becoming mingled one with the other, have necessarily been heightened in a country where the grand aspect of nature renders the mind prone to reverie and melancholy.

Hence John Davis, though he flattered himself he was a strong-minded man, did not fail, like all his countrymen, to possess a strong dose of credulity; and this man, who would not have recoiled at the sight of several muskets pointed at his breast, felt himself shiver with fear at the sound of a leaf falling at night on his shoulder.

Moreover, so soon as the idea occurred to John Davis that the White Scalper was a demon, or, at the very least, a sorcerer, it got hold of him, and this supposition straightway became an article of belief with him. Naturally, he found himself at once relieved by this discovery; his ideas returned to their usual current, and the anxiety that occupied his mind disappeared as if by enchantment; henceforth his opinion was formed about this man, and if accident again brought them face to face, he would know how to behave to him.

Happy at having at length found this solution, he gaily raised his head, and took a long searching look around him at the landscape he was riding through.

He was nearly in the centre of a vast rolling prairie, covered with tall grass, and with a few clumps of mahogany and pine trees scattered here and there.

Suddenly he rose in his stirrups, placed his hand as a shade over his eyes, and looked attentively.

About half a mile from the spot where he had halted, and a little to the right, that is to say, exactly in the direction he intended to follow himself, he noticed a thin column of smoke, which rose from the middle of a thicket of aloe and larch trees.

On the desert, smoke seen by the wayside always furnishes ample matter for reflection.

Smoke generally rises from a fire round which several persons are seated.

Now man, in this more unfortunate than the wild beasts, fears before all else on the prairie meeting with his fellow-man, for he may wager a hundred to one that the man he meets will prove an enemy.

Still John Davis, after ripe consideration, resolved to push on toward the fire; since morning he had been fasting, hunger was beginning to prick him, and in addition he felt excessively fatigued; he therefore inspected his weapons with the most scrupulous attention, so as to be able to have recourse to them if necessary, and digging the spur into his horse's flank, he went on boldly toward the smoke, while carefully watching the neighbourhood for fear of a surprise.

At the end of ten minutes he reached his destination; but when fifty yards from the clump of trees, he checked the speed of his horse, and laid his rifle across the saddle-bow; his face lost the anxious expression which had covered it, and he advanced toward the fire with a smile on his lips, and the most friendly air imaginable.

In the midst of a thick clump of trees, whose protecting shade offered a comfortable shelter to a weary traveller, a man dressed in the costume of a Mexican dragoon was lazily seated in front of a fire, over which his meat was cooking, while himself smoked a husk cigarette. A long lance decorated with its guidon leaned against a larch tree close to him, and a completely harnessed horse, from which the bit had, however, been removed, was peaceably nibbling the tree shoots and the tender prairie grass.

This man seemed to be twenty-seven or twenty-eight years of age; his cunning features were lit up by small sharp eyes, and the copper tinge of his skin denoted his Indian origin.

He had for a long time seen the horseman coming toward his camp, but he appeared to attach but slight importance to it, and quietly went on smoking and watching the cooking of his meal, not taking any further precaution against the unforeseen visitor than assuring himself that his sabre came easily out of its scabbard. When he was only a few paces from the soldier, John Davis stopped and raised his hand to his hat.

"Ave Maria Purísima!" he said.

"Sin pecado concebida!" the dragoon answered, imitating the American's gesture.

"Santas tardes!" the new comer went on.

"Dios les da a Vm buenas!" the other immediately answered.

These necessary formulas of every meeting exhausted, the ice was broken, and the acquaintance made.

"Dismount, Caballero," the dragoon said; "the heat is stifling on the prairie; I have here a famous shade, and in this little pot cecina, with red harico beans and pimento, which I think you will like, if you do me the honour to share my repast."

"I readily accept your flattering invitation, Caballero," the American answered with a smile; "the more readily because I confess to you that I am literally starving, and, moreover, exhausted with fatigue."

"Caray! In that case I congratulate myself on the fortunate accident that occasions our meeting, so pray dismount without further delay."

"I am going to do so."

The American at once got off his horse, removed the bit, and the noble animal immediately joined its companion, while its master fell to the ground by the dragoon's side, with a sigh of satisfaction.

"You seem to have made a long ride, Caballero?" the soldier said.

"Yes," the American answered, "I have been on horseback for ten hours, not to mention that I spent the morning in fighting."

"Cristo! You have had hard work of it."

"You may say so without any risk of telling an untruth; for, on the word of a hunter, I never had such a tough job."

"You are a hunter?"

"At your service."

"A fine profession," the soldier said with a sigh; "I have been one too."

"And you regret it?"

"Daily."

"I can understand that. Once a man has tasted the joys of desert life, he always wishes to return to it."

"Alas, that is true."

"Why did you give it up then, since you liked it so much?"

"Ah, why!" the soldier said; "through love."

"What do you mean?"

"Yes, a child with whom I was so foolish as to fall in love, and who persuaded me to enlist."

"Oh, hang it!"

"Yes, and I had scarce put on my uniform, when she told me she was mistaken about me: that, thus dressed, I was much uglier than she could have supposed; in short, she left me in the lurch to run after an arriero."

The American could not refrain from laughing at this singular story.

"It is sad, is it not?" the soldier continued.

"Very sad," John Davis answered, trying in vain to regain his gravity.

"What would you have?" the soldier added gloomily; "the world is only one huge deception. But," he added with a sudden change of his tone, "I fancy our dinner is ready—I smell something which warns me that it is time to take off the pot."

As John Davis had naturally no objection to offer to this resolution of the soldier, the latter at once carried it into effect; the pot was taken off the fire and placed before the two guests, who began such a vigorous attack, that it was soon empty, in spite of its decent capacity.

This excellent meal was washed down with a few mouthfuls of Catalonian refino, with which the soldier appeared amply provided.

All was terminated with the indispensable cigarette, that obligato complement of every Hispano-American meal, and the two men, revived by the good food with which they had lined their stomachs, were soon in an excellent condition to open their hearts to each other.

"You seem to me a man of caution, Caballero," the American remarked, as he puffed out an immense mouthful of smoke, part of which came from his mouth, and part from his nostrils.

"It is a reminiscence of my old hunter's trade. Soldiers generally are not nearly so careful as I am."

"The more I observe you," John Davis went on, "the more extraordinary does it appear to me that you should have consented to take up a profession so badly paid as that of a soldier."

"What would you have? It is fatality, and then the impossibility of sending the uniform to the deuce. However, I hope to be made a *Cabo* before the year's out."

"That is a fine position, as I have heard; the pay must be good."

"It would not be bad, if we received it."

"What do you mean?"

"It seems that the government is not rich."

"Then, you give it credit?"

"We are obliged to do so."

"Hang it! but forgive me for asking you all these questions, which must appear to you indiscreet."

"Not at all; we are talking as friends."

"How do you live?"

"Well, we have casualties."

"What may they be?"

"Do you not know?"

"Indeed, I do not."

"I will explain."

"You will cause me pleasure."

"Sometimes our Captain or General entrusts us with a mission."

"Very good."

"This mission is paid for separately; the more dangerous it is, the larger the amount."

"Still on credit?"

"No, hang it; in advance."

"That is better. And have you many of these missions?"

"Frequently, especially during a pronunciamento."

"Yes, but for nearly a year no General has pronounced."

"Unluckily."

"Then you are quite dry?"

"Not quite."

"You have had missions?"

"I have one at this moment."

"Well paid?"

"Decently."

"Would there be any harm in asking how much?"

"Not at all; I have received twenty-five ounces."

"Cristo! that is a nice sum. The mission must be a dangerous one to be paid so highly."

"It is not without peril."

"Hum! In that case take care."

"Thank you, but I run no heavy risk; I have only to deliver a letter."

"It is true that a letter—" the American carelessly remarked.

"Oh! this one is more important than you fancy it."

"Nonsense!"

"On my honour it is, for it concerns some millions of dollars."

"What is that you say?" John Davis exclaimed with an involuntary start.

Since his meeting with the soldier, the hunter had quietly worked to get him to reveal the reason that brought him into these parts, for the presence of a single dragoon on the desert seemed to him queer, and for good reason; hence it was with great pleasure that he saw him fall into the trap set for him.

"Yes," the soldier continued, "General Rubio, whose asistente I am, has sent me as an express to meet Captain Melendez, who at this moment is escorting a conducta de plata."

"Do you mean that really?"

"Do I not tell you that I have the letter about me?"

"That is true; but for what purpose does the General write to the Captain?"

The soldier looked for a moment cunningly at the hunter, and then suddenly changed his tone.

"Will you play fair?" he asked him, as he looked him full in the face.

The hunter smiled.

"Good," the soldier continued; "I see that we can understand one another."

"Why not? those are the conditions that suit Caballeros."

"Then, we play fair?"

"That is agreed."

"Confess that you would like to know the contents of this letter."

"Through simple curiosity, I swear to you."

"Of course! I felt assured of that. Well, it only depends on yourself to know them."

"I will not take long then; let me hear your conditions."

"They are simple."

"Tell me them for all that."

"Look at me carefully; do you not recognize me?"

"On my honour, I do not."

"That proves to me that I have a better memory than you."

"It is possible."

"I recognize you."

"You may have seen me somewhere."

"Very likely, but that is of little consequence; the main point is that I should know who you are."

"Oh, a simple hunter."

"Yes, and an intimate friend of the Jaguar."

"What!" the hunter exclaimed with a start of surprise.

"Do not be frightened at such a trifle: answer me simply; is it so or not?"

"It is true; I do not see why I should hide the fact from you."

"You would be wrong if you did. Where is the Jaguar at this moment?"

"I do not know."

"That is to say, you will not tell me."

"You have guessed it."

"Good. Could you tell me, if I wished you to lead me to him?"

"I see no reason to prevent it, if the affair is worth your while."

"Have I not told you that it related to millions?"

"You did, but you did not prove it."

"And you wish me to give you that proof?"

"Nothing else."

"That is rather difficult."

"No, it is not."

"How so?"

"Hang it, I am a good fellow; I only want to cover my responsibility; show me the letter, I ask no more."

"And that will satisfy you?"

"Yes, because I know the General's handwriting."

"Oh, in that case, it is all right," and drawing a large envelope from his breast, he said as he showed it to the American, though without loosing his hold, "Look!"

The latter looked at it closely for some minutes.

"It is really the General's handwriting," the soldier continued.

"Yes,"

"Now, do you consent to lead me to the Jaguar?"

"Whenever you like."

"At once then."

"Very good."

The two men rose by mutual agreement, put the bits in their horses' mouths, leaped into their saddles, and left at a gallop the spot which for several hours had afforded them such pleasant shade.

CHAPTER XXIX
THE BARGAIN

The two adventurers rode gaily side by side, telling one another the news of the desert, that is to say, hunting exploits, and skirmishes with the Indians, and conversing about the political events which for some months past had attained a certain gravity and alarming importance for the Mexican government.

But, while thus talking, asking each other questions, the answers to which they did not wait to hear, their conversation had no other object save to conceal the secret preoccupation that agitated them.

In their previous discussion, each had tried to overreach the other, trying to draw out secrets, the hunter manoeuvring to lead the soldier to an act of treachery, the latter asking no better than to sell himself, and acting in accordance with his wishes; the result of the trial was that they had found themselves of equal force, and each had obtained the result he wanted.

But this was no longer the question with them; like all crafty men, success, instead of satisfying them, had given birth in their minds to a multitude of suspicions. John Davis asked himself what cause had led the dragoon to betray his party so easily, without stipulating beforehand for important advantages for himself.

For everything is paid for in America, and infamy especially commands a high price.

On his side, the dragoon found that the hunter put faith in his statements very easily, and, in spite of his comrade's affectionate manner, the nearer he approached the camp of the border rifles, the more his uneasiness increased; for he was beginning to fear lest he had gone head first into a snare, and had trusted too imprudently to a man whose reputation was far from reassuring him.

Such was the state of mind in which the two men stood to each other, scarce an hour after leaving the spot where they had met so accidentally.

Still, each carefully hid his apprehensions in his heart; nothing was visible on the exterior; on the contrary, they redoubled their politeness and obsequiousness toward each other, behaving rather like brothers delighted to have met after a long separation, than as men who two hours previously spoke together for the first time.

The sun had set about an hour, and it was quite dark when they came within a short distance of the Jaguar's camp, whose bivouac fires flashed out of the gloom, reflecting themselves with fantastic effects of light on the surrounding objects, and imprinting on the rugged scenery of the prairie a stamp of savage majesty.

"We have arrived," the hunter said, as he stopped his horse and turned to his companion; "no one has perceived us; you can still turn back without any fear of pursuit; what is your decision?"

"Canarios! Comrade," the soldier answered, shrugging his shoulders with a disdainful air; "I have not come so far to shiver at the entrance of the camp, and allow me to remark, with all the respect due to you, that your remark appears to me singular at the least."

"I owed it to myself to make it; who knows whether you may not repent to-morrow the hazardous step you are taking to-day?"

"That is possible. Well, what would you have? I will run the risk; my determination is formed, and is unchangeable. So let us push on, in Heaven's name."

"As you please, Caballero; within a quarter of an hour you will be in the presence of the man you desire to see. You will have an explanation with him, and my task will be accomplished."

"And I shall have nothing but thanks to offer you," the soldier quickly interrupted him; "but let us not remain any longer here: we may attract attention, and become the mark for a bullet, which I confess to you I am not at all desirous of."

The hunter, without replying, let his horse feel the spur, and they continued to advance.

Within a few minutes they entered the circle of light cast by the fire; almost immediately the sharp click of a rifle being cocked was heard, and a rough voice ordered them to stop in the devil's name.

The order, though not positively polite, was not the less peremptory, and the two adventurers thought it advisable to obey.

Several armed men then issued from the entrenchments; and one of them, addressing the strangers, asked them who they were, and what they wanted at such an unseasonable hour.

"Who we are?" the American answered, firmly; "What we want? To come in as quickly as we can."

"That is all very fine," the other replied; "but, if you do not tell us your names, you will not enter so soon, especially as one of you wears a uniform which is not in the odour of sanctity with us."

"All right, Ruperto," the American replied, "I am John Davis, and you know me, I suppose; so let me pass, without delay. I answer for this caballero, who has an important communication to make to the Chief."

"You are welcome, Master John; do not be angry with me, for you know that prudence is the mother of safety."

"Yes, yes," the American said, with a laugh, "deuce take me if you easily get into a scrape for lack of prudence, gossip."

They then entered the camp without farther obstacle.

The border rifles were generally sleeping round the fires, but a cordon of vigilant sentries, placed at the openings of the camp, watched over the common security.

John Davis dismounted, inviting his comrade to follow his example; then, making him a sign to follow, he walked toward a tent, through the canvas of which a weak light could be seen flickering.

On reaching the entrance of the tent, the hunter stopped, and tapped twice.

"Are you asleep, Jaguar?" he asked, in a suppressed voice.

"Is that you, Davis, my old comrade?" was immediately asked from within.

"Yes."

"Come in, for I was impatiently waiting for you."

The American raised the curtain which covered the entrance, and glided into the tent; the soldier followed him gently, and the curtain fell down behind them.

The Jaguar, seated on a buffalo skull, was reading a voluminous correspondence by the dubious light of a *candil*; and in a corner of the tent might be seen two or three bear-skins, evidently intended to serve as a bed. On seeing the newcomers, the young man folded up the papers, and laid them in a small iron casket, the key of which he placed in his bosom, then raised his head, and looked anxiously at the soldier.

"Who's this, John?" he asked; "Have you brought prisoners?"

"No," the other answered, "this caballero was most desirous of seeing you, for certain reasons he will himself explain; so I thought I had better carry out his wishes."

"Good; we will settle with him in a moment. What have you done?"

"What you ordered me."

"Then you have succeeded?"

"Completely."

"Bravo, my friend! Tell me all about it."

"What need of details?" the American answered, looking meaningly at the dragoon, who stood motionless a couple of paces from him.

The Jaguar understood him.

"That is true," he said, "suppose we see of what sort of wood this man is made;" and addressing the soldier, he added, "Come hither, my good fellow."

"Here I am, at your orders, Captain."

"What is your name?"

"Gregorio Felpa. I am a dragoon, as you can see by my uniform, Excellency."

"What is your motive for wishing to see me?"

"An anxiety to render you an important service, Excellency."

"I thank you, but usually services are confoundedly dear, and I am not a rich man."

"You will become so."

"I hope so. But what is the great service you propose to render me?"

"I will explain to you, in two words. In every political question there are two sides, and that depends on the point of view from which you regard it. I am a child of Texas, son of a North American and an Indian woman, which means that I cordially detest the Americans."

"Come to facts."

"I am doing so. A soldier against my will, General Rubio has entrusted me with a dispatch for Captain Melendez, in which he gives him a place of meeting, so as to avoid the Rio Seco, where the report runs that you intend to ambush, in order to carry off the conducta."

"Ah, ah," the Jaguar said, becoming very attentive, "but how do you know the contents of the dispatch?"

"In a very simple way. The General places the utmost confidence in me; and he read me the dispatch, because I am to serve as the Captain's guide."

"Then you are betraying your Chief?"

"Is that the name you give my action?"

"I am looking at it from the General's side."

"And from yours?"

"When we have succeeded I will tell you."

"Good," he carelessly replied.

"You have this dispatch?"

"Here it is."

The Jaguar took it, examined it attentively, turning it over and over, and then prepared to break the seal.

"Stop!" the soldier hurriedly exclaimed.

"What for?"

"Because, if you open it, I cannot deliver it to the man for whom it is intended."

"What do you mean?"

"You do not understand me," the soldier said, with ill-concealed impatience.

"That is probable," the Captain answered.

"I only ask you to listen to me for five minutes."

"Speak."

"The meeting-place appointed for the Captain and the General is the Laguna del Venado. Before reaching the Laguna there is a very narrow and densely-wooded gorge."

"The Paso de Palo Muerto; I know it."

"Good. You will hide yourself there, on the right and left, in the bushes; and when the conducta passes, you will attack it on all sides at once; it is impossible for it to escape you, if, as I suppose, your arrangements are properly made."

"Yes, the spot is most favourable for an attack. But who guarantees that the conducta will pass through this gorge?"

"I do."

"What do you mean?"

"Certainly, as I shall act as guide."

"Hum! We no longer understand one another."

"Excuse me, we do, perfectly. I will leave you, and go to the Captain, to whom I will deliver the General's dispatch; he will be compelled to take me for his guide, whether we like it or not; and I will lead him into your hands as surely as a novillo taken to the shambles."

The Jaguar gave the soldier a glance which seemed trying to read the bottom of his heart.

"You are a daring fellow," he said to him, "but I fancy you settle events a little too much as you would like them. I do not know you; I see you to-day for the first time, and, excuse my frankness, it is to arrange an act of treachery. Who answers for your good faith? If I am foolish enough to let you go quietly, what assures me that you will not turn against me?"

"My own interest, in the first place; if you seize the conducta by my aid, you will give me five hundred ounces."

"That is not too dear: still, allow me to make a further objection."

"Do so, Excellency."

"Nothing proves to me that you have not been promised double the amount to trap me."

"Oh!" he said, with a shake of the head.

"Hang it all! Listen to me; more singular things than that have been known, and though my head may be worth little, I confess to you that I have the weakness of attaching remarkable value to it; hence I warn you, that unless you have better security to offer, the affair is broken off."

"That would be a pity."

"I am well aware of that, but it is your fault, not mine; you should have taken your measures better before coming to me."

"Then nothing can convince you of my good faith?"

"Nothing."

"Come, we must have an end of this!" the soldier exclaimed, impatiently.

"I ask for nothing better."

"It is clearly understood between us, Excellency, that you will give me five hundred ounces?"

"If by your aid I carry off the conducta de plata; I promise it."

"That is enough; I know that you never break your word."

He then unbuttoned his uniform, drew out a bag hung round his neck by a steel chain, and offered it to the Captain.

"Do you know what this is?" he asked him.

"Certainly," the Jaguar replied, crossing himself fervently; "it is a relic."

"Blessed by the Pope! As this attestation proves."

"It is true."

He took it from his neck, and laid it in the young man's hand, then crossing his right thumb over the left, he said, in a firm and marked voice—

"I, Gregorio Felpa, swear on this relic to accomplish faithfully all the clauses of the bargain I have just concluded with the noble Captain called the Jaguar: if I break this oath, I renounce from this day and for ever the place I hope for in Paradise, and devote myself to the eternal flames of hell. Now," he added, "keep that precious relic; you will restore it to me on my return."

The Captain, without replying, immediately hung it round his own neck.

Strange contradiction of the human heart, and inexplicable anomaly; these Indians, for the most part pagans, in spite of the baptism they have received, and who, while affecting to follow ostensibly the rules of the Catholic religion, secretly practise the rites of their worship, have a lively faith in relics and amulets; all wear them round their necks in little bags, and these perverse and dissolute men, to whom nothing is sacred, who laugh at the most noble feelings, whose life is passed in inventing roguery, and preparing acts of treachery, profess so great a respect for these relics, that there is no instance of an oath taken on one of them having ever been broken.

Anyone who pleases may explain this extraordinary fact; we content ourselves with telling it.

Before the oath taken by the soldier, the Jaguar's suspicions at once faded away to make room for the most perfect confidence.

The conversation lost the stiff tone it had up to the present, the soldier sat down on a buffalo skull, and the three men, henceforth in good harmony, quietly discussed the best means to be employed to prevent a failure.

The plan proposed by the soldier was so simple and easy to carry out, that it guaranteed success; hence it was adopted entirely, and the discussion only turned on points of detail.

At a rather late hour of the night, the three men at length separated, in order to take a few moments of indispensable rest between the fatigue of the past day and that they would have to endure on the morrow.

Gregorio slept *a pierna suelta,* to employ the Spanish phrase, that is to say, straight off the reel.

About two hours before sunrise, the Jaguar bent over the sleeper and awoke him; the soldier rose at once, rubbed his eyes for an instant, and at the end of five minutes was as fresh and ready as if he had been asleep for eight-and-forty hours.

"It is time to start," the Jaguar said, in a low voice; "John Davis has himself rubbed down and saddled your horse; come."

They left the tent; they found the American holding the soldier's bridle, and the latter leaped into the saddle without using his stirrups, in order to show that he was quite fresh.

"Mind," the Jaguar observed, "that you employ the utmost prudence, watch your words and your slightest gestures carefully, for you are about to deal with the bravest and most skilful officer in the whole Mexican army."

"Trust to me, Captain. Canarios! The stake is too large for me to run any risk of losing the game."

"One word more."

"I am listening."

"Manage so as not to reach the gorge till nightfall, for darkness goes a great way toward the success of a surprise—and now good-bye and good luck."

"I wish you the same."

The Jaguar and the American escorted the dragoon to the barrier, in order to pass him through the sentries, who, had not this precaution been taken, would have infallibly fired at him, owing to the uniform he wore.

"When he had left the camp, the two men looked after him so long as they could distinguish his dark outline gliding like a shadow through the trees of the forest, when it speedily disappeared.

"Hum!" said John Davis, "That is what I call a thorough scoundrel; he is more cunning than an opossum. What a fearful villain!"

"Well, my friend," the Jaguar answered, carelessly, "men of that stamp are necessary, else what would become of us?"

"That is true. They are as necessary as the plague and leprosy; but I stick to what I said, he is the most perfect scoundrel I ever saw; and the Lord knows the magnificent collection I have come across during the course of my life!"

A few minutes later, the border rifles raised their camp and mounted to proceed to the gorge, where the rendezvous had been made with Gregorio Felpa, the asistente of General Rubio, who placed in him a confidence of which the soldier was in every respect so worthy.

CHAPTER XXX
THE AMBUSCADE

The Jaguar's measures were so well taken, and the traitor to whom the guidance of the conducta was entrusted had manoeuvred so cleverly, that the Mexicans fell literally into a wasp's nest, from which it was very difficult, if not impossible, for them to escape.

Although demoralized for a moment by the fall of their Chief, whose horse was killed at the beginning of the action, they still obeyed the Captain's voice, who, by a supreme effort, rose again almost simultaneously, and they collected round the string of mules laden with the treasure. They boldly formed a square, and prepared to defend courageously the precious depôt they had under their guard.

The escort commanded by Captain Melendez, though not large, was composed of old tried soldiers, long habituated to bush-fighting, and for whom the critical position in which their unlucky star had brought them, possessed nothing very extraordinary.

The dragoons had dismounted, and throwing away their long lances, useless in a fight like the one that was preparing, seized their carbines, and with their eyes fixed on the bushes, calmly awaited the order to begin firing.

Captain Melendez studied the terrain with a hurried glance, and it was far from being favourable. On the right and left steep slopes, crowned by enemies; in the rear, a large party of border rifles ambushed behind a barricade of trees, which, as if by enchantment, suddenly interrupted the road, and prevented a retreat; lastly, in front, a precipice about twenty yards in width, and of incalculable depth.

All hope, therefore, of getting safe and sound out of the position in which they were beset seemed taken from the Mexicans, not only through the considerable number of enemies that surrounded them, but also through the nature of the battle-field; still, after carefully examining it, a flash burst from the Captain's eye, and a gloomy smile passed over his face.

The dragoons had known their commander a long time, they placed faith in him; they perceived this fugitive smile, and their courage was heightened.

As the Captain had smiled, he must have hopes.

It is true that not a man in the whole escort could have said in what that hope consisted.

After the first discharge, the bandits appeared on the heights, but remained there motionless, satisfying themselves with attentively watching the movements of the Mexicans.

The Captain profited by this respite which the enemy so generously offered him, to take a few defensive measures, and amend his plan of battle.

The mules were unloaded, and the precious boxes placed right away at the rear, as far as possible from the enemy; then the horses and mules, led to the front, were arranged so that their bodies should serve as a rampart for the soldiers, who, kneeling and stooping behind this living breastwork, found themselves comparatively sheltered from the enemy's bullets.

When these measures were taken, and the Captain had assured himself by a final glance that his orders were punctually executed, he bent down to the ear of no Bautista, the chief arriero, and whispered a few words.

The arriero gave a quick start of surprise on hearing the Captain's words, but recovered himself immediately, and bowed his head in assent.

"You will obey?" Don Juan asked, as he looked at him fixedly.

"On my honour, Captain," the arriero answered.

"Very good," the young man said gaily; "we shall have some fun, I promise you."

The arriero fell back, and the Captain placed himself in front of the soldiers. He had scarce taken up his fighting position, when a man appeared at the top of the right hand bank; he held in his hand a long lance, from the end of which fluttered a piece of white rag.

"Oh, oh," the Captain murmured, "what is the meaning of this! Are they beginning to fear lest their prey may escape them? Hilloh," he shouted, "what do you want?"

"To parley," the man with the flag answered laconically.

"Parley," the Captain answered, "what good will that do? Besides, I have the honour of being a Captain in the Mexican army, and do not treat with bandits."

"Take care, Captain, misplaced courage is frequently braggadocio; your position is desperate."

"Do you think so?" the young man said in an ironical voice.

"You are surrounded on all sides."

"Bar one."

"Yes, but there is an impassable abyss there."

"Who knows?" the Captain said, still mockingly.

"In a word, will you listen to me?" the other said, who was beginning to grow impatient at this conversation.

"Well," the officer said, "let me hear your propositions, after which I will let you know my conditions."

"What conditions?" the bandit asked in amazement.

"Those I intend to impose on you, by Jove."

A Homeric laugh from the border rifles greeted these haughty words. The Captain remained cold and impassive.

"Who are you?" he asked.

"The Chief of the men who hold you imprisoned."

"Prisoners? I do not believe it; however, we shall see. Ah! you must be the Jaguar, whose name is held in execration on this border?"

"I am the Jaguar," the latter answered simply.

"Very good. What do you want with me? Speak, and before all be brief," the Captain said, as he leaned the point of his sword on the end of his boot.

"I wish to avoid bloodshed," the Jaguar said.

"That is very kind of you, but I fancy it is rather late to form so laudable a resolve," the officer said in his sarcastic voice.

"Listen, Captain, you are a brave officer, and I should be in despair if any misfortune happened to you; do not obstinately carry on an impossible struggle, surrounded as you are by an imposing force; any attempt at resistance would be an unpardonable act of madness, which could only result in a general massacre of the men you command, while you would not have the slightest hope of saving the conducta under your escort. Surrender, I repeat, for you have only that way of safety left open to you."

"Caballero," the Captain said, and this time seriously, "I thank you for the words you have spoken; I am a connoisseur in men, and see that you are speaking honourably at this moment."

"I am," said the Jaguar.

"Unfortunately," the Captain continued, "I am forced to repeat to you that I have the honour to be an officer, and would never consent to deliver my sword to the leader of banditti, for whose head a price is offered. If I have been mad and idiotic enough to let myself be drawn into a trap, all the worse for me—I must accept the consequences."

The two speakers had by this time come together, and were conversing side by side.

"I can understand, Captain, that your military honour must, under certain circumstances, compel you to fight, even under unfavourable conditions; but here the case is different—all the chances are against you, and your honour will in no way suffer by a capitulation which will save the lives of your brave soldiers."

"And deliver to you without a blow the rich prey you covet."

"Whatever you may do, that prey cannot escape me."

The Captain shrugged his shoulders.

"You are mistaken," he said; "like all men accustomed to prairie warfare, you have been too clever, and your adroitness has carried you past your object."

"What do you mean?"

"Learn to know me, Caballero; I am a cristiano viejo; I am descended from the old Conquistadors, and the Spanish blood flows pure in my veins. All my men are devoted to me, and at my order they will let themselves be killed to the last without hesitation; but whatever may be the advantages of the situation you occupy, and the number of your companions, you will require a certain time to kill fifty men reduced to desperation, and who are resolved not to ask quarter."

"Yes," the Jaguar said in a hollow voice; "but in the end they are killed."

"Of course," the Captain replied calmly; "but while you are murdering us, the arrieros have my positive orders to cast the money chests to the bottom of the abyss, to the brink of which you have forced us."

"Oh," the Jaguar said with an ill-restrained look of menace, "you will not do that."

"Why shall I not, if you please?" the officer said coldly. "Yes, I will do it, I pledge you my honour."

"Oh!"

"What will happen, then? You will have brutally murdered fifty men, with no other result than that of wallowing in the blood of your countrymen."

"Rayo de Dios! This is madness."

"Not at all; it is simply the logical consequence of the threat you make me; we shall be dead, but as men of honour, and have fulfilled our duty, as the money will be saved."

"All my efforts, then, to bring about a peaceful settlement are sterile."

"There is one way."

"What is it?"

"To let us pass, after pledging your word of honour not to molest our retreat."

"Never! That money is indispensable to me, and I must have it."

"Come and take it, then,"

"That is what I am going to do."

"Very good."

"The blood I wished to spare will fall on your head."

"Or on yours."

They separated.

The Captain turned to his soldiers, who had been near enough to follow the discussion through all its turnings.

"What will you do, lads?" he asked them.

"Die!" they answered in a loud and firm voice.

"Be it so—we will die together;" and brandishing his sabre over his head, he shouted, "*Dios y libertad Viva México!*"

"*Viva México!*" the dragoons repeated, enthusiastically.

While this had been going on, the sun had disappeared below the horizon, and darkness covered the earth, like a sombre winding-sheet.

The Jaguar, with rage in his heart at the ill success of his tentatives, had rejoined his comrades.

"Well," John Davis asked him, who was anxiously watching for his return, "what have you obtained?"

"Nothing. That man is a fanatic."

"As I warned you, he is a demon; fortunately he cannot escape us, whatever he may do."

"Then you are mistaken," the Jaguar replied, stamping his foot passionately; "whether he live or die the money is lost to us."

"How so?"

The Jaguar told his confidant in a few words what had passed between him and the Captain.

"Confusion!" the American exclaimed; "In that case let us make haste."

"To increase our misfortunes, it is as dark as in an oven."

"By heavens! Let us make an illumination. Perhaps it will cause those demons incarnate to reflect, who are croaking there like frogs calling for rain."

"You are right. Torches here!"

"Better still. Let us fire the forest."

"Ah, ah," the Jaguar said, with a laugh, "bravo! Let us smoke them out like musk-rats."

This diabolical idea was immediately carried out, and ere long a brilliant belt of flame ran all around the gorge, where the Mexicans were stoically awaiting the attack.

They had not long to wait; a sharp fusillade began, mingled with the cries and yells of the assailants.

"It is time!" the Captain shouted.

The sound of a chest falling down the precipice was immediately heard.

Owing to the fire, it was as bright as day, and not a movement of the Mexicans escaped their adversaries.

The latter uttered a yell of fury on seeing the chests disappear one after the other in the abyss.

They rushed at the soldiers; but the latter received them at the bayonet's point, not giving ground an inch.

A point-blank discharge from the Mexicans, who had reserved their fire, laid many of the enemy low, and spread disorder through the ranks of the assailants, who began falling back involuntarily.

"Forward!" the Jaguar howled.

The bandits returned to the charge more eagerly than before.

"Keep firm, we must die," the Captain said.

"We will," the soldiers repeated unanimously.

The fight then began, body to body, foot to foot, chest against chest; the assailants and assailed were mixed up and fought more like wild beasts than men.

The arrieros, though decimated by the bullets fired at them, did not the less eagerly continue their task; the crowbar scarce fell from the hand of one shot down, ere another seized the heavy iron mass, and the chests of money toppled uninterruptedly over the precipice, in spite of the yells of fury, and gigantic efforts of the enemy, who exhausted themselves in vain to breach the human wall that barred their passage.

'Twas a fearfully grand sight, this obstinate struggle, this implacable combat which these men carried on, by the brilliant light of a burning forest.

The cries had ceased, the butchery went on silently and terribly, and at times the Captain could be heard sharply repeating—

"Close up there, close up!"

And the ranks closed, and the men fell without a murmur, having sacrificed their lives, and only fighting now to gain the few moments indispensable to prevent their sacrifice being sterile.

In vain did the border rifles, excited by the desire of gain, try to crush this energetic resistance offered them by a handful of men; the heroic soldiers, supporting one another, with their feet pressed against the corpses of those who had preceded them to death, seemed to multiply themselves in order to bar the gorge on all sides at once.

The fight, however, could not possibly last much longer; ten men only were left of the Captain's detachment; the others had fallen, but every man with his face to the foe.

All the arrieros were dead; two chests still remained on the edge of the precipice; the Captain looked hurriedly around.

"One more effort, lads!" he shouted, "We only want five minutes to finish our task."

"*Dios y libertad!*" the soldiers shouted; and, although exhausted with fatigue, they threw themselves resolutely into the thickest part of the crowd that surrounded them.

For a few minutes, these men accomplished prodigies; but at length numbers gained the mastery: they all fell!

The Captain alone was still alive.

He had taken advantage of the devotion of his soldiers to seize a crowbar, and hurl one chest over the precipice; the second, raised with great difficulty, only required a final effort to disappear in its turn, when suddenly a terrible hurrah caused the officer to raise his head.

The border rifles were rushing up, terrible, and panting like tigers thirsting for carnage.

"Ah!" Gregorio Felpa, the traitor-guide, shouted gladly, as he rushed forward; "at any rate we shall have this one."

"You lie, villain!" the Captain answered.

And raising with both hands the terrible bar of iron, he cleft the skull of the soldier, who fell like a stunned ox, not uttering a cry, or giving vent to a sigh.

"Whose turn is it next?" the Captain said as he raised the crowbar.

A yell of horror burst from the crowd, which hesitated for a moment.

The Captain quickly lowered his crowbar, and the chest hung over the brink of the abyss.

This movement restored the borderers all their rage and fury.

"Down with him, down with him!" they shouted, as they rushed on the officer.

"Halt!" the Jaguar said as he bounded forward, and overthrew all in his way; "Not one of you must stir; this man belongs to me."

On hearing this well-known voice, all the men stopped.

The Captain threw away his crowbar, for the last chest had fallen in its turn over the precipice.

"Surrender, Captain Melendez," the Jaguar said, as he advanced toward the officer.

The latter had taken up his sabre again.

"It is not worth while now," he replied, "I prefer to die."

"Defend yourself then."

The two men crossed swords, and for some minutes a furious clashing of steel could be heard. All at once, the Captain, by a sharp movement, made his adversary's weapon fly ten paces off, and ere the latter recovered from his surprise, the officer rushed on him and writhed round him like a serpent.

The two men rolled on the ground.

Two yards behind them was the precipice.

All the Captain's efforts were intended to drag the Jaguar to the verge of the abyss; the latter, on the contrary, strove to free himself from his opponent's terrible grasp, for he had doubtless guessed his desperate resolve.

At last, after a struggle of some minutes, the arms that held the Jaguar round the body gradually loosed their hold, the officer's clenched hands opened, and the young man, by the outlay of his whole strength, succeeded in throwing off his enemy and rising.

But he was hardly on his feet, ere the Captain, who appeared exhausted and almost fainting, bounded like a tiger, seized his adversary round the body, and gave him a fearful shock.

The Jaguar, still confused by the struggle he had gone through, and not suspecting this sudden attack, tottered, and lost his balance with a loud cry.

"At length!" the Captain shouted with ferocious joy.

The borderers uttered an exclamation of horror and despair.

The two enemies had disappeared in the abyss.

[What became of them will be found fully recorded in the next volume of this series, called "THE FREE-BOOTERS."]